VACANCY

a love story

TRACY EWENS

VACANCY

a love story

Book design by Maureen Cutajar
www.gopublished.com

ISBN: 978-0-9976838-1-3 (print)
ISBN: 978-0-9976838-0-6 (e-book)

For Michael.
Who never laughs at my lighthouse and loves me even when
I'm in my scratchy sweater.

Chapter One

Hollis Jeffries wasn't exactly a religious person. She had gone to church a few times as a child, mostly holidays, and attended a Lutheran grammar school, but that was it. She seldom prayed as an adult, yet now, as the curtains of the large window overlooking Tomales Bay were ripped open to let in the ruthless light of late morning, she found herself offering up the same feeble plea she was certain so many other "heathens," as her grandmother would say, cried in similar situations.

Dear Lord, please make this jackhammer going off in my head stop and I promise never ever ever to wash down an entire bag of cheese popcorn with two bottles of Prosecco again.

She wasn't sure why they bothered, she or the other heathens, because God had no time for poor little privileged pity parties. Hopefully, God was busy with bigger, more far-reaching issues, but as Hollis raised her forearm to cover her eyes, she wished this once he, or maybe she, would make an exception.

"Rise and shine, Tiny Tots. You didn't check into the Betty, and even if you had, your twenty-eight days are up," her uncle said in a voice that sounded a lot like the jackhammer, but more madras shorts and springtime flowers. Come to think of it, even without a hangover, her uncle often sounded like springtime flowers. The man was entirely too peppy, entirely too positive, and entirely too much. Hollis once again called on her recently rediscovered deity.

"Dear God!" She gingerly rolled onto her side.

"Shower's running, and once you're dressed, we're heading to the market."

Taking in a breath and letting it out slowly, Hollis precariously opened one eye to find her uncle holding out sunglasses—big, obnoxious sunglasses with rhinestones on the sides. *Where would a person even buy those?*

"Water," she croaked.

"Put these on first and then we'll get you sitting up for water. No sense drooling on yourself."

Hollis thought she nodded as she took the glasses, but she couldn't be sure. By the time Uncle Mitch hooked his arm through hers and began pulling her up like a child after a long nap, she was swatting at his hands until he stepped back.

"Yeouch, you've got claws."

"What time is it?" Hollis asked as her legs now dangled over the side of the bed. With her toes barely grazing the warm wood floor of her beach cabin, she tried to rationalize how at the age of thirty-four she was still stupid enough to drink too much.

"Eleven thirty," her uncle answered, now keeping his distance.

"In the morning? As in almost afternoon?" Easing the sunglasses onto her nose, Hollis was certain her head weighed a hundred pounds all by itself. She once watched a documentary and learned that the brain was 2 percent of a human's body weight, and it was a testament to the neck and the spinal cord that it managed to hold the whole thing upright. This morning, her spinal cord was struggling through the haze of wine and white cheddar because she felt like one of those bobbleheads vendors peddled at sporting events.

When she could finally lift her head, Hollis found her uncle surveying what she already knew was a hot mess. She scratched her head and took a slow drink from the water glass he'd carefully placed in her hands. At some point, she was going to need to get her shit together, get back to her life. It had been over a month since the second biggest failure of her thirty-four years, but this time, no amount of wine or junk food could disguise that she had no one to blame but herself. She continued to check in with the office, but she didn't have a plan. She couldn't recall a single moment in her life when she had not had a plan.

Yesterday, she'd spent the better part of an hour-long conference call listening to Reese Winterford, one of their project managers who liked to think he was the boss, confirm that the lead programmer for the game Fat Pigs, Zeke Walderblast—she couldn't make this stuff up—had, in fact, not been arrested as previously reported. He was "hanging" in Mexico with some friends and detained for possession of Aunt Mary.

"I'm sorry. Did you say he was detained with his Aunt Mary in Mexico?" Hollis had asked, rubbing the bridge of her nose.

"No, he was in Mexico when he was busted for possession of Aunt Mary," Reese clarified over laughter.

Hollis searched her brain then quickly Googled Aunt Mary. A type of marijuana. Right.

"Hollis, do you know what Aunt Mary is?" Megan liked to lurk in the background during conference calls, sort of like a sulking, bitchy party guest. She was Reese's boss.

"Yes, thank you, Megan. I may not smoke it, but I'm well aware. While he was puffing on his Aunt Mary, did he find any answers? Did it help him figure out why a nine-year-old was able to discover a flaw in his game after one afternoon of playing?"

"No. He said he's doing a lot of meditation and has a massage scheduled for tomorrow. He's hoping that will clear out his chi." Reese had to be smirking. Hollis could actually feel the bastard through the phone.

"His what?"

"Chi. His life force."

"Fan-damn-tastic." She bit into her second oatmeal cream pie. "Any idea how blocked his life force is?"

"He said he'd call us in a few days."

Hollis licked her fingers, having finished the entire cookie, pie, whatever in less than three bites. "Anything else? How are the investors holding up? I spoke with Greg on Monday. He'll be on vacation for a couple of weeks. I bought us some time. How are the rest of them?"

"We're burning platform here," creepy, lurking Megan added. "Zeke needs to finish this and fast. If we can't do something to move the needle on this soon, they're pulling out. They want it all functioning and the disaster-recovery plans in place by the end of the third quarter or they're pulling funding."

"That gives us about four months to get our ducks in a row. I suppose the silver lining is that he's not in jail. I'm guessing jail is not good for the chi."

Strained laughter again.

"How long will you be out of pocket?" Reese asked.

Hollis, who had been pacing her cabin, finally caved under the stupidity spilling from her phone. She'd used the "out of pocket" in e-mails before but never understood the phrase. If she was "out of pocket" when she was away from the office, did that mean when she returned she was "in pocket?" Why did all of this corporate crap sound so ridiculous when her feet were bare? Dropping to the edge of the bed, she rubbed her face. "I'm not sure."

Silence.

"What? It's a few days," Hollis said, trying to deflect.

"Thirty," bitch-face Megan clarified.

"Whatever. I'm working remotely. That guy in accounting was out for three weeks while his damn dog had surgery. Back up."

"Should we be worried, Hollis?" Megan had become a ginormous pain in the ass ever since she'd lost the partnership position to Hollis about a year before. Hollis was entrenched in the corporate culture as much as the next pair of expensive shoes, but Megan Tiffany was on a whole other level. She was known to say things like "in the brown" and "let's not boil the ocean" instead of "let's not waste time." She was the true definition of kiss ass.

"Megan, you can worry if you'd like, but I would direct your angst toward making sure the Plimpton and Inc. merger goes through without a hitch. You don't need to worry about me." Hollis heard some mumblings and was certain she'd hit her target.

Megan cleared her throat. "I suppose you're right. With the hot water you've landed us in, we need all the leverage we can get."

Hollis opened the wrapper of another oatmeal cream pie and felt the "go screw yourself" perched right on her lips, but since her "leverage," as Megan put it, was in short supply these days, she decided to chomp into her junk food instead. Hollis had worked hard to make sure she always had the upper hand, but this last bump had shaken all she knew to be normal. Megan was right—it was not something Hollis would ever say out loud, even alone in her cabin—but it was true. Hollis had screwed up royally, taken her eye off the ball, failed to "see the granular," as Reese enjoyed saying.

After a few less-heated exchanges and an agreement to "circle back around" again on Friday, Hollis ended the call and walked to the restaurant to see if her wine order had come in yet. The box had been sitting on the bar, and that was precisely why she was now playing host to her uncle and his jackhammer backup singers dancing around her cabin.

"Someone likes oatmeal snack cakes." Mitch plucked the wrappers from Hollis's bedside and threw them in the wastebasket. "All right, let's get you up and at 'em." He handed Hollis two Tylenol, which she promptly swallowed. She hoped there was a way to fix this mess and fast because there was no way she was failing without a fight.

Matt Locke opened The Bean fifteen minutes early because Mr. Trumble had been standing outside for almost a half hour holding three jars of something. Even though he had been helping out with his parents' coffee shop for a little over two months now, Matt still couldn't predict what bounty from Mrs. Trumble's garden would end up in the jars, but it was guaranteed to be interesting. He'd asked Poppy, the manager who was currently out on maternity leave, the first time Mr. Trumble handed him jars and was told, "It's a weekly thing. You'll get used to it." He had gotten used to it and had even grown to like Mr. Trumble, so with the coffee brewed and pastries arranged in the three glass-covered displays, Matt pulled the dairy from the refrigerator and flipped the sign.

"Morning, Matt." Mr. Trumble handed over the three jars.

"Morning." Matt had no idea what Mr. Trumble's first name was, and it was never offered.

"The missus did something crazy cool there for you. Spicy cauliflower and carrots in one and the other two are smoking hot okra. Do you do okra?"

Matt smiled. He'd never quite thought of it as "doing" okra, but according to Poppy, since Mr. Trumble retired a couple of years ago he'd been watching way too much reality TV and enjoyed being "hip with his lingo."

"Yes, I like okra. Thank you."

He nodded. "Welcome. So, what's good in the pastry case, bro?"

Matt walked behind the counter and set the jars down. He would add them to the others he'd placed out of sight in the storage room later. A mother and daughter arrived, accepting the "after you" gesture of a cop in uniform as they filed in behind Mr. Trumble, who appeared like he might take well into the afternoon choosing his breakfast.

"Scones. There are a couple of orange cranberry ones that I think you and Mrs. Trumble might enjoy." Matt tried to move him along. When his mother called him to ask a "little favor," he had agreed to stop by and help out in Poppy's absence, but once his dad hurt his hip, stopping by had turned into nearly full-time. Most of what Matt was working on at his own company could be done remotely, so he didn't mind, but the pace of things, the slower, lazy-day way that floated freely throughout the cove, was an adjustment. He'd grown up around coffee but never worked a shop for any extended period of time. Matt was reluctant to return, especially to Tomales Bay, but now that he'd been at it for a while, he had to admit he was enjoying himself.

Mr. Trumble hesitated for a minute and then smiled. "Sweet, those are it. Two of 'em and your usual brews."

"Great. Be right with you, folks. Good morning, Officer Hernandez."

"Morning. Do you have any coffee cake today?"

"I do." Matt put the scones in two separate bags, knowing that was Mr. Trumble's preference, and poured two medium roast coffees—one with a Sweet'N Low and a splash of cream, the other black.

Paying with singles and change as he usually did, Mr. Trumble commented that he and his boys played poker and he was nearly "baked," but he managed to pull through. Matt knew "baked" meant something else entirely, but he wasn't going to say anything. Instead, he smiled as Mr. Trumble gathered up his bags, stuck brown plastic plug sticks in his coffee, and left.

Matt met Officer Greg Hernandez for the first time the summer he turned seventeen, the year he was allowed to drive his own car up to the cove for their summer stay. His parents wouldn't be up for another week, but Matt had worked the roaster with his dad the Saturday before and convinced him he could be trusted. Matt could still conjure up the restlessness of seventeen, a time when hours felt like days and one week was a lifetime.

He'd finished his last final early and used his lunch period so he would be done by Thursday. The old blue Nissan, with the dent on the rear bumper, a little reminder from backing into a cart pole in the Safeway parking lot when he was learning to drive, was packed to the windows. He drove the first hundred miles listening to a playlist she'd sent him and the last forty-five minutes with his windows down feeling the ocean breeze on his face as if she were sitting right next to him. It was one of his best memories made perfectly movie worthy when the lights and sirens appeared in his rearview mirror about fifteen minutes from Mitchell's Cove.

Officer Hernandez, then quite a bit younger, had requested license, registration, and proof of insurance. It was all painfully professional and Matt's heart was drumming in his chest with equal parts nerves and frustration at being so close to seeing her. As Matt impatiently waited for the inevitable ticket, Officer Hernandez informed him how fast he was going and asked why he was in such a hurry. It had felt pointless, glancing up into the officer's dark, almost machine-like, neutral face, his eyes invisible behind the standard-issue mirrored cop glasses, but back then Matt was more compulsive. He remembered rubbing his neck as he tried to decide how much to share, and also because one of the springs of his seat poked through the upholstery and into his back. Matt never missed that car, not one day.

"I'm sorry. I know it's wrong to speed, but I finished all of my finals and I'm excited to see my girl." He had tried to maintain eye contact even behind the mirrored shades. His father had drilled into him that eye contact was the key to winning a person over and when Officer Hernandez spoke again, Matt offered thanks to his dad.

"Understood. These turns can be tricky as I'm sure you know, Mr.... Locke"—the officer glanced at his license and then back at him—"so if you're planning a long life with this girl, you might want to take it easy." He handed back the paperwork with a stern nod followed by a smile.

Matt had been stunned. He sat waiting for something else: the reprimand, the call to his parents. No way it was this easy.

"You better get going. It's never good to leave a pretty girl waiting," he said and then patted the top of the Nissan.

"Yes, right, sir. Thank you." Since a cop was watching, Matt checked left and then right, exactly the way the driving manual had instructed, and pulled back out onto Highway 1. After kissing Hollis that night and then kissing her some more, he had told her all about being pulled over as they walked to the pier. Matt knew it was one of the few moments growing up when he'd looked at an adult and known they must have been a kid at one point too.

About a week into that summer, Matt had noticed Officer Hernandez's patrol car parked in one of the cutouts in the road near the 76 gas station one night. He brought him a cup of coffee and some of his mother's maple cake, and that was the beginning of their friendship.

Nothing too heavy, it was simply a mutual understanding of the journey every guy took toward becoming a man. Matt learned over time that Officer Hernandez was married to "the love of my life" and they had a son and a daughter both in high school too.

Matt stood facing Officer Hernandez on the other side of the counter and was struck by how many years had passed. He still slowed down when he saw that patrol car, but lately it was to wave. Matt wondered if Greg, that was his first name although Matt never used it, saw the years too, if he noticed that Matt had grown into — what exactly had he grown into? Annoyed at the tension his moment of reflection stirred, Matt returned to the present because most of the past, anything that took place in this little corner of the world at least, reminded him of her. It was an ache that had dulled to manageable but never quite went away.

"How was Ruby's wedding?" Matt asked, warming up the coffee cake.

"Great, she looked beautiful and I managed to get her down the aisle without disgracing the father-of-the-bride title."

Matt smiled. "I'm sure you made her proud."

"It's a tough business. I read some article that this guy in Florida started having a heart attack while he was walking his daughter down the aisle."

Matt's eyes widened.

"The man finished the walk, handed his girl to her fiancé, then walked to the side of the church and quietly called 9-1-1."

"Wow."

"I know, wedding heroes, right? Who knew?"

Both men laughed, and Matt handed him his coffee and cake. As was routine, Greg tried to pay and Matt wouldn't take his money.

"Thanks, Lead Foot." He turned back right before the door. "Hey, I noticed your girl is back in town."

Matt tried to smile, unable to meet his eyes. "She's not my girl anymore and you know it."

"Eh, you never know where that road out there will take you." Their eyes met and Officer Hernandez lifted his coffee cup in a toast.

"Tell her I said hello." He flipped his sunglasses down over his eyes, smiled, and was gone.

Matt shook his head and turned to wipe the counter.

His girl. Had Hollis ever truly been his girl? All these years and Matt still couldn't answer that question. It had seemed about as perfect as a love story could be, but great love should be effortless, shouldn't it? There was never anything effortless about Hollis and she eventually left him, or he stopped trying. Matt was never sure which it was and it certainly didn't matter anymore. Between Hollis arriving at the cove and his father coming home from surgery next week, things were bound to get complicated. Matt didn't do complicated. Even with his business back home, things were streamlined and he liked it that way. Poppy would be back part-time next week and he'd be closer to wrapping all of this up and getting back to a life he understood.

By the time the door tinkled again with arriving customers, Matt slipped the memory of a time so simple, so happy, back where it belonged.

Chapter Two

By Wednesday of the following week, Hollis was beginning to think that her days as a reclusive binge-eating drunk were numbered. Uncle Mitch might patiently humor her for a little while longer, but as she finished listening to a staff meeting, her head throbbed, this time thanks to a party-size bag of Doritos and a great bottle of Fumé Blanc. Hollis knew none of this was the answer. The cabin, the drinking, the pity party, none of it would get a Bob Marley-loving asshat named Zeke to fix his pigs. None of it would stave off her utter embarrassment should Dobbins Capital, the company she'd given her life to for the past eight years, find out exactly why they'd brokered tens of millions of dollars for Pretty Boy Games in the first place. She knew there wasn't enough wine, that all the junk food in the world wouldn't help, but she was stuck, more stuck than she had ever been in her entire life. She'd dropped her guard, and damn it, she knew better. Hollis had "taken her eye off the ball," as most of the men she worked with would say—the same guys who would be clamoring for her job once she was fired.

Fired. Holy shit, the mere word drove her to drink, but that was exactly what she would be if she didn't figure something out and quickly. Gently rubbing her temples and downing another two

Tylenol, she sent out e-mails to her assistant asking for follow-up on the three consultants Hollis had asked her to contact first thing on Monday.

The word "fired" ran through her head again as Hollis took a shower and pretended she was not already wondering how early was too early for wine. She needed a few more days to decompress, that's what she was calling it now, and then she would fix all of it. She would not be fired. That wasn't going to happen.

"Doesn't housekeeping come in here?" she asked later that day after the headache subsided and she ran a finger along the dust of her uncle's office bookshelves.

He sat propped back in his chair, feet up on a desk that appeared to be a gorgeous antique but for the fact that it was covered from corner to corner with more paper than Hollis had seen since 1998. *Did the man not know about scanners, shredders, electronic anything?* Uncle Mitch was reading an invoice, or something that looked like an invoice on an almost transparent piece of pink paper, and eating an apple clutched in his other hand. "No. Housekeeping doesn't come in here. They will eventually, but I need to go through some stuff first. I'll get to it. You know anything about space heaters?"

Hollis pushed the scraggly-looking cat that appeared to have come from nowhere off the one other chair in the room, an armchair with green velvet upholstery and twirled wooden arms, and sat. "Space heaters, as in, having a backyard party on a chilly night?"

"Yeah, I'm thinking we should order some for the patio so we can fit more people during the busy season."

"Okay, are you finding you need more room? Do you have long waits for dinner?"

"No." He took another bite and tried to catch the juice trickling down the side of his mouth with the back of his hand.

Hollis was confused. "If you don't have an unmanageable wait, then I'm not understanding the need for extra space."

"I think it would be cool to have people outside at night."

"That's another thing entirely. If you're buying the heaters as an added benefit to your customers, then it's what the business world calls a 'loss leader.' Which, depending on your clientele, could be a great move. For example, if you are pushing a certain dish, the ambiance of outside dining could be a win-win and you'll make up the initial outlay for the heaters. What's your marketing strategy?"

Her uncle sat up, apple between his teeth, looking like one of those luau pigs on the postcard her sister Meg sent her from Hawaii a couple of years ago.

"My what?" he asked through the apple.

Hollis shook her head and grabbed a stack of papers sitting on the small table next to her. "Honestly, sometimes I'm not sure how you keep this place going." Scanning the top bill in a paper-clipped group of maybe eight, Hollis noticed the stamped red warning. "This is sixty days past." She flipped through the others. "All of these are."

Her uncle leaned over as if to check which stack she had, finished his apple, and threw it in the overflowing trash can by his desk. "Those are set-asides."

"What is a set-aside? Before you start considering heaters, I think these need to be brought current, don't you?"

"Yes. Set-asides are the bills that can be paid online, or more accurately, they prefer to be paid online. I need to get them loaded. I bought a new computer." He stood gesturing to the still-unopened box behind his desk. "It's taking me a minute to get it set up. I'm on it, though." He took Hollis by the arm. "Now, let's find something for you to do. We need to get into the storage unit and start airing out the umbrellas and summer seat cushions."

"When?" She stood, bills still in hand.

"Well, ideally, I'd like to get all of it aired out today. The spring and summer stuff was put away after the season and we have Party on the Pier in two days so—"

"I'm not talking about the stupid seat cushions. When are you going to get things set up and those bills paid? Some of these are suppliers. Aren't you concerned they'll cut you off?"

"No." He took the stack of bills from her hand, set them on his desk, and guided her from his office.

Few people "guided" Hollis, but her Uncle Mitch had a way about him that made things feel like a fun dance rather than a directive.

"Why not let me worry about that, okay? What you need to do is get the key to the storage unit. It's on the SpongeBob SquarePants key chain right behind the register in the restaurant."

"Don't you think my particular skill set would be better served by helping you with the business end of things?" she asked as they walked out onto the patio that joined the office and the dining area.

Surrounded by the mid-afternoon warmth, Uncle Mitch pretended not to hear her, something he'd perfected when she was a little girl, although friendly ignoring was usually reserved for Hollis's father. Uncle Mitch and his younger brother had been complete opposites, at least in the ways a young girl would notice. Her uncle's hair was a couple of inches past his collar and he rarely wore socks while her father had a standing every-six-weeks appointment with his barber and Hollis could count on both hands the number of times she'd seen her father's feet. They shared the same mother, which was about all they had in common.

"I'm sure you spend enough time with computers. Seat cushions are what you need. I need them too, so what was it you said back there? It's a win-win."

"I came down here because Mom made me and now you want me to be some… seasonal helper? How about I go back to my cabin, pretend the sink in the kitchenette isn't dripping incessantly, and return to my fermented grapes. That, my dear uncle, is what's referred to as a win-win."

"That sink is on the repair list. I'm—"

"On it?" Hollis raised her eyebrow.

"You always were a smart-ass, ya know. Repairs are done every other week. I think this is the off week for that. I found a new maintenance guy and he gave me a schedule. It's somewhere."

"Did he e-mail it to you? Do you want me to contact them and ask—"

"Nah, you won't have time for that. There are tons of cushions."

There were three couples having lunch and one man sitting at the bar when Uncle Mitch pulled her into the cool air-conditioning of the restaurant. Reaching behind the bar, he produced a single key attached to a yellow plastic square with eyes and tiny legs. Hollis had heard of SpongeBob but had never actually seen him. As Uncle Mitch handed her the key, she wondered if there would be a SpongeBob question on her quarterly skills assessment review at Dobbins. Or if there would be anything at all from her little let's-play-high-school-summer-job experience. *Doubt it. This whole thing is a mistake.*

Running away from commitments never solved anything. Years of parental lectures had taught her that. Besides, it was the middle of the week. She should be back at home ordering her usual veggie on dark bread with half the hummus from that take-out place with the tiny daisy in their logo. She should be eating at her desk, doing all that was possible to keep from becoming a ridiculous cliché. Having shunned female contemporaries for wearing their skirts too short or flirting during budget meetings, Hollis imagined the fun they'd have if she couldn't find a way to fix this, if the whole ugly mess came out.

She needed to get back, and she would be ready soon. Maybe next week she would be... less stuck. It had been over a month and she thought by now she would be pushing back through the imposing glass doors of Dobbins Capital with a great tan and a fail-proof plan, but instead, she currently had an uneven sunburn, was wearing the same shorts she'd slept in, and was nowhere near even a maybe-could-work plan.

"All right, so you're going to go up Miller and take a left before you get to the laundromat. Treasure Chest Storage is two streets past, on the left," Uncle Mitch said right when Hollis was wondering if it had been two or three days since her last shower.

"Treasure Chest? I thought it was Store More?"

"Used to be. New owners."

"Dumb name." Hollis took the key dangling from his finger.

He shrugged. "Maybe you can help them with their marketing plan."

She rolled her eyes. "How am I getting there?"

This time, he pulled a full set of keys from the front pocket of his teal shorts embroidered with what looked like marlins or swordfish.

Where does the man find these clothes?

"You can take the truck." He pointed through the door to a truck that looked like something an antique shop might put out front to hold flowerpots or a sign announcing a sale.

"That runs?"

"She's perfect, but third to fourth is a little sticky, so be kind." He threw her the keys and Hollis caught them. He smiled.

"Why do men insist on referring to their cars or trucks as women?"

"Well, I suppose for some men it's because they ride —"

"Oh, wow, I'll stop you right there." She walked through the blue paint-chipped screen door that slammed on the rumble of her uncle's springtime laughter.

Matt disconnected from a concept meeting that had gone thirty minutes too long. He missed work—the hum of his office and even his partner's bad jokes. Matt looked at his phone, and it no longer mattered what he was missing because he was late. Poppy was back today and they'd hired a new employee she insisted on training when they'd spoken on the phone last week. He said he would be there to help handle the morning rush, so Matt grabbed his keys.

His parents had hired Poppy almost three years ago. She'd worked as a mechanic with Eddie at the garage, so when Matt's mother told him they hired her, he was surprised. According to his parents, once Poppy and Eddie were married, she decided for the sake of their marriage that she couldn't work with him anymore. While Matt had questioned why someone with her automotive skills would choose to make coffee, his mother said, "She's ready for a change," so they'd hired her and she turned out to be "the best manager we've ever had," his father had raved one night when Matt was over at their house for dinner.

Poppy was about ten years younger than Matt, almost another generation, which was particularly glaring when they were talking music or social media. She had a tattoo of a campfire with a stick and a marshmallow on her shoulder blade. It was visible when she wore a tank top, which was basically all the time. Matt's parents didn't seem to mind. He liked that about them. As far as parents went, his had been cool. The fact that they were in the service industry, and coffee no less, kept them connected with people. They enjoyed sharing stories and being that place where people gathered. Everyone was accepted, appreciated even, within the walls of The Bean locations. Once they were at home, though, with their own son, that same open acceptance was in short supply.

The Bean was laid-back, open, and surprisingly airy for such a small space. The exposed ductwork and weathered concrete walls gave it an urban feel in a beachside town of less than six hundred. Of his parents' ten locations, "the cove," as they'd come to call it, was his favorite. The building used to be the garage of one of the great houses built into the hill on the non-ocean side of Highway 1. The house burned down in the fifties, but the separate garage survived. It was used to store materials when the demolition team removed the charred house and allowed the natural vegetation to grow over, but once the work was done, the garage was left vacant. Matt's parents bought the space in 1992 from the preservation society that now owned the land. Matt was ten and practically grew up shuffling back and forth when his parents could get up from the city during the remodel of the garage and the initial opening. Once things were up and running, they would come to the cove for most of the summer while his father managed his new "baby" and made sure it was as successful as the others.

Each location had been the same; his childhood was speckled with memories of falling asleep on couches while his parents painted or getting up early before school and waiting while his dad opened one of the shops because some "damn college kid" hadn't shown up for work. The smell of coffee and the copper shine of the espresso machine came to mean home, but Matt had never wanted to go into the family business, no matter how successful.

Once accepted by Stanford, early decision, Matt wanted to be the "next big thing" in the tech world. His parents were less than delighted, and it was never made clearer than when Matt's father coined the famous Locke family phrase "Stanford Shmamford." At the time, it felt like a slap and Matt often wondered if that moment was when he realized that hard work and extra effort didn't necessarily guarantee the gold star of approval. He wasn't one to blame, but it was possible that when instead of congratulations or "We're proud of you, son," his parents went on with life, business as usual. Matt had downshifted into the background again.

Hollis had told him over and over again he needed to "give it maximum effort" when they were in college, but what good would it have done him? Because of his career choices, his parents treated him as if he'd proclaimed he wanted to hunt aliens. They saw no point in going to a "fancy school" or learning how to "play with computers" when they'd built a perfectly good business for him to take over. It's possible that mentality took some of the wind from his sails.

By his freshman year in college, Matt was pursuing his dream alone, which was fine because he was technically an only child and he understood alone. His mother still sent care packages and Matt made friends. He met Bradley, his business partner, when he'd tried to cheat off Matt from the back row in Economics their sophomore year. Matt waited, hopeful his parents would eventually come around and even if they never did, he had Hollis.

She was already at Stanford a semester before Matt arrived because she'd finished high school in three and a half years, graduated valedictorian. Matt smiled even though his chest thumped at the memory as the morning fog burned off and he walked up the hill toward The Bean. She was something back then, a force that he'd never known before or since if he were honest with himself. Not sure how he'd allowed her back in, Matt made an effort to focus back on his parents.

Sondra and David Locke had done their best not to appear excited when he dropped out of college, and they smiled at the ribbon cutting when he and Bradley opened Pilot Programs, but his father remained a little scratchy because things hadn't worked out the way he planned. Recently, though, they were happy Matt had "taken an interest," as his mother explained it to his father. *Was there a choice this time around?*

Truth be told, he'd always found their business interesting; it probably shaped him, making him the kind of person to want his own company one day, but that commonality was never enough for his father. He wanted a "coffee man" for a son, he'd exclaimed to their neighbors during a block party Matt attended while home from college for a visit. Matt had brushed him off with humor but had often wondered if things might have been easier had his brother survived to share the responsibility, and more importantly, the guilt… if John would have grown into the type of man capable of filling their father's relentless need for a coffee heir.

"Hey there, boss man," Poppy said.

Matt balked at the title but was grateful for the diversion away from memory lane. He walked into the morning energy of people on their way to work or the beach and some customers already plugged in at the tables scattered around. He joined Poppy behind the counter.

"Are you hopped up on espresso yet?"

"Already on the second round," she said, blinking her eyes as if she was one quiet moment away from a nap.

"Not sleeping?"

"What's sleep?"

Matt helped take orders until there was a lull and Poppy pulled out her phone to show him pictures of the adorable and super tiny baby Hannah. As Poppy flipped through photos, his eyes locked onto a picture of Hannah asleep on Eddie's bare tattooed chest. Matt took the phone from Poppy and tried to smile while something wiggled its way open in his chest. There was a look in Eddie's eyes and for a split second, Matt tried to picture his life cluttered with toys and visits to the park. It felt like a memory and a brand new sensation all rolled into one. Matt found a polite smile and nodded to Poppy as he handed back her phone.

"Wow, she's incredible."

Poppy beamed and slid her phone into the back pocket of her jeans before asking a balding man in front of them if he wanted a hot or iced latte. Matt turned away from her for a moment, his back to the forever-forming line of customers while his mind tried desperately to avoid the trap of "what if."

Chapter Three

The uneven wood of the floor creaked as Hollis stood barefoot before the full-length mirror that hung on the bathroom door. She had not put on a dress since well before she'd arrived at Tomales Bay. In fact, the one she was pulling over her just-showered and almost-finished-peeling body was purchased from a new shop she'd spotted on her way back from the storage unit the other day. It was cornflower blue and nothing about it said modern-day Hollis Jeffries, which might be why she liked it. Before she thought too much about it, she put on some lip balm, pushed her still-wet hair off her face, and looked around for her trusty flip-flops. They were by the front door, still sandy from her walk on the beach that morning. Wiggling her toes in the grit as she slipped them on, Hollis finished her glass of wine and grabbed a light sweater.

When was the last time she'd had her feet in the sand before arriving at Mitchell's Cove again? Why didn't she ever go to the beach or "frolic in the sun," as her mother would have put it? Hollis took in a slow breath and told herself this was no time for deep introspection. Uncle Mitch was counting on her to arrive early and help fill the ice buckets. *Ice buckets. Focus on the tasks at hand, Hollis.*

Despite her best efforts, stupid introspection returned as she stepped out into the surrounding blue of predusk. Maybe she shut off the things she couldn't control. Maybe the warm sand and steady waves were part of a time in her life when she was with him, and the moment she closed that chapter, life suddenly became too fast for flip-flops.

That was a shame, she thought, because while it was true that most of her memories of the cove were built around him and a broken heart had kept her away, the feeling she had walking along the path that led away from the cabins felt solitary. She'd grown up on this cove, spent lazy days with her parents and her sisters. Sure, she'd fallen in love, but she'd also learned how to sail and snorkel. She had read her first Jane Austen book on the patio of her uncle's restaurant while trying to avoid chores and made s'mores for the first time around a dwindling fire after her parents had hosted a clambake for visiting friends. Meg broke her wrist when she slammed it on the dock doing a cartwheel into the water. Hollis remembered running for help. She taught Sage to jump off the dock without holding her nose during their second summer and directed Annabelle's first puppet show in the restaurant after closing. There were life stories of her own that had nothing to do with him. Whether she had come here to escape or to find parts of herself she'd given up to become who she was now, she would need to remember that Mitchell's Cove was so much more to her than one person. No matter how important he had seemed at the time, it was fine that he was living here now, Hollis thought, because she was no longer a silly young girl.

The music grew louder as she approached the pier and saw the pops of light as they broke through the hazy mist. Hollis smiled, her cheeks warm from the wine, and felt the moisture seep into her pores like one of those balms they put on her anytime she was feeling stressed and went to her favorite spa in the city. This was better: more nourishing and free. Not much in her life was free anymore.

Party on the Pier took place the second Saturday of each month. The entire pier was flanked with colorful lights as local merchants set up tables, offering everything from barbecue to candy-covered pretzels. Dex and the Drowned Rats were warming up at the end of the pier behind a makeshift dance floor. Dex must be pushing sixty, Hollis thought as her uncle made eye contact and gestured for her to follow him into the kitchen.

POP, as the locals called it, went as far back as Hollis could re-member, and sometimes her family would make a special trip up on the off-season for the party. Hollis hadn't been to a POP for over twelve years, but she followed the pictures on Uncle Mitch's social media. From the safety of her city office, she'd seen two marriages during a May and June POP and a bon voyage for Laura Cray when she went to college three years ago. Last Christmas, there had been a Santa look-alike contest. Beards and bellies from all over the bay area came to compete, and Hollis had liked and commented on Uncle Mitch's Facebook post: a photo of him center pier surrounded by all the Santas.

Pictures were great, she thought, but as Hollis wheeled out a cart holding two large ice buckets, it hit her that she'd been away far too long. There was no substitute for standing on the pier as the sun burst rose and orange before dipping into the bay after a long sum-mer day. A photograph could not capture the feel of an ocean breeze or the salty taste of a kiss long overdue. Hollis jerked upright as she filled the bins with cold cans of soda and bottles of water and looked around, wondering if anyone could see the regret.

Hollis dried her hands and felt like a bit of a shame. She'd been away for so long that as the crowd began to gather along the pier and locals waved to one another, she didn't seem to belong. Like someone who'd crashed a party and was waiting to be tapped on the shoulder and asked to leave, she bowed her head, smoothed the red-and-white checkerboard tablecloth, and turned to face the water and that sunset she'd missed for so many years. Hollis wanted to announce that she knew the back roads that led to Bodega Bay and she remem-bered Pete's Fish and Chips before they had a patio. She felt a need to justify that she belonged, and despite her absence, she was still part of the history, the easy comfort of her cove.

Is that why you're here, is it the comfort, Hollis? There it was again, introspection. Who knows and who cares? Hollis thought, laughing at herself. None of this soul searching was going to get her where she needed to be, which was back on top, eye to eye again with her colleagues behind her imposing desk. She didn't need answers anymore; she needed a way forward.

First, she needed a drink.

"What's so funny?" Uncle Mitch asked, coming up next to her and handing her a plastic cup of lemonade.

Hollis looked down at the cup. "Nothing. I was thinking. I'm amazed Dex and his other lovely tatted-up contingent are still a band. This looks like lemonade." She tilted the drink toward him.

"Those guys are legends, and it *is* lemonade."

"It's well past appropriate drinking time."

Her uncle nodded and focused his attention on the band.

Hollis sipped her lemonade. It was sweet, tangy, and severely lacking a kick of something more. Her uncle was definitely hinting. If she wasn't careful, he'd start making her eat kale next.

"I see you've brought on some seasonal help, Mitch."

Hollis closed her eyes. She knew the voice, felt it way down in places she often ignored. Matthew Everly—middle name also his mother's maiden name—Locke came into her life the summer between fourth and fifth grade. He had skinny legs and wore navy-blue Vans with a hole in the toe. They had been paired up the first morning of Junior Sailing. Hollis had only sailed once before, but it still counted. Matt was a newbie.

"Have you ever done this before?" he had asked her, all big blue eyes and summer-bleached, overgrown brown hair.

"Have you?" eleven-year-old Hollis had shot back.

"No. I was hoping you were worse than me, though."

She had smiled politely and zipped up her life jacket in the way she imagined all the expert sailors did. "That will never happen."

His head tilted in confusion.

"That I'll be worse than you. Not gonna happen." She'd thrown a life jacket at him and stepped on the small Laser sailboat.

Matt turned out to be a more than decent sailor, and they'd been friends ever since. She would tell him later that his honesty was what first drew her to him. He had been drawn to her bite. "I love the bite," he'd said all the years she'd known him.

"Yeah, I brought in the top brass to help me out this season," Uncle Mitch said and patted Matt on the shoulder. "Tiny Tots here has an MBA. She's a big deal now."

Hollis cringed. She was sure she'd never heard "Tiny Tots" and "MBA" mentioned in the same sentence and hoped she never would again.

As if some gear had turned, they all faced the band, now well into the first guitar solo of the night.

Matt glanced at her. "So I've heard," he said, with a familiar charm the little hairs on her neck registered as dangerous. For as long as she'd known him, Matt had a warmth that drew people to him.

When she was a little girl, they'd lived in an old house in San Rafael. Her room had a big closet. One day, while playing hide-and-seek with Sage and Meg, Hollis had noticed a wire in the back of her closet. It was big and hung from the corner like a reluctant snake. No longer worried about the game, she stacked a few books and reached up to touch it, but before she made contact, she was frightened by the pull. That was how she described it to her mother moments later when she ran downstairs. It was as if the wire was pulling her in, daring her to touch it. The energy was palpable and it scared her so much she forgot all about her sisters, who were still hunting for her, and ran to find an adult.

Turned out the contractors had overlooked the wire and left it live with a voltage that could have killed her. Her father had frantically shut off the electricity, cut the wire back, and capped it as a precaution until the workers arrived the next morning. Hollis remembered her heart was still thundering almost an hour later at dinner. Part of her had wanted to touch it, give herself over to the energy even if it stole her life, but her mind, her common sense had kicked in just in time.

Matt was like that wire. A draw so enticing that the possibility of her heart stopping in her chest had not mattered. There was a time when what they were together meant more than anything she could ever be on her own. "You are my 'split-apart.' The half that makes me whole, Locke-ness," she had whispered to him one night when they'd pitched a tent on the beach and cooked chicken on the rocks over a fire. He was the great love, the big one they write epic romance novels about. That was, until once again her common sense kicked in and she ran.

"Good to see you without the fuzzy slippers this time, Holls. Where you been hiding?" he asked, oblivious to her memory.

Her jaw tightened and Hollis turned, ready to ask him why he wasn't behind his table serving coffee where he belonged, but when her gaze locked on his, she lost her words.

Matt's eyes should have been brown. Everything about his face said brown eyes, and yet indicative of the man himself, he was effortlessly given soulful blue eyes. In fact, all of the features on his face should have read average, ordinary. His nose was a little too wide, his eyes a little too big. He had small ears, noticeably small, but all of it together was more than she'd ever encountered in another man. She was her true self with Matt from the moment she'd met him. Unlike so many people she'd known in her life, Matt didn't lie. He was almost incapable because most of his secrets were right there in those eyes.

"I'm not hiding. I'm drinking," was all she managed. It was a weak comeback, but the heat off his all-too-close shoulder was not helping her find her bite. Obviously, the man could still piss her off and trip her up in equal measure. Hoping for some balance, she turned her attention back to the band because looking at him was certainly not the answer.

Matt laughed, the ass. "Is that so? Is that why you're here? Mitch, are you working a detox program for the upwardly mobile these days?"

Her uncle almost cracked up too, but instead turned and left as if he had something important to tend to.

"It's nice to know, along with everything else, that you haven't changed, Matt."

"Yeah, well you know us townies, we like consistency."

"Do you have something you need to get off your chest? Because I can recommend a top-notch therapist."

"We don't exactly have time for all of my issues, Holls, and besides, it's a party. No sense bringing down the mood." He took a sip of his drink, which looked way more exciting than lemonade and God, she could use some liquid courage right about now.

Turning to leave at the same time Matt did, Hollis found herself face-to-face with the one man capable of seeing right through her as the Drowned Rats began their version of "Barracuda." The corner of his mouth curled into the faintest snicker. "Now this song seems appropriate," he said, his mouth so close to her that had he not been so smug, she might have been tempted. Instead, her jaw again clenched in anger as she left and walked toward the edge of the pier. She felt him come up behind her, keeping his distance. Typical.

"Have you missed me?" she teased, because it certainly wasn't like anything she could say would make her life worse at this point.

"No."

Hollis laughed. "Fair enough."

They stood in silence surrounded by noise.

"How's married life?"

"Good."

He was surprised she knew. Under all his casual hands-in-the-pockets ease, after so many years, she could still read the paragraphs hidden in that one-word response.

"Did you think about me?" she asked because she found she wanted to know.

"Every day for a while."

"Me too, but then it fades, right?"

"No."

By the time Hollis turned, he was gone.

Seven of the eight cabins at Mitchell's Cove were named after dogs. Matt couldn't remember if they were all dogs owned by Hollis's grandfather or the family's dogs, but each one had a dog name, and weird ones like Miss Kitty and Lil' Earl. Matt never kept the names straight, but when the Jeffries were in town for the summer, they stayed in the Bunny Blue cabin. He would probably remember that forever. It was appropriately blue and next to the Innkeeper's Cabin where Mitch lived year-round. Earlier when Matt was setting up, he noticed Hollis wasn't staying in the usual family cabin. She waltzed out of the last one, farthest from the restaurant—it was green and called Mr. Boots maybe—wearing that practically see-through summer dress.

Why the hell did he even care? Other than the cabins, nothing else was the same. Except for her bite, that was still there. He'd expected it, looked forward to it even, but did she honestly ask him if he had thought about her after she left? Had she stood on their pier, dark curls teasing the tan bare skin his hands remembered, and asked him that? *What kind of sick, twisted—*

"Hey, Matt, where's the sugar?" Thom, the guy that did the landscaping for almost everyone in Tomales Bay, asked.

Matt was refilling the sugar while he replayed the conversation with Hollis over and over again. Screwing the top back on, he handed the sugar canister across the table.

As POP 2016 wound down, people stopped by for something to either sober them up or keep them awake until the Drowned Rats played their last song. Matt took orders, made coffee, and tried not to notice how the moonlight danced along the pier. When it reached Hollis, spilled along her bare shoulders, for an instant Matt wanted to be that light. Then he would have a reason to tangle in her hair, kiss all the spots she left exposed, and surround her in a glow that would captivate her once and for all. The line at his table dwindled, and Matt had nothing else to focus on except her. How could a woman who—if town gossip was right, and it often was—had been "boozing it up and stuffing her face with junk food in the Mr. Boots cabin at Mitchell's Cove" still be practically luminous? How was that fair?

Matt's father and Poppy normally worked Party on the Pier. He'd come up a few times to support his parents, but back then, the ease and comfort of the cove had turned sour and painful, so he often stayed away. That was years ago and things had healed somewhat, but he must have a death wish because he'd told Poppy to take the night off. It was better that he stay busy because he knew if there was the slightest chance, she would be drawn to the pier like the proverbial moth to the flame.

Party on the Pier was a good time, and Matt loved the energy of the event even if it reminded him of Hollis. The first time he had danced with her was at POP. So was the last time, he realized as he stood watching her now. Stupid fool, but he couldn't help it.

Hollis finished up dancing with her uncle and made her way toward him. He didn't think she'd bother coming around again, but he should have known better—she'd never been one to leave a conversation hanging. She hadn't put him in his place yet, which meant she wasn't done. Matt pretended he didn't see her and started packing things up for the night.

"Ahem." Hollis stood in front of his table as if she were any other customer. Matt adjusted his mental armor and looked up. It had never mattered how long they were apart; Hollis Jeffries stole his breath.

"So was it a total crash and burn or simply a temper tantrum?" he asked, hoping to start a fight because that was easier than swirling in the way she smelled or the way the breeze twisted her hair across her cheeks.

"What?"

Her jaw clenched—the tiniest dent below her cheekbone gave it away. In that moment, Matt went from grown man to stupid teenager. "What brings your fine city ass back to our little neck of the bay?"

"Woods, neck of the woods."

"Yeah, I modified it."

"Dumb."

"Thanks. So?"

"I... will not be discussing... anything with you."

She was almost pulsing with agitation and, for reasons Matt would need to examine another time, it was thrilling to have her right in front of him all pissed off. He fed the fire. "Huh, so total crash and burn. That's what I thought."

Her stormy gray eyes he would know anywhere narrowed into a piercing glare. "Do I look like an idiot? Forget it. Don't answer that. I know what you're doing. You think if you get me all riled up that I'll blabber on and make a fool of myself."

Matt shrugged. "Still worried about what people think, Holls?"

"Grow up. Junior high is over. I'll have an espresso."

"Funny, I figured you for espresso."

Her brow furrowed. "Um, because it's been my drink since I was sixteen."

"You didn't drink espresso at sixteen."

"Yes, I did."

He shook his head.

"Where is my drink?" Hollis leaned forward as if he was hiding it somewhere, and the sun-soaked smell again put a chink in the armor.

Matt handed her a small paper cup, but when she reached for it, he didn't let go. "You drank a small Americano with a splash of whole milk. You never drank espresso straight. You must have needed something a little stronger for your new life."

"Water and milk. Same thing."

"No, very different."

"The base of the drink is the same. Why are we arguing about this?"

"Because your drink is different."

Hollis sipped and then shook her head. "This is some of your symbolism garbage, isn't it? I'm different. That's what you're trying to say, right?"

He shrugged again. If it was true some things never changed, she still hated his shrug.

"You too, you're different too."

"How so?"

"You used to be honest. Instead of picking at me, come out with it. What is it you have to say?"

He smiled. "We should probably leave dead dogs where they are."

"It's let sleeping dogs lie. They're not dead."

"Whatever."

"Thanks for the drink." She downed the last bit of espresso, crumpled her cup, and turned to leave.

"Are you happy, Hollis?"

When she turned back to him, for an instant he thought he saw pain, but then it was gone. Their eyes held until it seemed she couldn't take it anymore. Hollis was probably born tough and from what he read and heard from colleagues, she'd gone on to become an incredibly successful negotiator. He had never known her to back down, but something was different. Something buried deep came to the surface, and then the unspeakable happened— she let him win.

Christ, Holls, tell someone what's wrong.

She nodded in answer to his question but said nothing.

"I'm glad." Matt dropped his gaze and continued folding up the tablecloth as she walked away.

Apparently, she had pinned him perfectly too. He no longer dealt in honesty.

Chapter Four

*H*ollis hosed off the tables on the patio of the restaurant the following morning. It was cloudy, and the white-capped dark blue bay stood in contrast to the sunshine-speckled ripples of the day before. She found the ocean fascinating, whether it was the vastness of the open sea, the powerful crash of high tide, or the tucked-away wonder of a small inlet. The ocean had so many faces, so many lives, and yet everything was connected, made from the same salty water she'd splashed at her sisters when they were young.

The wind picked up and water from the hose sprayed her feet. There was no point in washing the deck anymore if it was going to rain. She turned the water off and coiled the hose. Uncle Mitch was at his new computer, which was no longer in the box. Hollis could see him through the office window off the shared patio. She thought about marching into his office to make sure he knew how to organize his e-mail and she wanted to show him the schedule she'd been working on with the staff, but instead, she stopped and pulled the bag from the trash barrel by the patio door. She tied it then noticed the checkered tablecloths now bundled and tied together sitting on one of the patio chairs.

As rain began freckling the ground, Hollis grabbed the dirty bundle of linens with one hand and the trash in the other before she turned back to the office window. It had never before occurred to her that a person or place wouldn't benefit from her involvement one way or another. She'd invariably assumed her way was the best and that most people needed her help. As the rain started coming down faster, Hollis stood for a moment, a bit transfixed, watching her uncle pecking away at his new computer in the warm golden light of his desk lamp. The sky darkened and she wondered if anyone truly needed her or if that was a story she told herself.

Hollis shook her head because she was being absurd. Of course she was needed: she had a master's in business, people loved her and if they didn't love her, they feared her, which was great too. She heaved the trash bag into the dumpster. That was the problem with this place, she thought, too much time for feeling and thinking. And now it was getting wet. There was nothing more melancholy than a perpetually sunny summer place drenched in rain. The sky opened up and it began to pour. Hollis ran inside the restaurant and was grateful Party on the Pier had made it under the wire, not that it would ever be canceled on account of rain. Save the time that Benny, the volunteer fire chief, collapsed with a hernia, Party on the Pier was a rain-or-shine tradition.

The years she'd stayed away continued circling through her mind like some kind of sweeping epic with its own soundtrack. Her last summer had been 2004, or the beginning of the end, as she had come to call it. At first, she and Matt played like nothing had happened that summer, but no matter how many times they'd walked the pier or taken a drive, she couldn't find her way back to what they were or the focused young girl she was before. After less than a month at the cove, Hollis couldn't take it anymore and returned home early. She had applied for early graduation and left Stanford the following December. The last time she saw Matt before this summer, he'd looked like a man standing too close to a cliff's edge. He loved her—that's what he'd said—he wanted to be with her for the rest of his life—he'd said that too—but when she told him she didn't know how they would work, that things would never be the same, she would remember forever the way his big blue eyes glossed over.

"If you don't want this, Holls, then go find what makes you happy. I want you to be happy." At the time, it had seemed like a get out of jail free card, but by the following month when she'd moved into her own place in San Francisco, she began to wonder how it had all been so easy for him. Why hadn't he demanded she stay? Why hadn't he fought for them? Hollis grinned at the thought of him demanding anything as she took a seat and watched the storm from the comfort of a brown leather chair cozied around the fireplace in the restaurant. Matt didn't work that way, he never had. He was the guy who started off studying and fizzled by the end of the semester. He was up for anything so long as there wasn't drama or too much effort involved. They were quite a pair back then. She never asked for anything because she was her own one-woman juggling act, and he never offered much past what was comfortable.

Hollis became more driven than ever once she moved back to the city. After a year of working as an entry-level analyst, she returned to Stanford and earned her MBA. She'd lived off campus and purposely avoided places that reminded her of Matt and their life together. She completed her master's in just over a year and started interning for Bridgewater Capital. It was a small firm and Hollis was a sponge, soaking up each opportunity. She'd lived her life with such single purpose for the last twelve years that it almost felt like a blur. Kind of like when someone, after a tragic accident, says the last thing they remember was leaving the house. Maybe not quite that dramatic, but all Hollis knew for certain was that after she left Matt, things were shaky for a while and then it was like a switch went off somewhere. She "was the job," she told every boss she'd ever had, but now, as she curled her legs under her and heard the first crack of thunder, Hollis wasn't even sure what that meant. How could a person be a job? People weren't jobs, were they?

"Did I ever tell you about the time your dad and I went camping?" Uncle Mitch set a tray with two cups and a pot of coffee on the iron table next to her that doubled as a magazine rack. He took a seat in the leather chair opposite her and poured.

"Which time?" Hollis asked with gentle sarcasm she was sure her uncle would miss. She wasn't in the mood for a chat but took the offered cup anyway.

"The one where we... ya know, I might as well tell it again."

Hollis shook her head. "Might as well," she said, still mocking as she added some cream.

"Does anyone work here?" A guy in navy-blue shorts and bad top-siders stood near the hostess station across the open dining room. His haircut was too short on the sides, Hollis noted, and he should have rethought tucking his shirt in. The guy looked like an asshole, even in the rain, which was hard to do. Most people looked vulnerable, a little wet-puppy in the rain. Not this guy. Hollis had fine-tuned and reliable asshole radar. Sure, it had malfunctioned a few months ago, leading to what her boss had started calling the "debacle," but her radar was working now and it was definitely ringing alarms with this guy.

"No," Hollis answered back, projecting across the empty space, then took a sip of her coffee.

Uncle Mitch snickered under his breath as he stood and promptly ran to help the man right as the shock of Hollis and her smart mouth started to wear off and Asshole's scowl turned to rage. He reminded her a little of Liam from Pretty Boys Gaming, the company Zeke owned with two of his friends. That name, she thought now, and the stupid sweaters he wore. *Radar must have been broken with that one, huh?* Hollis sighed because hindsight was, in fact, crystal clear.

"Maybe we should keep you in the office after all," her uncle said when he returned, still smiling.

Hollis held up her coffee mug in a toast. "I could probably work myself to friendly, but I'd need some Kahlua in this coffee and I'm on the wagon. Don't you have a hostess?"

"We're in between lunch and dinner. It's never busy so I can handle it myself."

"If I were being Ms. Hollis Jeffries instead of Tiny Tots with the ass of my shorts still wet from the rain, I would advise that you are not adequately staffed and that no customer, no matter how bad his haircut, should be waiting around or asking if someone works here."

"Yeah, well thank God you are, Tiny Tots."

"I'm serious. I've been here for a few days."

"Over a month."

"Whatever. Why do people keep bringing that up? A month is not a lot of time."

"Time flies when oatmeal cookies are involved."

"Pies, oatmeal cream pies, and there's a difference. Anyway, I've noticed things are a little shabby around here. Are you having trouble?"

"Shabby is *in* around here. No one wants completely together, it's the beach and these are cottages."

"I disagree. Guests may want the feel of shabby, but they still want soft sheets, great pillows."

"What's wrong with our sheets?" Uncle Mitch poured them both more coffee.

"Nothing if I'm in a dorm room or camping in the woods. Your cabins aren't cheap, so I think some upgrades may be in order. After you pay those late bills, that is."

"Okay, well we can look at that, maybe add it to our action plan."

"Look at you, remembering it's not called a thingamadoodle."

Her uncle nodded. "Yeah, well some terminology never dies, no matter how hard I try."

Hollis was curious. "What did you do before you took over these cabins from Grandpa?"

Sipping his coffee, her uncle met her eyes. "I was in the circus."

She nodded and saw something in his eyes that for the first time had her wanting to hug him instead of the other way around, but he looked out at the rain and the look was gone.

"Because if money is tight, I'm sure Dad will—"

"Your dad never wants to deal with this place. His ass has been in a twist ever since I said I didn't want him to redesign all the cabins. They don't need to be redesigned. Maybe they need a little TLC, and we can work on that."

"Do you have investors?"

"Tots, put the briefcase away. I'm fine."

Hollis sipped her coffee, which was delicious now that she bothered to taste it. Coast Roast. Matt's dad roasted the best coffee ever and with each sip, Hollis wished she hated coffee. Even something as simple as a cup of coffee had a memory attached to it. Hollis closed her eyes and refused to let Matt back into her mind. She'd thought about him all last night while she pretended to sleep. By the time the sun rose, she was all thought out.

"What was I saying? Oh right, the camping story."

Uncle Mitch rambled on in exuberant animation while Hollis laughed and realized she hadn't done enough of that before coming back to the cove. *Is there much to laugh about in your life, Hollis? Great. You can shut up now, Introspection.*

Mitch stood and went to the front of the restaurant once more to give directions to a young girl in a pink slicker drenched from the downpour that looked as if it might be letting up soon. When he returned and finally finished the camping story, Hollis was rewarded with the lesson that "sometimes rain is a gift." She thanked him for that little "pearl of wisdom" and made a mental note to grab one of the small brown bags of coffee from behind the bar for her cabin. She added to that note that she needed to laugh more. Coffee and laughter, maybe that's what Zeke and his chi needed too. She highly doubted it. The sun parted through the dark cotton sky as Hollis returned to the back patio and waited for her uncle to dream up more "tasks."

Matt was never sure if he loved Tomales Bay or San Francisco Bay more. When he was in high school and hell-bent on picking a favorite, his mother said he didn't need to choose. "Each bay speaks to a part of you. Both are important." He supposed she was right. As he crossed over into the city, he realized if Tomales filled him up, San Francisco emptied him out. He'd woken up early having promised his mother he would help get his dad settled after hip surgery. It was raining, which Matt normally enjoyed, but his father would no doubt arrive cursing everything, including the rain. After stopping for bagels and grabbing a few stems of lilacs from the flower vendor up the street for his mother, Matt unlocked the front door of the home he'd grown up in, a brownstone on King's Street in the Potrero Hill section of San Francisco. He shook off his coat and hung it on the hook by the door.

His father loved to say they lived in the "last quiet part of the city" and his mother often commented that they had "a sprinkling of gay couples, which added some style to the neighborhood, but not overboard like the Castro District." His parents were born and bred in San Francisco and while he'd never known them to be politically correct, they had tremendously open minds for their age and they were good people. Matt picked up the mail that had been strewn in the entryway after being pushed through the brass mail slot. He pulled back the curtains from the front window where his mother's orchids sat on a semicircular table. She had three orchids and swore the reason they weren't dead like her friend Sibi's was because she talked to them and was sure to water them every ten days. "Sibi waters hers too much. Rots the roots right off the poor babies," she often said.

After dropping the bagels off in the kitchen, putting the flowers in water, and pushing the button on the coffee maker, Matt returned to the living room and noticed they'd finally replaced his dad's La-Z-Boy with a new and improved leather model. He smiled and thought about his father, how much he'd likely hated being in the hospital and undoubtedly aggravated each staff member he came in contact with to ensure a speedy discharge. Matt had no idea what to expect or how much pain his father was going to be in. Maybe he should have brought lunch too. Taking his hands from his pockets, he climbed the stairs caged by a yellow-and-oak banister. Right before he reached the second-floor landing, he remembered his mother telling him the cleaners had set up the room off the dining room as a bedroom for his father until he was healed and able to climb to their bedroom again.

The idea of spending more than a passing hour with his father was unnerving to begin with, but right after surgery, it would probably prove to be close to fatal. Matt felt guilty the minute the thought entered his head, but not before acknowledging it was the truth. Before he could check on things in the makeshift bedroom, he heard the taxi pull up at the side door off the kitchen. Matt had a contractor turn the three side steps leading from the alley to the house into a small, low-incline ramp. It would be weeks before his father could climb the front steps on his own, the doctor had said, and Matt didn't want him embarrassed by someone having to carry him. Thankfully, the clouds had parted when he opened the side door.

"What in sweet Jesus is this?" his father's voice bellowed from outside the house.

Matt looked down. *Let the grumbling begin.*

"Are you responsible for this?" he barked, looking pale and visibly worn out from the short trip home.

"I told him to. Now stop it and put both hands on the walker. Be careful, it's slippery." His mother rolled her eyes at Matt and helped guide her husband toward the ramp. After a stumble and several complaints, they arrived at the landing.

"Good to have you back, Dad." Matt gave him a one-handed hug as his mother took a picture of them in the doorway on her iPhone.

"I'm sure. Now you can get back to your penthouse," his father grunted as if he were saying something under his breath, but it was loud enough for all to hear.

Matt stood back to allow him into the house.

"Aw, Matty, you bought bagels and lilacs." His mother put a black bag down and leaned in to smell the flowers. "Thank you, honey," she said in soft contrast to the grumbling and kissed him on the cheek. Her hair was a little shorter and she smelled like soap—she usually did.

Right as Matt was going to comment on her haircut, his father declared, "I'm going upstairs to rest."

"Oh no"—she took three large strides toward him and gently turned the walker—"we set you up down here."

"In the servants' quarters?"

His mother smiled. "We don't have servants' quarters. Doctor says you can't climb stairs until he sees you back in his office, so you're in there until next Tuesday."

Huffing and shaking his head slowly, his father hesitantly walked toward the small room at the back of the house. Matt felt a tinge of pity for his father. He was a big man, but he'd lost weight and was so frail at the moment. Of course, Matt knew his dad would be back in "fighting shape," as he liked to say, in no time. It was hard to see him down since most of Matt's childhood memories were of his father working, and working hard. If something needed to be done at one of their shops, it didn't matter what time of day or what he was doing, his father would get it done. Birthday parties, Sunday dinners, Matt's own rehearsal dinner the night before his wedding: if something needed to be dealt with, his father dropped everything. It was a work ethic, his mother had often claimed to soften any sense it was an obsession, but now that Matt was older, he understood. His parents had ten shops; that didn't come easy.

"How about I help you get settled?" Matt grabbed his father's bag off the table and started to follow behind.

"Nah, I'm not an invalid. Sit with your mother," he said over his shoulder, one hand lifting quickly off the walker to dismiss him.

They would surely have to help him into bed, but he let him go for now.

"Why do you back down?" his mother asked, pulling some prescription bottles from her purse and pouring a glass of water.

"From him? I wasn't aware there was any other way to deal with Dad. I'm not going to beg him or be somewhere I'm not wanted."

"Did you ever think sometimes people don't realize they need you? That it's your job to help them figure that out?"

"No." Matt stuck a bagel in his mouth and sat at the kitchen table.

"Well, it's true. Your father is stubborn. He doesn't realize he's vulnerable."

"Correction. I'm a huge disappointment because I went out and made money, a sin worse than all sins, except maybe divorce, which I've also managed. So, I think it's best if we try to tolerate each other because I'm his only child, only son, and"—his mother quietly gasped—"his only *living* son, sorry, Ma. So he doesn't even get a do-over with another kid. It's a tragic tale."

"Stop it. Your father is very proud. He's not—"

"Good at showing it. Right. I seem to attract people with that particular block."

His mother shook her head, put some pills in her hand, and took the water into his father's makeshift room. When she returned, she sat across from him at the small table. "How are things at the shop?"

"Good. I've added some new pastries and a couple of prints I had made of the roasters. Poppy is back part-time."

"She sent me pictures of the baby. So precious."

Matt could feel the baby talk coming on, as it often did with his mother. "When are you going to get married again?" "I wish I had some grandchildren." He decided quickly to cut that off before she even started.

"She is a beautiful baby. I should get going. Do you need me to help you get him into bed?"

She shook her head. "The nurse will be here in a little while and I can handle your father. Thank you for the flowers and for opening the house."

"You're welcome. I'll call you later." Matt kissed his mother on the cheek, put his coat over his arm, and closed the door behind him.

He'd done what he was asked to do and nothing more. Leaving before polite conversation turned into a list of his shortcomings was self-preservation, and he couldn't control his father any more than he could control the weather. As if on cue, the sun burned through the clouds and Matt climbed into his car.

Chapter Five

Hollis remembered Patty Cranston became addicted to her mother's prescription pills their sophomore year in high school. Her dad was said to be some kind of music producer and she'd started clubbing early in life. Hollis never hung out with Patty and at the time thought for sure the story was mostly rumor. But she did remember Patty was sent to a rehabilitation hospital called The Happy Orange something-or-other. It was a "positive" place for teens with addiction and once Patty was clean, she started sending pictures to her friends back at school and saying the program had "saved" her life.

Standing on the back patio of the Innkeeper's Cabin, paintbrush in hand, Hollis began to wonder if she was at the grown-up version of The Happy Orange because this had turned into some kind of rehab program.

"You're dripping," her uncle said.

"Oh, sorry." She felt the droplet of paint squish between her toes. Hollis set the paintbrush on top of the can of "Caribbean Sunset" paint and used a paper towel to wipe off her foot.

"Sage is getting married in Napa," she said, looking out over the water.

"I heard." Her uncle was propped back up again, this time with his feet on his teak table, reading the newspaper.

"In two months. I thought Garrett's sister would get married first. Isn't that how it works?"

He peeked over the paper. "How what works?"

Hollis picked up the paintbrush and started another slat. "The order of things. Makenna is Sage's friend. I've met her once. She's marrying Travis. He asked her before Garrett asked Sage, so shouldn't they go first?"

Mitch set the paper down completely this time and shook his head. "Hollis, I don't think there are rules for this sort of thing. Doesn't Kenna have a child?"

"Yeah, so?" She scooted the paint can over with her foot to reach the rest of the slat.

"Maybe that's a little more complicated. Why do you care?"

"I don't, but two months isn't long and I'm not sure if that's enough time."

"For her or you?"

"For her. I'm fine." Paint dripped onto her toes again.

He tried not to smile and handed her another paper towel.

"Crap. Why the hell am I doing this?"

"You said you wanted to help." He leaned forward, resting his elbows on his knees as if he was watching some fascinating freak show.

"I said no such thing."

"Are you sure?"

"Positive. You set up this 'whole work around the place and do things other than my actual job.' I was perfectly fine in my cabin washing down my sugar with wine."

"I'm almost positive you offered to 'help out' when you arrived." He used the finger quotes and even though his T-shirt said, *Keep Calm and Paddle On*, she still wanted to punch him.

Hollis cursed when the paintbrush slid a little too far into the can and she got paint on her hands. "Two months. Can she even get a dress in that time?"

"I'm sure she can. Maybe she'll wear your mom's." He handed her the entire roll of paper towels this time.

She tried to figure out why the idea of Sage wearing their mother's wedding dress bothered her. It's not like she had plans to get married. Sage was welcome to it, wasn't she? *Maybe you want to get married? Oh shut up, will you? No more thinking.*

Uncle Mitch looked startled and concerned. This was it, she was talking to herself. More accurately, she was arguing with herself. If she was going to be carried off in the happy jacket, she might as well start drinking again, Hollis thought.

"Who's going to be her maid of honor?" her uncle asked.

"Both of us, Annabelle and me, which is stupid, don't you think?" Hollis plopped down at the table and felt a bit like a petulant child. She couldn't remember the last time she'd felt childish, happy, or otherwise.

"No. I think it's nice. What about Meg?"

"She's not going to make it, are you kidding? She's probably in some hut in the middle of nowhere. Especially since it's so soon. I think maybe I should tell Sage to postpone it."

He guffawed. "I love how you assume she would just do that because you say so. Sure, postpone her happiness because you're in a funk... what happened to you back home, Tiny Tots? Are you ever going to tell me?"

"My stuff has nothing to do with this."

Eyes still on her, he waited for her to say more.

"Speaking of marriage, Matt is married. I'm sure you already knew that," Hollis said. The abrupt change of subject along with the shake in her voice rang pathetic as Hollis scrambled to discuss anything other than her failure. Of course, thoughts of Matt were right there waiting to leap from her mouth.

"I... did know that. Did he tell you he was married?" Uncle Mitch asked with an awkward expression usually reserved for secret keepers.

Hollis paused at his look. *What am I missing?* "I read about it in the newspaper."

"Oh, well, sure. Years ago. So, back to my question—Why are you here, Tots? What happened at work?"

Shit! Hollis glanced toward the bay as if there were answers out there. "It's a long story."

"I have a big patio, lots of fence to paint."

He gestured back to the paint can. Hollis glared at him and grabbed his iced tea from across the table.

"Let's start with this question: Were you fired?"

"No."

That was all she was willing to offer and the simple shift in conversation to her work, her reality, was all it took to make Hollis uneasy.

"Okay, you quit?"

"No. I've been working. I have my laptop. I needed to step back. Stress, it was stress." Hollis stood up, restless to do something other than sit there and be interrogated, but not wanting to paint. Giving in, she crouched to the paint can and started on the bottom part of the three slats she'd managed so far. Painting was definitely not one of her core competencies, as her boss would put it.

"Sure, let's go with stress for now. Do you remember that movie *The Karate Kid*?"

Hollis shook her head.

"Oh, it's a classic. Maybe we can rent it while you're here. This kid wants to learn karate because boys keep beating him up, so he goes to Mr. Miyagi and the guy puts him to work fixing things around his place. Sort of like this."

"Am I the karate kid in this little story?" she asked, wiping her forehead while trying not to get paint in her hair.

He nodded.

"I know a little karate." She returned to painting.

"Well, there you have it. I am Mr. Miyagi and you are the student. What was his name? Cute kid... Ralph. The actor's first name was Ralph. You can be him."

"Yikes. Will lunch be provided if I let you call me Ralph?"

"Sure. I'll feed you once you can catch a fly with my chopsticks." As he returned to his paper, Uncle Mitch looked amused with himself and his reference to a movie the majority of the world had probably forgotten.

Hollis painted in silence and against all logic, thought about whether or not she was happy. Damn him. "You happy, Holls?" What kind of question was that after all this time? She supposed she'd opened it up with her "Did you miss me?" stupidity, but that was a direct question. Happy was such a broad term. Was she happy before this latest screw up? She thought she had been, but with the warm sun on her face and paint ruining her one decent pair of flip-flops, she wasn't sure. Maybe she'd simply shut down and convinced herself she was happy.

Hollis shook her head. She needed to stop thinking before she turned into the homeless lady she often noticed on the Muni back home, complete with unitard and purple cowboy boots. Actually, she at least played a tiny ukulele and clapped for herself after each song. Hollis could barely paint a fence. When the last dribble of paint snuck down the brush and onto her wrist, she gave up.

"I need to get some work done, so karate kid is over until tomorrow."

"Internet is down."

"What? Why?" Hollis turned.

"I'm having a new router put in so the guys needed it down until about three."

"Why does it take that long?"

"Hey, you put it on the action plan." Her uncle stood and took the paintbrush from her. "Matt has Internet at the coffee shop." He raised his eyebrows.

Hollis huffed, returning to sulky-child mode, shook her head, and walked inside.

"Since you're going to be out, could you stop at Kerensky's and pick up my order?" Uncle Mitch called after her.

"What's in the order?" Hollis asked at the door.

"More paint and some varnish for the chairs. I can't remember what else, but he has it all boxed up for me."

"Sure." Hollis grabbed the truck keys hanging on a hook near the front door of his cabin and walked out. Needing the comfort of her laptop and hoping there would be good news any day, she tried not to panic. She was at least a few more weeks away from cowboy boots and a ukulele. Maybe.

Matt handed over control of the register to Poppy, who had just started her shift. He was emptying coffee grounds, a part of filling in that he liked because the smell reminded him of being young. A lot of things about being at the cove did that, reminded him that inside all of his important adult meetings and the trappings of a grown-up, he was still a kid who used to sweep behind the counter for ice cream money. Tying the bag closed, Matt glanced up when the bell jingled and the front door of the shop flew open.

Hollis walked, more like stormed, into The Bean with all her affected corporate purpose and Matt's warm, sentimental mood instantly turned to aggravation. She should have left Tomales Bay by now. Why was she still hanging around? The hesitant lilt of her voice when she asked if he'd missed her had been on repeat in his head. She was messing with him and Matt wasn't in the mood. When she took a seat at the table under the oversized clock, his mind somehow couldn't process adult Hollis in his parents' place. The one version that seemed right running through that door was sun-bleached, seventeen, and flinging herself into his arms. This woman was on a couple of IPOs away from complete bitch, and Matt imagined the furthest thing from her mind was getting anywhere near his arms. Fine by him.

"Do you have Internet in this place?" she asked, digging in her bag with self-importance, which was amusing considering she had what appeared to be paint on her shirt.

Matt finished wiping down the counter by the window, taking his time because he was confident it would piss her off. "We do."

Hollis pulled out her laptop and placed it on the table as if it were an extension of her arm and began tapping away at the keyboard.

"What? You need a password? Who still does that?" She looked at him with the wild eyes of someone rarely unplugged.

"We do."

Fingers poised midair, she raised her eyebrows like she could somehow command him that way. Matt returned two chairs to their original tables and picked up a straw wrapper off the floor.

"Are you going to tell me what it is?"

"Are you going to ask me nicely?"

"No."

He shrugged. "Then no."

Hollis shook her head as she dropped her hand to the table. "Fine. Locke-ness, could you please pretty please with extra caramel sauce on top, tell me the stupid password for your Wi-Fi, which was obviously installed before the new millennium?"

At the sound of the nickname she'd had for him, Matt froze, all potential jibes vanishing. He gave her the password and walked away.

Maybe today was a good day to count the sugar packets, he thought, rubbing the back of his neck. He joined Poppy, who was carefully sweeping crumbs off a display behind the counter.

"Who's that?" she asked, brushing her hands over the trash.

"Who?"

Poppy put her finger to her lips. "Hmm, let's see, the gorgeous brunette wearing the Tori Burch flip-flops. She didn't get those in this town and she was giving you an impressive death stare. One more time, boss man. Who is that?"

"Hollis Jeffries."

"Wow, she even has an out-of-town name. Hollis, it's different."

Spot-on choice of words. Matt willed himself not to entertain exactly how *different* Hollis was and instead continued chatting as if that would calm the racing of his pulse. "Your name is Poppy, that's different."

"True, but I have stretch marks and am still wearing an elastic waist. That hair is salon gorgeous disguised in a ponytail and I haven't seen you this electric, well, ever."

"I'm not electric. That's not even... what does that mean?"

Poppy rang up two people and turned to fill a ceramic travel mug with decaf. "Electric, sparky, alive I guess. She's someone, I can tell, because my hormone super powers are still raging."

Matt laughed and felt his shoulders loosen a little. "Her uncle is Mitch Jeffries. She used to come here with her family, probably long before you were even born. That's how I know her."

"So what happened with you two?"

"Why do you think something happened?" Tension returned. Poppy's eyes widened and she smiled.

"Those super powers are strong. We dated and broke up toward the end of college."

"Bad one?" She winced.

"Is there ever a good breakup?"

"Not really. Wait, she's Mitch's niece. Eddie is letting him keep her car in that small garage he has off the restaurant. I guess she was sort of messed up when she got here. Was that your doing?"

Matt shook his head and turned to look at Hollis. "I haven't seen her in almost twelve years. I'm in the clear."

"Huh, well, she looks incredible now."

Yes, she does, he thought but did not say. The line grew and Poppy was busy. Hollis's back was to him as she typed and spoke into the headphones dangling from her ear. Why the hell was she back, sitting in his coffee shop, still working, and looking like she was waiting for her overpriced lunch to be delivered from The Sentinel?

It wasn't his business. This was temporary for both of them, he kept reminding himself. Poppy would be back full-time in a couple of months and Hollis would surely sort out her situation by then, if not before, and be on her way. "She was sort of messed up," he heard Poppy's words again in his head. Whatever it was that brought her back must be powerful because he'd never managed in all these years to lure her back, not that he'd tried all that hard.

Hollis squeezed the cord and removed her headphones. Matt grabbed his coffee cup and, like those idiots on YouTube who try to feed a bear then wonder why they lose an arm, he went to sit with her.

"Are you ever going to tell me why you're here?" Matt drank his coffee and tried for the same casual tone he'd mastered when talking to potential clients.

"Probably not." Hollis didn't even look up from what she was typing.

"I guess that's better than a flat out no."

"Are you going to tell me about your wife?"

"No."

She looked up. "No probably?"

He shook his head.

"Any kids?"

"No."

"One-syllable answers, wow. You know the first year of my master's program I had this professor who preached if you wanted information from someone, you needed to be willing to share information. It was obvious advice and the class was boring, but somehow you're bringing it all back."

"Who told you?" he asked. He gripped his coffee cup with both hands because it felt like they were starting to shake.

"I read that you were getting married. There was an announcement, don't you remember? When was it? Like two years after we graduated?"

Matt knew it sounded sick, but when her sarcasm drifted briefly into pain, his heart felt somehow vindicated. Like it was possible he wasn't alone drowning in his stupid feelings.

"Two thousand and six," he answered, now looking into the last small pool of coffee at the bottom of his cup.

"Well, there you go. Didn't waste much time, did ya?" She returned to typing. "It's been great catching up, thanks for stopping by, now if you'll excuse me."

Matt stood, prepared to leave, but he quickly sat back down, desperate to relieve them both from the chill of the conversation. "I thought you would come back."

Hollis stopped typing but kept her fingers on the keys. Her eyes slowly met his and there she was, no corporate training or bitter wit. He was looking into the shining, shocked silver eyes of his Hollis, and then she was gone.

"You told me to be happy."

"I wanted you to be happy, but I thought you would go and then come back to tell me you couldn't do that without me. Eventually." He felt like his chest was going to cave in. He wasn't supposed to share this with her. Ever.

"Is that why you asked me if I was happy the other night? Because I never came back?"

Ding. Hollis hesitated for a minute, her eyes still on him, and then like an addict she checked her laptop screen.

With her focus somewhere else, Matt tried to back away from the whole conversation. "I guess. I don't know. Forget it. I'm glad you're happy."

Hollis closed her laptop. "Classic, Matt. Let's tie this all up with a nice bow so we don't need to deal with it anymore, right? You're in big trouble, buddy, because I can't even find the bow that goes around my clusterfuck of a life. How about this?" She leaned in and he could see the dare in her eyes. "No. No, I'm not happy. I'll do you one better. I don't even know what that means anymore. I thought I was following all the steps to happy, but it appears none of it has worked because when you're—" She shook her head and unplugged her laptop. Cords dangling, she made her way to the door then turned back. "Are you happy, Matt?"

"No," he said after a moment of hesitation. *She said she wanted honesty.*

"You should probably talk to your wife about that," she said and walked out.

Kerensky's Hardware made small-town hardware stores look big. Kerensky went by his last name. He was sort of like Madonna, if Madonna wore overalls, had a tape measure clipped to her pocket, and a wax pencil behind her ear. His store had three rows of old-school aisles complete with handwritten price signs and small plastic paint buckets fastened with zip cords to hold "odds and ends," as Kerensky often called them. The aisles were so narrow Hollis almost had to turn sideways, so the home improvement men who made up most of his clientele all but shimmied to the back service counter. They didn't seem to mind and she didn't blame them. It was impossible to care about a little scooting in a place that reflected such obvious character, complete with three wheelbarrows attached to the wall. When Hollis was little and her dad would bring her into Keren-sky's, she'd stare up at those wheelbarrows. Did he ever sell them, and if he did, how hard was it to get up there and unfasten them? She'd asked Kerensky one day and he explained that they were "For display, darlin'. The ones we give customers are in the back."

Standing at the back counter looking up at the wheelbarrows now, the little girl in her that she often kept tied up was still fascinated. *That's ridiculous*, she told the Hollis in her head, the one still in braids and braces. *Look at the sophistication of the businesses with which you currently work. We are talking about wheelbarrows hanging from a smudged white wall? Please, grow up.*

Kerensky smiled, most likely because Hollis was gazing off into nowhere and arguing with herself again. "Done and paid for. Great to see you, Little Miss Hollis." He tilted a wood bowl toward her. "Too grown up now for a lollipop?"

She looked in the bowl and before she knew it, her fingers were searching through Dum Dum "lollies," as Annabelle called them, looking for grape, her favorite. Once she found it, she tore the wrapper off, threw it in the brown plastic garbage can to the side of the counter, and enjoyed the rush of sweet that filled her tongue. Little Braids Hollis stuck her tongue out at adult Hollis and she smiled, allowing herself a moment of young.

"Thank you. May I use your restroom?"

"Sure, back through there, you know where it is. I'll load this stuff up for ya." He hoisted the box on one arm and grabbed the paint with his other hand.

Right as Hollis pushed the gold sticker that read *Toilet* on the bathroom door, her phone vibrated. It was Reese, so she threw the half-licked Dum Dum in the bathroom trash because it was grown-up time. She was certain the call was prompted by an e-mail she'd sent explaining her schedule for the next few weeks. Walking past the tiny sink and into the single stall of the bathroom, Hollis answered.

"This is Hollis."

"Hey, long time no talk. You're pissing people off here, Jeffries. I mean first the sloppy vetting of these pretty boys and their crazy man, and now it seems like you're what? On an extended vacation?"

Hollis sat on the toilet and looked down at her feet. The soles of her flip-flops were starting to separate, and fence paint had all but taken over what used to be an every-two-weeks pedicure. It was difficult to find her badass with her running shorts down around her knees while she stared at a bathroom wall with the endorsement, *Oscar the Grouch for Pres*, scrawled in black pen, but she had extra reserves of attitude specifically for these types of situations.

"I'm sorry, is there something you need, Reese?" Hollis asked, hoping the bathroom echo wasn't obvious.

"I need a lot of things, and if it was up to me, I'd join you wherever you are, sweets, but Megan and the boss are not so forgiving."

"And you've been chosen as a liaison? Sort of like a little errand boy to check up on me?"

Hollis stood. She was angry to the point that she no longer cared if he knew where she was, so she flushed.

"Hey, don't get all scratchy with me," Reese exclaimed, oblivious as usual. "Megan asked me to call you and she's merely answering to the big boss. You remember how it is, don't you? She wants me to get a *real* ETA. Her words, not mine."

"I think my e-mail about an hour ago was clear. I'm not in the office for the next few weeks, but I will be working and attending meetings per usual. As for your nasty, meddling bitch of a boss, tell her I don't report to her and she can shove her fucking ETA up her perpetually tight as—"

Hollis lost her words as she opened the stall door to a woman, slightly younger than her, and a little girl of six or seven. Hollis was never good at guessing ages of children. From the look on both of their faces while the mother held her hands over the girl's ears, the specifics hardly mattered.

Hollis hung up on Reese, slid the phone into the pocket of her shorts, and began washing her hands. She glanced up in the mirror at the mother, who was still glaring at her.

"Are you even going to apologize for your... disgusting language in front of my child?"

Hollis shut off the water and turned for a paper towel. "I am sorry.

That was the office, and you know how people can be."

"No, I don't," the woman said.

"You didn't wash your hands the right way," the little girl added. "Three minutes in very warm, soapy water."

Who in the world had three minutes to wash their hands? Hollis thought but did not dare say. Instead, she smiled at the petite blond girl with the bumblebee on her T-shirt and turned the water back on.

The mother sent her miniature hygiene analyst into the stall and stood by the closed metal door as if that extra level of protection made her Mother of the Year. She was still glaring. *Lady, give it a rest!* Somehow guilted into still scrubbing her hands, Hollis wondered which useless government agency came up with three minutes and why this little girl bothered filling her tiny mind with such stuff. Shouldn't she be thinking about sandcastles and swing sets? "There are Dum Dums on the counter!" she wanted to yell. Maybe the child was so pent up at an early age because her mom was a nasty bitch in comfort shoes. Hollis grabbed for another paper towel and continued rationalizing her own behavior until the mother spoke again.

"You obviously have no moral compass if you walk around spewing things like that in public places. I'm sure you don't care one bit about me, nor do you care what my daughter hears. You probably don't even have kids. I'm so tired of you out-of-towners thinking you own the place."

Hollis was ready to say something, poised to fire back, but she couldn't speak. The words that would have put this obviously nothing-to-do-on-a-workday woman in her place, that would have told her exactly who she was dealing with, were right there on Hollis's lips, but—*Maybe taking people down, making them feel less than is why you have no one at work to help you with your current situation?* stupid self-reflection's voice said. Hollis dried her hands, quietly apologized one more time, and left the bathroom.

After waving to Kerensky, who was now helping another customer, Hollis climbed into her uncle's truck. She went to pull out of the lot, but her hands were shaking. She had that feeling a person gets when she's narrowly missed a collision and needs a minute to collect herself before continuing to drive. Hollis was a vice president of one of the largest venture capital firms in the country, she managed assets in the billions, but standing in that dingy bathroom, she had no words because the simple fact was that she was wrong. She'd lost control with Reese. If she was honest with herself, she'd lost control of everything over a month ago and right there in the hardware store, a stranger called her out.

If she was ever going to rescue herself from this... predicament, she needed to think about doing things differently, approaching her life from a different angle. Maybe she needed help. No. Help would require disclosure, and that was not an option.

Alone in a truck she would not have been caught dead in a few weeks ago, Hollis tried to conjure up every kick-ass affirmation she'd ever told herself. If her personal code had allowed it, she would have cried, but crying, as her mother told her when she was seventeen, never helped get anyone anywhere—certainly not a woman.

Chapter Six

*T*he long Memorial Day weekend brought out the Jeffries clan in full force, minus Meg, of course, who had recently left Africa for Canada where she was now tracking and photographing the "illusory spirit bear," their father had explained over a group text message. Hollis showered, shaved, and thought about blowing out her hair for about a minute before deciding wavy mermaid would have to do. Shortly after tidying up her cabin and stepping out to walk over to the Innkeeper's Cabin, she saw Sage exit a rental car, followed closely by her fine-looking and evidently stupid-in-love new fiancé. Even from a distance, Hollis could see her sister's happy as bright as the afternoon sun.

"My God, look at you. Regular sex is working for you, sis," Hollis called out, swallowing back so many emotions she almost choked.

Sage blushed, and Hollis loved her so much it was a little painful. Sometimes she felt like she had all of these pieces of her heart spread out over so many people that it was easier to hide behind ambivalence than it was to acknowledge the truth of her feelings. There were moments Hollis understood why people wanted to be alone: it was easier. Loving was hard work.

"Wow"—she bumped shoulders with Garrett when they met—"Look at you go, Farmer G, rush wedding. It's almost shotgun. I'm so proud."

They laughed, as people often did when Hollis was on and entertaining, and Garrett put his arm around her. "I hear the circus is on tour. Not a bad place to set up a tent for a while."

Hollis nodded, taken by the warmth of his arm and the concern that filled his eyes. "Indeed. I'm cleaning the elephant sh— poop these days, but I'm hoping to fold myself back into the box again very soon."

"I think you look incredible out of the box." Sage touched Hollis's hair and then pulled her into a hug.

"Thanks, sis." Hollis swallowed that same relentless love lump again. "If this wedding is because there's a bun in the oven, you can go ahead and thank me for the baby making. I did buy the naughty book after all. You're welcome," she said to Garrett.

"There's no bun." Sage smacked her arm and looked to Garrett. "We don't want to wait."

Yeah, right.

Garrett put his arm around his future wife, and Hollis was so happy the big lug had finally figured things out. It gave her hope for her own happily-ever-after. Eh, not really, but it was a wonderful day, so why not get all mushy?

"Kenna was supposed to be next," he explained as they walked toward Uncle Mitch's front door. "But she and Travis are taking Paige to Yellowstone, and then she's spending a week with Adam's parents over summer break. They don't seem to be in a hurry. We are." Garrett kissed Sage and if it had gone on for a second longer, Hollis was going to turn away and find them a room. Middle One was definitely pregnant.

"I like the adventure part of the wedding, at least what I've heard from Mom. Ceremony at the barn and then we're flying to Napa?" Hollis asked.

Sage nodded and before Hollis could ask for more details, their uncle sprang through his front door wearing blinding orange shorts and a lavender polo. He looked like some crazed fan who didn't care if the team colors looked good, he was wearing them. After open arms and lots of hugging, any conversation was lost as he interviewed

Garrett and pelted him with little anecdotes the rest of the family had long forgotten. Later, Uncle Mitch asked his "favorite niece" to whip up a batch of her sangria, and Sage obliged.

"She's the favorite? I cleaned toilet bowls for you," Hollis exclaimed, shaking her head at their uncle's exaggerated shrug and the laughter of her family.

Hollis walked out to the porch of the cabin and rolled her eyes at the still half-unpainted fence. Who would have thought painting would be her greatest failure? Well, at least as of that moment. She couldn't figure out why being around her family brought up her looming problems at work, but Hollis guessed it had something to do with the inherent pressure of being a Jeffries. Both of her parents were architects. Her two middle sisters Sage (Middle One) and Annabelle (Middle Two) were brilliant each in their own right. Sage was an engineer turned bartender, and Anna was an English professor at UC Berkeley. Their youngest sister, Meg, could have been the typical wild child, but in the Jeffries house that translated to a National Geographic photographer. The worldview her baby sister shared through her photographs often put the rest of their lives into rather harsh perspective.

Then there was Hollis. She was the oldest and with that came the pressure of being first, showing by example, and staying on top. It was often lonely from her family perch, but she was not about to give it up now. This morning, she'd already put in a call to a Santa Clara-based company that specialized in disaster recovery specifically with gaming companies. She felt confident they could help get Zeke back on track. If not, Hollis would have to visit the little turd herself.

She looked out over the bay toward the restaurant. They were busy for lunch and she hoped Uncle Mitch had staffed with the long weekend in mind. Still unclear on why she cared other than the cove was special and compared to what was currently spinning around in her head, filling rooms and hosing off patios was a cakewalk, Hollis closed her eyes to soak in the sun.

Her parents and Annabelle had arrived. Hollis could hear them from inside the cabin, but she stayed put because she wasn't exactly ready for the whole team and the looks of concern. It had been almost over a month since she'd seen Middle Two. Technically, Hollis had two middle sisters, so when they were little, she declared them Middle One and Middle Two after reading Cat in the Hat one afternoon. Eyes still closed, Hollis could hear Anna's flowery calm voice as everyone greeted each other and caught up. If Hollis was the megaphone of the Jeffries family, Middle Two was certainly the whisper, so when she joined her outside and gave her a big hug, Hollis held on a little tighter than normal. She'd missed Anna, needed her without even knowing.

"How are you?" her sister asked, still holding on.

Hollis nodded and gave no response. She squeezed her one last time. Anna would understand. She was the most emotionally available of all of them. The youngest tenured professor in the English department, she taught nothing but Shakespeare and was forever trying to convince their family and anyone else who would listen that Shakespeare was "totally accessible" and "really not that difficult at all." That was crap because everyone who wasn't holed up with dusty and musty leather tomes of "jibber jabber," as their father liked to tease, knew Shakespeare was a better-left-at-high-school pain in the ass.

"My heart is ever at your service," Anna said as they pulled apart, and Hollis looked into her sister's dark eyes. All the Jeffries girls had some version of their father's silver-gray eyes, but Annabelle's were the darkest, almost the color of wet concrete, which was ironic because she was the most fairy like. Gentle and often in her head unless she was quoting something or humming a song no one recognized, Annabelle Jeffries was the closest to magical Hollis had ever been.

"Honestly? Bill even has a quote for your sister's latest crash and burn?" Hollis asked, smarting a little as she used Matt's words from the Party on the Pier.

Annabelle nodded. "Bill, or Will as I like to tell my students, understood every facet of the human experience."

"Great. Maybe I should read *Taming of the Shrew* while I'm here at summer detox."

"Maybe *The Tempest*."

"Isn't that the one on the island? The one you took me to with the guy from *Star Trek*?"

Anna chuckled. "Patrick Stewart, who is a classically trained and phenomenal actor."

"And... also from *Star Trek*."

"Yes, I suppose. You are correct. We did see *The Tempest* in the city. You fell asleep right after intermission."

"That's because you wouldn't let me get an espresso at the break. All those waves and tinkling music without caffeine." Hollis leaned on the white railing of the patio.

Anna pulled off the overnight bag still on her shoulder and set it on one of the Adirondack chairs. "So, Garrett seems nice."

"He is. She's in love. He's in love. It's all good."

"And how are you?"

"Well, he is a great guy, but I don't think they're looking for a third wheel."

"Not what I meant." Anna leaned shoulder to shoulder with Hollis and looked out over the bay too.

"I know. I'm fine, good. I even painted this railing, fence, whatever it's called. I painted it... well, some of it." Hollis nodded and extended her hands in a gesture of presentation. "You guys missed Party on the Pier. Don't worry, it was the same as usual. Everything here stays the same, doesn't it?"

"I don't know. You tell me. Is he here?"

"Who?"

Annabelle gave her a "don't be daft" look, and Hollis lost the ability to pretend.

"Yes. He works at his parents' coffee shop. He's married."

"Seriously?"

"Appears so. Well, he left Stanford, remember?"

"I do. None of that ever made any sense. I thought for sure you two would get married. You were inseparable and then... you weren't."

"Married? Oh Lord, that would have never happened. I'm not

exactly marriage material. It was college and we were—" Hollis was unsure how to finish what felt like an awkward defense, something a person might put up to try to get out of a speeding ticket. She could tell Anna wasn't buying it, so she stopped.

"Hollis, you were completely in love with him and the few times we saw him, he appeared to feel the same."

Hollis shook her head. "I think 'completely in love' is a little dramatic."

"So even after all these years, you're still not discussing him. Maybe I should go get some coffee and ask him myself."

"Be my guest." Hollis knew her sister would never be so bold, but the thought of it had her wondering what that scenario would look like. What *would* Matt say had happened to them?

Hollis looked out over the water and again tried to chase Matt from her mind. As if sensing the effort, he was suddenly right there in the center of the bay. *Dear sweet Lord!* So much for clearing her mind now. He and Toro, the resident all-things-water guy, were out on paddleboards in nothing more than low-slung swim trunks. Hollis had a sudden intake of breath at all that skin, a touch familiar, but mostly new. Her sister must have noticed because she followed her line of sight and being typical Annabelle discreet, she sighed, "Oh my."

"Yeah, he saved you a trip. He's right there on the water." Hollis pointed.

"Which one?"

"Anna, you're a college professor, this one should be easy. Do you remember Matt being a big dark Hawaiian guy?"

She shook her head, still entranced, and Hollis said, "Down girl, he's on the right."

"I'm not sure what went wrong, big sister, but Lord, either of those would be hard to leave behind."

"I need a drink."

"Uncle Mitch said you weren't drinking anymore." Anna pulled her eyes off the bay and put her bag back on her shoulder.

Hollis shook her head. Great, the entire family now knew she'd been on a bender that might have put some frat boys to shame. This was why she didn't share, this was why she did things on her own, Hollis rationalized and followed Anna back into the cabin. Before closing the screen door, she took one more look as Matt pushed a paddle into the glassy surface of the water, his body flexing and glistening under the afternoon sun. Oh my was right, she thought, turning to finally face her family.

"How long will she be in Canada?" Annabelle asked hours later as the three of them sat out on the pier, legs dangling.

"She didn't say, but she won't be able to make it back for the wedding." Sage was now lying on the dock.

"She sent a Mother's Day card and some weird box thing that holds worry dolls, I guess." Hollis added with a "what the hell?" face she often reserved for Meg.

"Well, at least she thought to send something." Sage, the nice sister, added.

Hollis leaned back on her hands as the sun set around them and the water gently lapped against the pier. It was quiet, each of them most likely in that belonging-to-something moment sisters often shared and not for the first time, they missed Meg.

"She'll be home for Christmas this year, that's what she told Mom," Annabelle offered, breaking the silence. "I think she said she'll even be home for the Big Game."

Sage, who had the misfortune of sitting between Hollis and Annabelle, rolled her eyes. "Oh, come on. Not tonight, please."

It was too late, Hollis already had six fingers up indicating the number of times Stanford had beat Cal in a row. Six years of undefeated victory, and Hollis took every opportunity to rub it in her sisters' faces. All three of them attended UC Berkeley, the school of their parents, even though Hollis had paved a perfectly decent path for them by attending the rival school. She had thought at least one of them would follow in her footsteps, but they all chose Cal Berkeley, so Hollis had to be diligent any time there was mention of their house divided.

"We didn't lose the game, we ran out of time," Anna said, reaching across to pull Hollis's fingers down.

"Wait, that's not Shakespeare." Hollis giggled like they were kids.

"I know. It's in the faculty lounge. The new football coach put it up. It's Vince Lombardi."

"What, you losers don't have any of your own coaches to quote so you have to borrow from Vince?"

"Hollis," Sage warned and smirked at the same time.

"Don't laugh at her," Annabelle set her half-finished glass of sangria down on the pier, probably so she wouldn't throw it at Hollis.

"You know what I don't get? You don't even like football. Every year, we watch the game and you have no idea what is going on," Hollis said.

"That is not true. I can follow along and even if I can't, who cares? I don't like to lose, and I have to represent."

"Oh my God, it's too late for all of you. I'm sorry you went to the wrong school."

Sage and Annabelle shook their heads.

"I think this could be our year," Sage said. "I read an article in the paper. We have a new receivers coach."

Hollis shook her head, realizing it had felt like forever since she'd even read a newspaper. "Oh, well, there you have it, Middle Two. This is the year," she mocked.

She and Sage looked to Annabelle, who suddenly appeared lost and ready to go in.

"Anna?"

"What?"

"Receivers, care to join in the conversation?"

Annabelle shook her head and while Sage visibly tried not to laugh, Hollis lay back on the pier and felt the same satisfaction she felt when she used to kick Annabelle's ass in checkers. It was normal for sisters to have a healthy competitiveness, but maybe the Jeffries women were crazy. It was entirely possible, Hollis thought as she waited for Anna to strike again. It was silent, the calm before the storm. She'd made Anna blush, so this was far from over. Right as she remembered seeing Matt on that paddleboard, her sister tapped into her creepy mind-reading ability and made her move.

"Sage, you remember Matt, don't you?" Annabelle said in that crisp distinct professor voice Hollis hated.

"I do. Well, I do now that Hollis and I bumped into him a couple of months ago. Is he still around?" Sage asked, now baiting Anna.

Damn middles, they're ganging up again.

"He sure is. In fact, we saw him out on the water earlier today. He's a bit more... developed than I remember him when we were growing up. Hollis, Matt's development, do you care to join the conversation?"

Hollis laughed—she couldn't help it. She couldn't decide which was funnier: her sisters' exaggerated conversation as if they were talking to a kindergarten class or picturing the look on Matt's face if he'd heard them calling him "developed." Matt's face. It occurred to her she could no longer call up his expressions or the look of him, certainly not the older him. Which was probably a good thing because she wasn't going to be around long enough to need that information.

Annabelle was reveling in having turned the tables, and this time, Sage joined her.

Hollis put her hands over her head in mock surrender.

"That's right, give up. I win." Annabelle was kicking her feet and doing a seated victory dance.

She almost made it too easy. Hollis reached an arm behind Middle Two and gently but firmly pushed her into the water.

Anna surfaced, hands flailing now for a different reason. "You... that was... shoot, you are... incorrigible!"

"Oh, a two-point word even soaking wet. Well done, professor," Hollis said.

Sage reached out a hand to help her back up on the dock. Hollis would have offered, but no way she was giving Anna that opportunity. Soaked to the bone, her sister glared at her, looking little more than eight years old.

"Now what kind of example would I be setting for my young, impressionable sisters if I gave up that easily?"

Anna looked to Sage, who ran into the cabin to get a towel. When she returned, they sat laughing as Middle Two dried off and once again accepted defeat.

Sage stood. "Okay, well, now that there appears to be a truce, I need to go rescue Garrett from Dad and Uncle Mitch. When I was getting the towel, they were breaking out the camping trip albums."

"Oh, shi—oot. Hurry before they get to the trip where you cut your own bangs. The man will run." Hollis sat back up as Sage flipped her the pinky and walked back into the house. One night, around the dinner table, Meg had said something that started an argument—none of them could remember what it was now—but that was the first night Annabelle flipped everyone the pinky. When their mother asked her about the gesture, Anna had said it was the way people flipped each other off in Chinese. For some reason, not one of them ever fact-checked it. The gesture stuck and from that point on, anytime one of them was pissed at the other, joking or not, they flipped the pinky.

"Do you want to tell me what happened or when you're coming home?" Anna asked, wringing out the bottom of her blouse.

"Do you want me to push you in again?" Hollis tried to dodge the question.

"I'm serious. Tell me, please, so I can stop worrying." Her eyes had a way of soliciting the truth, even rimmed in smeared mascara.

Hollis took a deep breath and let it out slowly, as if that could somehow help her find the words. "It's not a big deal. I'm fine. We're having some issues with a new client. My new client."

"Okay. That doesn't seem like a reason to drop everything."

"I didn't. I'm still working. I needed some time."

"Is it helping?"

"The time?"

"Yes."

Hollis lay back on the dock and Annabelle joined her, both of them turning to face the other. "I think so, yes. It's helping."

Anna took her hand and they were again quiet.

"So, do you think paddling around on that board gave him that body?"

Hollis smiled and was again thankful for her sister. She knew there was no point in pushing because Hollis never asked for help. *Why was that?*

"I'm not sure, Anna. Did you want me to ask him?"

"Yes. Get on that, will you?" Annabelle stood up and without a word walked toward the house.

"Literally? Are you saying I should literally get on that?" Hollis asked, taking the upper hand again. Anna was great at eluding, so Hollis liked nothing more than being blunt to throw her off.

"Goodnight, Hollis."

"Goodnight, Middle Two. I love you."

"I love you too. Be sure to let me know if those swim trunks have a drawstring or Velcro when you take them off," Annabelle said quickly and closed the back door.

"Shit," Hollis said to no one, but still looked around like that crazy mother was going to appear to chastise her.

Anna had gotten the last word. Hollis should have held back the "I love you." That's what opened it up, she thought as she gazed up at the night sky now practically dripping in starlight. The last word, last laugh, the win—that's what it meant to share the Jeffries name. Hollis was again alone on the pier and wondered if those instincts ingrained in her had helped and hurt her in equal measure.

Chapter Seven

Matt and Toro paddled in right as the sun was setting and by the time they put their equipment away, the night air had turned chilly. It had been a perfect day to be on the water and it had been far too long, Matt realized. Toro Kapule, which literally translated to "the magic," had opened the kayak and paddleboard rental near Mitchell's Cove about seven years ago when he retired from surfing and moved to Tomales Bay. He'd taught Matt how to get the most from his board a few years ago and since Matt had been in town more lately, Toro made a point to go out with him as much as possible, as long as Matt agreed to bring the coffee. Coming from Hawaii, Toro was understandably a coffee snob, and he'd long ago dubbed the Coast Roast sold exclusively at The Bean locations to be the "Best coffee on the planet. Period." His name was fitting because Toro was one of the most fascinating people Matt had ever known. He remained completely focused and centered in a way Matt found next to impossible. He was a living, breathing example of every positive affirmation out there and on top of it all, he was probably twice the size of Matt and ripped like a superhero from the comic books he used to read as a kid.

Matt pulled on sweatpants and a hoodie in the makeshift hut near the boards.

"You bring coffee?" Toro asked on the other side of the curtain.

"Two pounds ground for a French press and a thermos is by my bag."

"Aw, yeah. Time to warm from within while watching the gift of that sunset. Thank you, my friend."

My friend. For some reason, those words stuck out for Matt every time Toro said them. Matt wasn't big on friends. Maybe it was the only child thing, maybe it had to do with running his own business. Whatever it was, he called very few people "friend." Matt had never minded being alone until he realized it was because he never *had* to be alone. Hollis had been with him for most of his life growing up and when they went to college. She'd been his best friend and when their love story didn't work out, he'd lost her touch and her friendship.

Sometimes, Matt wondered which was worse, and then glancing up to see her on the pier with her sisters, he knew that it was similar to which bay he liked more. There was one kind of pain in losing a lover and another in the loss of a friend. She'd been everything he ever imagined wanting in a person, not just a woman. The passion, the laughter, the endless debates and conversation... she'd pushed him and loved him in equal measure. When that was all taken away, he must have been in some kind of daze because try as he may, he still wasn't able to reconcile why he hadn't fought. Why he said he wanted her happiness and let her go. What kind of a man does that?

Matt heard a deep sigh and pulled the curtain open to see Toro with the thermos cup in his hand and his eyes closed.

"Juice of the gods."

"No. I keep telling you it's only my dad and a scary-looking roaster, but I know how you like to deify him."

Toro nodded and took another sip.

"How is the ACM?"

Matt shook his head. "Maybe you're part of the reason the 'Almighty Coffee Man' is such a pain in my ass."

Toro laughed, and he sounded a bit like a god himself. "If he's still able to give you a hard time, the surgery must have gone well. How's the hip?"

"He barely lets me get close enough to find out."

Toro's face grew serious as he pulled on a sweatshirt and poured another cup of coffee. "We should get him in the water."

Matt shook his head. "He'll never come up here until he's one hundred percent."

"We could go to him. My sister runs a health club in the city. She's a physical therapist."

"Thanks for the offer, but he's not going to work with your sister, and why would we want to put that on her?"

"Then I'll work with him. She can supervise, but I'll be in the water with him. He loves me." Toro grinned like a favorite child.

Matt knew he looked dumbfounded, but he was taken aback by the gesture. He was trying to picture his dad holding on to Toro's arm, which was the size of Matt's thigh, doing the dog paddle.

"What kind of stuff would you do with him? I honestly can't imagine he'll go."

"He needs to get that hip moving or his recovery is going to be twice as long. The water is a miracle worker."

"It's a great idea, but I'm not sure."

"I'll help you get him. We'll throw him over my shoulder if we have to. Once he gets in, feels the relief, he'll want to go."

"You sure about that? Are you sure you want to be aggravated?"

"Are you kidding? The man brings me home with his coffee every time I take a sip. Least I can do." Toro locked up his shop and walked with Matt toward Mitch's place, which seemed a little busier lately even with the Memorial Day weekend.

"I'll talk to my mom and get back with you."

"Okay"—Toro hopped in his yellow Jeep—"Don't wait too long. He needs you."

"Me? He needs you." Matt bumped fists and Toro drove away.

He needs you. The words floated around in Matt's head as if he'd never heard them before. His father was a bull: first job when he was fourteen and a climber ever since. He took care of business, his family, and needed no one as far as Matt could tell. He tried to remember a time when his father had asked for help other than chores. Had Matt always helped? He couldn't remember and in dismissing the question, he thought of Hollis. She hadn't needed anyone either. What did that say about him? Did he surround himself with people who never asked so he never had to give? Christ, maybe he should ask Hollis for the name of that top-notch shrink.

Walking toward the coffee shop to get his car, his thoughts again drifted to Toro's offer and the last time he'd seen his father in the water. He swam in the ocean constantly when Matt was growing up, taught Matt how to swim, and practiced sailing when he was older, but lately his dad had not done much, and maybe that was because he'd been in pain or maybe it was something else. Matt should probably ask; then he wondered why he hadn't. Waiting as two slow-moving cars from out of town passed before he crossed to the shop parking lot, he turned back to look at the bay.

The lights from Mitchell's Cove cut iridescent through the growing darkness, and the moon was a sliver overhead. His eyes found the pier. He had likely looked to that pier hundreds of times in the last dozen years, hoping for something, a flashlight beam, her, but he had never seen anything. Until now. Hollis was lying back on the pier, legs dangling with nothing and no one but the night sky and the dim glow coming off the cabins. For a minute, he thought he'd conjured her up, but her foot splashed the water and he knew she was real. His breath caught, and his heart, which had remained fairly quiet until about six weeks ago, begged to be heard.

Christ, she's still here? What happened to her, and what does she need? If he told the whole mess to Toro, would his friend argue that Hollis needed him too? He sure hoped not because he hadn't been very good at giving anyone what they needed for a very long time. Besides, Hollis wasn't his father. If their past was any sign of their present, the person most capable of helping Hollis Jeffries was the woman herself. Unless he should have looked closer. There was no point in rehashing any of this. However they had lost their way, it was over and done. Water under the pier, so to speak, he told himself, but his heart wouldn't shut up. *Maybe you should ask?*

Matt turned from the road back to her. It certainly couldn't hurt to try something different. Could it?

This time, she knew he was there even with her eyes closed, even though he hadn't said a word. It was his walk, a rhythm that she obviously had not forgotten. When they lived together sophomore year, she knew when he was in the hall outside their apartment before his keys ever jingled in the lock. Matt liked to tell her it was because their apartment was a dump and she heard him coming because the walls were paper-thin, but that wasn't it. His movements, like the man himself, were efficient. He expelled the least amount of energy. He knew his body, was settled in it, and with the exception of the gym teacher in high school who gave him a complex about his small calves, Hollis knew he was comfortable in his skin. She knew Matt Locke almost as well as she knew herself, still.

Allowing the crisp bay air into her lungs, Hollis slowly exhaled. "Shouldn't you be getting home to the missus?"

"We're divorced." He sat down next to her, pulled up the legs of his sweatpants, and hung his legs over the edge.

Hollis sat up, trying not to react. She was grateful for the darkness because the look on her face must have read shocked or relieved. *Relieved? You shouldn't be relieved,* introspection whispered. He was divorced. She imagined Matt to be a forever kind of guy, but it had been years and after reminding herself that she no longer knew him, her next thought was that he hadn't married the right woman.

"That was quick. You were married a week ago when I asked you at the shop. Remember, I said, 'How's married life?' and you said, 'Good.'"

Matt shook his head. "A virtual transcript of our conversation. I see you're still precise, huh, Holls?"

"Could you please stop calling me that?"

"Holls? Why? Everyone calls you that."

"Not like you do."

He found her eyes even in the darkness.

"How is mine different?"

"I don't know it's your voice or some weird thing you do with your breath. Stick with my full name, please."

"No."

She rolled her eyes as some sort of junior high defense to the pounding in her heart. "So, you said you were married last week."

"I lied."

"Why?"

"Because you were whipping around all full of yourself, and I wasn't in a sharing mood."

"Oh, speaking of things that haven't changed."

They both rocked their legs back and forth. When Hollis realized they were in sync, she stilled her legs.

"Obviously you're ready to share now. When did you get divorced?"

"Only lasted a year. Took us another six months to make things official. It's been about eight years now."

"I'm sorry."

"No you're not, and she remarried five years ago, has kids. She's fine too."

"Who is she?"

"You don't know her."

"It did seem a little strange that you were married so—" She shook her head and put a hand to her jittery stomach.

"Quickly after us? Yeah, it was a great idea. Call my parents if you'd like to continue talking about the failure that was my marriage."

"Where did you meet her?"

"Why are we discussing this?"

"I'm trying to make conversation. You started it with the big divorce reveal."

He leaned back on his hands. "I met her at work."

"At the coffee shop."

He started to shake his head then nodded. "Yeah, at the coffee shop."

"Huh." Hollis had a feeling there was something he wasn't telling her. She also found it strange that Matt would meet someone at The Bean, although his parents had multiple locations so maybe it was someone in management. It was not as if any woman would make sense, so she wasn't sure why her mind kept turning the thought around.

"I'm surprised you never had this airbrushed out." He reached over and ran a finger across the small scar on the side of her chin. There was nothing illicit in the gesture, but it felt intimate, as if the touch should make her blush, but Hollis didn't blush.

"Is your second toe still longer than your big toe, or did you have that... chiseled down?" he asked, leaning forward to get a look at her feet in the water when she didn't answer.

Hollis went from jumpy stomach at the warmth of his leg touching hers to annoyed in the time it took her to blink.

"It's not that much bigger." She scrunched her toes.

Matt nodded. "Still there."

She stood quickly, grabbed her flip-flops off the dock, and turned to leave. There were very few people with the ability to make Hollis so aware of her body—flaws and all. Matt was one of them, top of the list if she were honest.

"Where are you going?" he asked, getting to his feet.

"Anywhere but here. I had a great day with my family and I simply wanted to sit out here in the quiet. I'm not going to let you pull me down memory lane so we can talk about my toes. I don't care what you think anymore."

"Refresh my memory, because I don't remember you ever caring what I thought."

"Oh, this is rich. Tell me, when you replay the sad little movie reel of our past, are you the passive, abandoned victim?"

Matt held her eyes. "I don't know, Holls. When you replay it, are you the bitter, selfish bitch?"

It might have been easier if he'd actually slapped her. Hollis rarely fought fair. She should have remembered that when Matt allowed himself to get angry, he gave as good as he got, sometimes better.

She smiled and steadied her breath because she knew he'd like nothing more than to watch her get worked up after all these years. "Okay, well, it's good to know you've grown into an asshole. That makes this a whole lot easier."

Matt stood in front of her, blocking her retreat. "Makes what easier?"

She shook her head. There was nothing left to say. "Get out of my way."

"I'm not picking you apart." He rubbed the back of his neck and then stopped as if he knew that was a giveaway to his aggravation. Instead, he shoved both hands into the front pocket of his sweatshirt. "I guess I was checking," he said softly, and stood back to let her pass.

She didn't move. "Checking what?"

"You." He swallowed. "Making sure my memory was accurate, the things I know, knew, about you. I guess. I'm sorry. I'll keep my distance." He sat back down on the dock as if she'd already gone.

Hollis closed her eyes. He had a way of making her so angry one minute and right when she was ready to smack him, he'd soften. Never one to follow, Hollis stayed standing but didn't leave.

"I knew what happened would mess us up," he said, almost as though he were talking to himself. "I knew it would mess you up, but I didn't know how bad it was until you came back."

"What are you even talking about?" The anger surfaced again. "I'm great. Last year, I made over a million dollars in bonuses alone, and I ran another marathon."

"Like I said, worse than I thought." Matt looked up at her.

"Oh, go to hell." She dropped her flip-flops on the dock and sat next to him with her legs and arms crossed, as if that would protect her. It was a nice try, but the reproachful look on his face shot pain right through the center of her and this time, she shot back. "You're a dropout, a quitter in everything. Do you think you have room to judge me?"

"Now we're getting somewhere. Did I quit you?"

"Oh wow, yes, Dr. Fuc-nky Town Phil. Twelve years later, let's talk now. That's a great idea."

He raised his eyebrows in what looked like amusement, which pissed her off even more.

"Please tell me all about my issues and how you can fix me. Right after you deal with your own." She leaned into him, needing to make sure he heard every jab. "You're right, I am messed up. So are you whether you bother to notice it or not. It's there. Nothing will fix us, so your first instinct was right. Keep your distance." Hollis went to stand, but he touched her arm. Her entire body buzzed with an energy she had forgotten all about and had never been able to replicate.

"As much as I'd like to do that, you're here and I don't think I'm going to be able to stay away. Maybe finally talking about what happened will help."

"It's very cute that you think so, but no. Too much has happened. We are not those people anymore."

"I know. We're adult people now. We have experience and we know what it's like."

"What what's like?"

"To be without each other."

"We've been without each other for twelve years. Twelve years and you never... we left each other alone. It was better that way."

"I never what? Came for you? Fought for you?"

"I don't want to talk about this." She stood, kicking herself for allowing him to get to her.

"Why not?" he asked, standing and looking so gorgeous and vulnerable illuminated by the lights off the shore that she forgot to be angry.

"Because we've already dealt with it. We've moved past it, as all the books say."

"We haven't dealt with anything. I sure haven't. I'll give you that we've moved on, or at least moved over our past, but there's been no dealing, Holls. If there had been, I guarantee we wouldn't be here."

"Where would we be?" she asked, her eyes watering at the simple question and her mind demanding that they halt any ideas of crying immediately.

Matt looked as if he didn't know how to answer her, so there they stood sharing air, trapped somewhere between the past and what had become their present. Hollis knew what nighttime did to her. She had a habit of letting her inhibitions down, sharing secrets, and acting on regrets that lingered till the following morning. She couldn't be here with him, not on this pier, and not like this. That door was slammed shut and locked. He was still looking at her, and the pull threatened to bring her right into the depths of those eyes. Hollis had enough of her own mess at this particular moment. She still hadn't found a way back to her circus box, and nothing humming through her right now was going to make that any easier.

Matt leaned in and touched the side of her face as if again checking his memory, and she almost lost her balance. His exhale whispered the smell of coffee and sunscreen, and she wanted him in a way she thought she'd all but cried from her system. As his fingers traced down the side of her neck, she suddenly realized that she didn't want a memory or the past, she wanted the grown man. Her heart was desperate to know his stories, as if they could simply sit on the dock and share secrets like they did when they were teenagers.

Pull back, Hollis. You won't survive this again, her mind said, hoping to be heard over the thundering in her chest. "I should go."

"You should." His voice was barely audible above the rippling of the water.

"Do you want me to go?"

Matt nodded, but said, "From the second I saw you, Holls, I'm not sure I've ever wanted you to go."

Her chest ached and her eyes welled again. Now he speaks, she thought, now he gives her heart the words it so desperately needed back before it was broken, before they were broken. It wasn't fair. He was too late. Hollis allowed herself one more moment then turned and ran back to her cabin.

Chapter Eight

*H*ollis closed her eyes and saw him. She flipped onto her stomach and buried her face in the new down-blend pillows her uncle finally agreed to buy as an upgrade for each cabin, but it was no use. Too many thoughts of him swirled in her mind, and the memory of the night that proved to be the beginning of the end snuck past the barrier that had taken Hollis years to build. She took a deep breath, closed her eyes, and let herself go there.

She and Matt had fallen asleep in the living room during a last-minute cram session they had for a final the next day. It was the first semester of their junior year at Stanford. Matt had bought her two packages of Oreos, a gallon of milk, and some of those marinated mushrooms from the specialty market off campus. Salty and sweet, she could still remember craving it with a vengeance. A mere two days before, she'd stopped at the deli and asked for a brat, extra sauerkraut, and a chocolate milkshake with extra whipped cream. She hoped all of this would pass once she survived what would prove to be the hardest finals of her life. Otherwise, forget the freshman fifteen she'd managed to avoid—she would be on her way to gaining the junior thirty.

Before they'd both collapsed, Hollis had eaten most of the Oreos and all of the mushrooms until she felt sick while Matt snacked on a bag of nuts and two bottles of water. He was a pain in the ass even back then, she thought, now turning onto her back and pulling the covers under her chin.

At around three in the morning, the air conditioner in their cheap apartment had kicked on with a groan and a hiss. Hollis remembered sitting up on the couch, throwing her open book onto the floor, and knew. As clearly as she knew every detail of horizontal mergers, she knew something was wrong.

After it all fell apart, Hollis had replayed that moment around in her head dozens of times in an effort to figure out why in that instant it had clicked exactly like the dying air conditioner. It never made any sense, there was nothing that led up to her moment of clarity.

After a few minutes of trying to regulate her breathing and count-ing the days on her phone calendar one more time to make sure she wasn't being foolish, Hollis had found Matt asleep on the floor. His dark hair sticking up as he lay on his back, sweatshirt bundled under his head, and his arms crossed over his face as if trying to hold in all of the coding and terminology he'd memorized over the past few days. Hollis rolled off the couch and crawled next to him. He groaned, rolled to his side, and pulled her in as if it were Sunday and they had all morning to wake up. Hollis couldn't breathe. She tried. She wanted to pretend what had woken her was ridiculous, but the nagging wouldn't leave her alone. She allowed herself one more tender moment and then woke Matt up.

"We need to get a pregnancy test," she said as he rolled onto his back again, eyes still closed.

"What?" Matt said, still half-asleep as his eyes cracked open. "What time is it?"

"Like three thirty, I don't know. Still dark, but I'm serious. Wake up."

He sat up. "Holls, you're freaking out because we've had like four hours of sleep in the last three days. You're delirious, not pregnant."

"How do you know? It's been ten days. I'm on the pill and that doesn't happen. I get to the end and I get my period every month. That's how it works. Late never happens. Something is wrong."

"I thought we decided it was because you were sick last month. Student health gave you the Z-pack, remember? That probably threw everything off."

"I'm not sure what we were thinking because that makes no sense. Besides, I was two days late when we came up with that. This is day ten and no period. Why would an antibiotic even mess with my period? It was a stupid explanation."

Matt huffed and reached for his laptop. Hollis was starting to sweat.

He typed something and then said, "Okay, right here," as he read off the screen, "Antibiotics can sometimes render birth control pills ineff—"

He stopped reading and the room began to spin.

"Holls, did you tell student health you were on the pill?"

She shook her head.

"Why not?" He looked up from his computer.

"I don't think they asked. Why?"

Matt closed his laptop and stood. He ran his hand over his face as if that might give him a few more hours of sleep and grabbed his wallet and keys.

"Where are you going?"

"To get a test."

Hollis stood and the ground felt uneven.

"Do you think?"

He took her hand. "Maybe. We need to find out. You have your Hawthorne final in less than three hours, so you might want to get in the shower while I'm gone." He turned to leave.

"Matt."

He looked back, blue eyes under heavy lids and still so handsome.

"Nothing. Hurry."

When he leaned in and gently kissed her, Hollis had no way of knowing that would be the last time they were ever going to be exactly as they were—two tired college students in love and on the brink of so many plans. Remembering now, Hollis wished she had known once Matt walked back through that door a half hour later that everything would change. Maybe she would have held him tighter before waking him up, kissed him longer, although knowing her twenty-one-year-old self, probably not.

By the time she stepped in the shower after gawking at the third positive test, she had already started sorting, prioritizing, and planning her way forward. Looking back on it now, she was so young, sheltered, and unsure how to navigate from which pizza she wanted on a Friday night to raising a child. Everything was suddenly two inches from her nose and then when everything fell apart, the love of her life had told her to "be happy" and stepped aside.

Matt couldn't sleep. He was never one to blame others, but this one was all on her. His heart, normally quiet, was now rushing and filling his mind with possibilities.

Don't start this crap, you're too late, his mind tried to assert some reason. It had been twelve years and if she wanted him the way her eyes seemed to for a moment, she would have been in touch. The simple act of sitting with her, trying to reach her, had him reeling with the frustration of a missed opportunity that he now somehow felt entitled to.

She'd arrived back at the cove polished and perfect. He knew from the occasional mention in the industry, or one of his late-night Google searches, that she was successful. She was the dynamo he knew she'd become once he cleared out and gave her room to grow. She was where she belonged, and yet when he saw her sitting there on the pier with what looked like paint on her toes, no makeup, and her wavy hair, Matt wanted her.

It was bad enough wanting the memory, that had nearly killed him, but this was different. He wanted the imperfection of who she was now. How was that possible? They barely knew each other, and somehow it all felt better than the memory. Even in all her pissed-off fury and drama, she was still like coming home, finding what was missing, or any other Hallmark card sentiment. He'd worked hard to plug up all those missing pieces a long time ago, but turned to a damn puddle the minute she sat next to him on their pier.

Maybe all of it was a sign telling him to go home, back to the city where they were mixed up with millions of other people practically destined never to set eyes on one another ever again. He needed to get away from this beachside movie set with its setting sun and the glistening water. Hell, even the coldest heart would go all Hallmark here. Once he returned home, things would slip back to normal. All he needed was a little pollution or some obnoxious commuters. Maybe Poppy could come back full-time earlier. He could ask her tomorrow.

Matt rolled over and held the extra pillow over his head. *That's a great idea—ask the new mom if she can work a full-time job a few weeks early because you can't seem to get over a woman who literally dropped you and the life you thought you knew over twelve years ago.* Matt moaned into the pillow. Why was he still letting her stroll right into his heart? *Wasn't once enough? What kind of idiot gets third-degree burns and puts his hand back in the fire because the flames are so warm and pretty?*

Throwing off the covers, Matt got into the shower. He was done trying to sleep. "From the first time I saw you, Holls," he said, and he could hear his own voice loud and clear in the echo of the bathroom. He bumped his head on the tiled shower wall. *Jesus Christ! What the hell is wrong with me? Grow up, man. Move on.*

After drying off and throwing on a pair of jeans, he grabbed a bottle of water and sat at the small round table in the dark kitchen. He touched his computer and the screen illuminated. God, he missed his den at home. There was a vintage arcade Pac-Man and a pool table, so Matt wasn't sure his home office qualified as a den, but that's what the realtor called it when she showed him the apartment, so it stuck. Any time Bradley came over, he loved saying, "Let's retire to the den." He was nuts. Innovative and a genius under pressure, but wearing two different socks to client meetings, liked to sit on the floor during staff meetings, nut. Matt was the straight guy to Bradley's crazy and often wondered if that need to keep order came from being an only child.

When he was growing up, his friends would get into all kinds of trouble, and Matt was the straight guy then too. His parents were working so hard it never occurred to him to give them anything else to deal with, so he did his homework, never snuck out, and rarely drank when he was staying at someone else's house. His don't-rock-the-boat mentality may have left him a little pent up in comparison to his friends. Sitting at his computer now, updating the latest development calendar, Matt knew he sounded like some kind of misfit. That was why he steered clear of talking about himself.

It was awkward when some potential client asked, "Well, you know how we guys are when we're young, right?"

Matt wanted to say, "Actually, my childhood was fairly uneventful," but instead he usually smiled and agreed with that guy nod he'd perfected from watching his father deal with vendors. He supposed uneventful wasn't entirely true. When he was four, his older brother by three years was killed by a drunk driver. That came with some baggage or a few colorful issues, but no one wanted that story at a cocktail party. What would that sound like? "Yeah, things get wild. Like the time my brother went to the science museum with his friend and the mom's car was T-boned by some asshole who had one too many. The mom and my brother's friend lived. John, my brother, died." Matt shook his head in the darkness and thought maybe Bradley wasn't the sole crazy one after all. Anyone who knew Matt had lost his brother asked the same question: "Do you miss him?" No. He was four. He hardly remembered him, but again, that's not something a normal person said. Maybe normal was overrated. Walking to the small living room window that looked out toward the bay, Matt wondered where all of this late-night analysis was coming from and promptly answered his own question.

"Hollis," he whispered to the night. She'd brought it all back and made him question why, in the presence of so much "no, don't go down that road again," he wanted her. Why was it so easy for him to soften and hand her his stupid heart all over again? Was he some kind of glutton for punishment because his brother died? Or a sad divorced guy incapable of real love and destined to roam around until the one woman who destroys him every time circles back around? That had to be it. Matt ran a hand over his tired face and sat on the couch to watch the sunrise even though that too reminded him of her.

The sun, how did she manage to take over the sun too?

Chapter Nine

*H*ollis enjoyed a good sweat. At least she used to in her gym at home, but in the open air, with the cove stretched out behind her, it was hard to focus on her music, her heart rate, anything. It was like the minute she pulled into town, all the structure she thought she had went right out the window. Back home, she clocked four miles on her treadmill before her first shot of espresso, all while watching the news and answering e-mails. "Heart, mind, and soul" was part of her parents' doctrine growing up, although her mother hated it when Hollis called it a "doctrine."

"It makes us sound like scientists or something," she would say. "We are simply human beings trying to raise exceptional human beings," her mother routinely added with a smile. When Hollis was younger, especially during her high school years, that often translated to "We are exceptional and therefore expect you to be the same or better." In her angry adolescent head, she heard her mother adding, "As if it's possible to be better than we are," followed by a sadistic laugh. After a few decent fights, Hollis outgrew hearing her mother as the lord of darkness and realized the agenda her parents were pushing led somewhere. Hard work was the key to success and as Meg often said, "Hollis drank the Kool-Aid." She was the oldest. It was her job to set an example, to be a role model for her younger sisters. Not that she'd been doing much of that lately.

Hollis finished running the loop and felt it in her knees as she came down the last hill toward the cabins. Soaked to her socks, she had to admit her body was happier. She'd been a slug for a few weeks now, but last night she'd recalled what her Pilates trainer liked to preach. "It's all fun and games until the jeans no longer fit." Hollis had liked the phrase so much she'd put it on her fridge at home.

Home. She hadn't thought about her apartment or the things in it until last night when she was drowning in his eyes, as if twelve whole years hadn't passed between them. There she was barefoot, on their pier, and hanging on his every word one more time.

She'd awakened this morning before the sun as if her mind grabbed her heart and said, "Okay, so as punishment for that little stunt, missy, five miles. Get your ass on the road."

Exercise had worked before, so there was no reason it shouldn't set her straight this time. Her parents were in *Bunny Blue*, Sage and Garrett probably cuddled up in *Bojangles,* and Annabelle thankfully opted for their uncle's couch because since Hollis put that new ad online and cleaned up the Yelp reviews, Mitchell's Cove was rarely vacant these days. Her family would leave after breakfast, but there was no hurry. They never hurried when they were here. In fact, most of Hollis's hang-out-and-relax family memories took place at the cove— it was one of those places that allowed for afternoon naps and where watermelon counted as a meal. Not much slowed the Jeffries clan down, but the cove did.

As Hollis approached her cabin, she heard soft music coming from Toro's hut. Calm, peaceful, Stevie Wonder, "Don't You Worry 'Bout a Thing" music. Hollis used the towel draped over the front gate of her cabin to dry her neck and arms.

Maybe Toro would take her out on the paddleboard, or she could get a kayak for an hour. That sounded restorative, and Hollis needed all the restoring she could find now that she felt a new leaf about to turn. She didn't want to go back inside the cabin, back to what had become a little sad. She felt restless and wanted to keep moving, keep sweating. Walking along the path, Hollis tried to remember when doing her job had turned her into a person she almost couldn't tolerate. When had the winning and the climbing won out over what was right and wrong? She reluctantly thought of the mean mom at the hardware store. While she still saw no need to wash her hands for three minutes and would still reserve the occasional "shit," "fuck," or both for toe stubbing and stupid people, she remembered one thing the woman had said: "Where is your moral compass?"

Was it possible Hollis had dismantled her life, her persona, on purpose? It's not like she hadn't made mistakes before... she had. Granted, she had never allowed herself to be screwed, so to speak, quite like this, but she was made of tough stuff. Wasn't she? Either way, she wasn't fired or even asked to take a break. Looking back at the moment she walked out, Hollis wondered if she was simply waiting for the right excuse. She shook her head because that was ridiculous. Why would someone with everything do that?

She hadn't planned on coming to Mitchell's Cove. In fact, when she first arrived on her parents' doorstep, she wasn't thinking beyond her mother's chocolate cake, a few days of wine, and someone else figuring out dinner. That had turned into a couple of weeks, which then grew into flip-flops and junk food, but now Hollis wondered about the compass. When she was young, she'd had one; right and wrong were clear, almost rigidly so. Now she couldn't tell whether anything was absolute.

Now, almost two months had passed and instead of feeling the need to return, she was thinking this might be where she dropped her compass. If she could find it, get it going again, maybe it wouldn't matter whether Zeke ever coded another line again or if everyone knew what she had done. The cove held bittersweet memories, some of them hard to swallow given her current yucky phase. The world she'd created in the city over the last twelve years stood in glaring contrast to the freshness of the sand and her favorite pier in all the world. Hollis threw the towel over the bench outside the restaurant and began running again. She would visit Toro after another lap, but right now, she still had some things to burn off.

Coach Kurt.

Hollis remembered her high school field hockey coach right as her quads gave up and her legs shifted to other muscles. She needed to finish up soon, but it was appropriate that Coach Aaron Kurt popped into her head. Initially, there hadn't been enough interest in a girls' field hockey team, so while they waited, Hollis and two other girls played with the boys. Coach Kurt was ahead of his time because when they were out on the field, male or female, they were all his players. Workouts were the same, and expectations were too. Hollis had loved it all: the challenge and being treated as an equal. The boys, of course, gave her grief, but she was so pumped up by the competition that she barely noticed. Once they couldn't get a rise from her, they stopped teasing. There were times Hollis was discouraged because while she could practice with the boys, she was still on the bench during games.

Coach used to sit next to her and say, "Someday, Jeffries. You'll wake up one day and your someday will be here, I promise."

Hollis shook her head and had replied that it should be now, that she should be out there and able to play like the boys. He'd grinned and said, "Every athlete will tell you patience is far more powerful than impatience. Work on that while you're sitting here."

Then he'd go back to coaching his team. The following year, there were enough girls for a team and by Hollis's senior year, they were state champions. She loved her parents, but now during what was turning into her sweaty scraping-the-bottom-of-the-barrel moment of reflection, it occurred to her that other people in her life had provided practical guidance without the pressure. Hollis came from a successful family, and that brought with it all sorts of baggage that probably screwed up her compass the older she grew and the higher the stakes became.

Coach Kurt had no motive other than to help out another kid on the bench. As Hollis came to a stop and put her hands on her knees, she was grateful for him, grateful for the advice, no strings attached.

Kayaking to Dillon Beach had cleared Matt's head, leaving the faint trace of her that inevitably lingered. He was back in his right mind, which was a good thing because when Hollis came around the tent, dripping in sweat and calling after Toro, he almost swallowed his tongue. That body, all of it tight and shining with sweat, her hair pulled back with pieces wet and curling around her neck, everything he'd managed to settle down suddenly yelled, "Please. Can we still have it?"

"He's not in yet." Matt untied Toro's dog and walked over, trying to face her like a man. Hands on her hips, Hollis was still catching her breath.

"Were you running?"

"No," she met his eyes with that bite that he never could resist.

"Huh, then you have a serious perspiration issue there, Holls." Yes, he was making sure he used her nickname every chance he could now that he knew it affected her. *What are you, in high school, moron?*

"What kind of dog is he or she?" Hollis asked.

"Beagle, and Scooter is a he."

"Seriously? He doesn't look like a beagle."

She was still breathing heavily, and Matt tried to control his thoughts. Wasn't it bad enough she was back? Did he need to also endure the tiny shorts and the sweaty, heaving chest?

"He only has three legs, maybe that's what's throwing you," Matt joked, hoping he would piss her off and she would leave to get some damn clothes on.

Hollis rolled her eyes. "Thank you, I can count his legs. No, I'm simply saying I pictured beagles bigger, in my mind."

"I find things are often bigger in my mind." *Don't go there, man.*

Hollis glared at him with a resolve Matt recognized as "whatever, asshole." Clearly they were back where they belonged. Maybe she had still been drinking too much last night and didn't even remember him spilling his heart all over their pier. Hope sprang eternal. From the looks of her, Hollis had put the booze down now and was probably as sharp as ever.

"I think he is a mix of beagle and some other little dog. I rescued him about a year ago. Toro adopted him."

"From here? How did he end up needing rescuing here?" Hollis crouched to pet Scooter.

"No, the city."

"Were you visiting your parents?"

"No, Twenty Questions. I was at home on a Saturday and Scooter was outside the shelter with a couple of other dogs. It was like an adoption fair thing. Toro wanted a dog. I called him and now Scooter here is one hell of a kayaker."

"Home. You don't live in the city." Hollis stood, looking confused.

She still had the same ability to order everyone's life for them based again on what she thought it should be in her mind.

"But I do." He grinned.

"I thought you said you lived here."

"I have been for a while. It's a long story, but I live in the city and commute when I have to."

"Where in the city?"

"What's with all the questions? Let me try. Where do you live in the city?"

"Financial district. Bush Street. It's less than a five-minute walk to work."

"Figures." Matt ran his hand through the loop in Scooter's leash and stuffed his towel in his bag.

"What's that supposed to mean?"

"I'm sure you know what that means. I've never understood that phrase. When people say, 'What does that mean?' they usually know exactly what the other person means. It's like a trap phrase, sort of like, 'excuse me?' but less abrasive."

"Okay, Mr. Philosophical. Are you still reading André Gide?" she asked as they walked along the shore and Matt lost his place in the banter.

He hadn't read Gide since he packed up his stuff and left Stanford for good. He hadn't read much of anything lately. It was as if somehow, the guy he was back then needed an ingredient that was no longer available. As uncomfortable as it would have been to admit it then, and as much as he tried to fight it, Hollis added something to his life, to him, that made him more interesting. She questioned and pushed. He loved pushing back. The challenge was so heady that once she was gone, things felt dim like the blinds had been drawn. Light had still snuck into his life over the past twelve years, but it was a dash here or a streak there. With Hollis, the windows were thrown open and there was no need for curtains ever again. Their life, the way they had loved each other, was as natural as a breeze or a rainstorm. By the time they hit their twenties, it was as if they'd loved each other all their lives. They practically had and that would explain why as hard as Matt had tried, he could never get back to reading Gide, never find that interesting guy that Hollis Jeffries was stupid in love with.

Somehow, in between all of their pushing and pulling, he must have become an obstacle, something she needed to discard so she could focus on shoving the pain or what happened way down. Matt never had any delusions about Hollis; she wasn't sappy or clingy. He loved that about her, but those very things that made her so singular were what had kicked him to the curb in the end. Hollis Jeffries used to leave him little notes around their apartment. He made her breakfast on Sundays and when she was anxious about a paper or presentation, she would bake. They made jokes about their teachers, liked completely different movies, and made love even after being up all night in the library. They couldn't get enough of one another back then, but the minute their life became messy and she couldn't see a clear path, she left and never looked back.

As the memories became too painful, Matt pulled himself back to the present in time for Hollis to prop her leg up on a nearby bench and bend to stretch. *What the hell? Was this some kind of penance for... my divorce? Or not fluffing Dad's pillows when they came home? What?*

"God, it felt great to run. I think I've eaten my weight in junk food and chowder and bread. There's so much bread here." Hollis looked lighter, less burdened. Matt supposed it was the endorphins from her run. He hoped they wore off soon so she could get back to bitchy-grumpy, because he wanted to pull smiling-in-the-sunlight Hollis into his arms and make up for all twelve years by the time the sun set. That was a very bad idea, but thankfully, his self-preservation instinct kicked in and helped Hollis find her way back to pissed.

"And alcohol," he said, with a smile that was preprogrammed a long time ago to slide right under her skin.

Hollis stopped mid-arm stretch and her brow wrinkled. "Yes. I've been doing some of that too. Are you a monk now, Matt? Did your ex take your man parts with her?"

He laughed and continued as Hollis left him standing on the sidewalk, her perfect ass all but flipping him off. The confidence, or the "brass" as his father would say, was intoxicating. Especially when he alone knew the insecurity that simmered right below the surface. She was funny but could turn like a lemon after a cool glass of iced tea. Matt was still smiling when he put his seatbelt on. He'd started the day feeling lousy and pent up, but after a few minutes of sparring with Hollis, he was ready to go.

Maybe she had been right all those years ago when she said they were split-aparts. Matt sure hoped not because she left him once and no matter how many summer days stretched out before them this time, she would leave again. It was simply a matter of time.

Chapter Ten

*H*ollis helped Candy clean Miss Kitty and Big Earl because they were expecting a ten o'clock check-in on those two cabins. As she walked into the bar to see if there were any more of those small plastic bags for the bathroom trash cans, she noticed Uncle Mitch and Matt sitting at a table near the patio. Perfect, Hollis thought. Wiping her arm across her forehead and hoping they wouldn't see her, she quietly slipped behind the bar and ducked to search through the basket under the register. All voices fell silent. So much for sneaking away. Hollis wanted to sit down in the cool air near the refrigerators and wait them out, but it was no use. She found the bags, threw them in her bucket, and stood to greet her uncle and her latest motivation to get her act together and get back to her life.

It was unfair how well just-rolled-out-of-bed worked on him. Hollis woke up lately looking like she'd had the crap beaten out of her until the cool water hit her face, but Matt somehow walked in the light. Despite his pillow-swirly head of dark hair, two days' worth of stubble, and a wrinkled gray T-shirt, she found herself wanting to climb into his lap.

That's perfect. Aside from the blatant stupidity of that idea, nothing says sexy like a woman who's recently had her hands in a toilet bowl. Leave, Hollis, now.

"Hey, Tots. Whatcha doing?"

"I helped Candy service Big Earl and Miss Kitty."

"At the same time?" Her uncle giggled.

Matt sat there, eyes shaded by sunglasses, with a blank expression similar to the one that used to glaze over his features anytime Hollis wanted to watch a movie with subtitles.

"You are hysterical, and so early in the morning. I'll let you two get back to... whatever it is you're doing."

"Why are you cleaning?" her uncle asked as she turned to leave.

"Because Chloe has strep throat and called in sick today. You have two early check-ins on the calendar and... those cabins aren't going to clean themselves."

"We have a calendar?"

She shot a fake grin in their direction. "We do now. You should check it out. Later gator."

"Why do you call her Tots?" Matt decided to participate.

Hollis shook her head, knowing her uncle would not hesitate to share the origin of her awkward and borderline inappropriate nickname.

True to form, he pointed to his own chest and gave an animated jiggle that had Hollis holding back a laugh.

"Seriously? Because of her—" Matt smiled. "How is it possible I never knew this?"

"Because when I was younger, he wasn't sharing it with the world," Hollis added, looking at her uncle.

"It's not as creepy as it sounds. Hollis came in from the beach one summer. How old were you?"

"Eleven. Can this please be over?"

"Right, she was eleven and there were some other girls on the beach with big boobs, well, big for that age. To make a long story short—"

"Too late." Hollis moved the bucket she was holding to the other hand before her arm went numb.

Uncle Mitch was enjoying himself. "I told her that lots of great stuff comes in small packages. Like—"

"Tater tots, which then grew into Tiny Tots. All done. Thank you for that. Matt, stop staring at my boobs."

"Sorry." He looked up.

"Okay, I'm getting back to work."

"Matt's driving down to Point Reyes to help with the oyster run for today because the oyster guy up and quit yesterday. Did you know he has a band?"

Hollis shook her head. "How would I know that?"

Her uncle shrugged. "He's also going to pick up some blue cheese too because the chef is making wedge salads tonight. Isn't that nice of him?"

"The chef, yes. I love a good wedge."

"I meant Matt."

"He's the salt of the earth." Hollis was almost to the door.

"I was thinking you could go with him since you've been cooped up here for a while."

Her back still to them, she closed her eyes. Her uncle had a way about him; Hollis liked to call it the Jimmy Buffett way. It wasn't something he put on, it was more about who he was. Everything was light and easy, sun and fun. All things were possible and nothing was ever complicated and if someone, namely Hollis, was focused or not in the mood for piñatas and drink umbrellas, they felt foolish in comparison. She had no idea how he did it, but nothing, nothing was a big deal to her uncle.

"I'll get those bags to Candy for you and help her finish up," he said, still waiting for a response.

"I'm not presentable." Hollis turned, holding out the bucket and looking down at her little wear-to-clean-a-toilet-bowl shorts and her navy-blue tank top with a fast-fading blotch she was certain was spilled bleach.

"We're getting oysters. Does that require a wardrobe change?" Matt asked, standing and folding his arms across that stupid chest of his that appeared to have grown over the years.

Screw you, Matt. Sideways.

She kept that thought to herself, which was a feat of Herculean strength, but she wasn't feeling all that powerful standing there without a bra on and holding a bucket, so she hushed her "sailor mouth" as her mother liked to call it and went with sarcasm instead.

"You are right. Thank you for pointing out my superficial tendencies."

"No problem."

Hollis lifted her arm, sniffed. "Let's do this."

Uncle Mitch laughed. "You two kids play nice. Take the truck. I gave Matt the keys."

"Fantastic." Hollis waved over her shoulder and walked out, shaking her nonsuperficial ass all the way to the truck.

There were worse things than spending the afternoon driving to Point Reyes with Hollis who, now that he took a closer look, was wearing next to nothing. He thought for a moment that he should be gracious and let her grab some clothes, but the very male part of him decided that wasn't necessary.

"What? It's not like I have any boobs, so it's not that scandalous."

Matt didn't realize he was staring. Shaking himself free from the very real urge to haul her into his lap, he pulled onto Highway 1.

"You have... boobs. Can we call them breasts?" he asked after a few moments of silence.

"No. That's stupid, they're boobs."

"I call them breasts."

"Great, and if they were yours, you could call them whatever you wanted to call them, but since I have to prop them up in a padded bra every morning, they're mine. My boobs."

"They're not in a bra now."

"Right, okay. Thank you for noticing."

"Anytime."

Hollis folded her arms across her chest, and Matt smiled.

The truck rattled a bit as they drove along the curves that cut through green and golden rolling hills. Quick postcard views of the ocean were around every turn. Matt loved this drive. Nothing but the hum of the road and the occasional bump of the center line when he corrected too late in a bend. Hollis rolled down the window and stuck her hand out to feel the wind. He did the same and the air traveled up his arm, cooling the heat of the sun on his face. From the corner of his eye, Matt noticed her pull her legs onto the bench seat of the truck. She looked up at the trees canopying parts of the drive, and Matt wondered how many lives those trees had seen. How many young lovers, arguments, and leisurely Sunday drives had the trees above them witnessed?

There were times life could make a person feel big and important. He was certain her big stage was pacing the length of a conference room in expensive shoes, but at the moment, curled in her uncle's truck with the windows down, Hollis seemed almost fragile. Nature, the ocean, the stars did that to a person. Matt's dad used to tell him anytime he was feeling too "big for his britches" that it was time for a trip to the seashore. Glancing at her, he wondered again why she came back.

"Let me get this out. I'm sorry about the pier. I was... it was the moonlight, I'm not sure," Matt said when it looked as if she might drift off to sleep.

"I think that's in a song, the moonlight bit." Hollis was now holding her legs to her body.

"O... Okay. Great. So you don't need to worry that I've been pining over you all these years. I'm fine."

"Good." She looked out the window. "So you take it back then?"

He quickly glanced at her again, his eyes returning to the road.

"When you said you never want to let me go, you're taking that back?"

"I guess." Matt downshifted as they came around a turn.

"Huh."

"Don't do that, don't one-word respond. That's my thing." He needed to focus on banter because the memories were strangling him.

Hollis, satisfied she'd gotten under his skin, grabbed a mint from the center console of her uncle's truck. Mitch always had mints. She took in a deep breath, and he could practically hear her mind moving like the pieces of a powerful engine.

Something about being in the cab of her uncle's old truck stirred things in Hollis. Even though the ride was rough and occasionally noisy, the smell of motor oil and wood mixed with a fair amount of dust made her feel safe. The fact that Matt was within touching distance and laughing as if they'd come from the movies and he was driving her home was equal parts joy and ache.

"Do you ever feel like life is short?" Hollis asked. "Because when I was younger it felt like everything took forever, but lately, someone has turned up the treadmill."

"There you are, no more one-word responses. Let the deep car ride discussions begin. Much better, all is right with the world."

"Shut up and answer the question."

"Yes and yes."

"Aren't you cute?"

"I try." Matt smiled. *Dear Lord, the sea air agreed with him.*

"Now try to use your big-boy words in an actual sentence, Locke-ness."

"Yes, I remember thinking things took forever. When I got my cast on sophomore year and I couldn't go in the water for like two weeks after we came to the cove, do you remember that?"

Hollis nodded.

"My parents getting older, that seems like it's rushing by. I swear they were forty last year." He quickly glanced at her again, and they both smiled.

"Uncle Mitch says it's probably my biological clock, which is such a stupid sexist thing to say. A woman's life doesn't suddenly speed up because she needs to reproduce. That's bullsh— eet fed to us so... there can be a baby clothes market."

Hollis was animated and wrapping up her point like it was a

presentation, but when she looked over at Matt he appeared lost, staring at the open road. She had not been in a car with Matt, or anywhere for that matter, in years but she knew instantly what was wrong. His eyes still on the road, she recognized that particular kind of stiffness.

"Sorry, I didn't mean to—"

"What?" He glanced at her quickly. "Didn't mean to what?"

"Bring up... I don't know. I didn't think and—"

"Is that what happened then? You didn't think?"

"What does that mean?"

"Is that why you shut me off? Why it became *your* pregnancy and eventually..."

Hollis felt a rage build in her that she'd forgotten she had on the subject. "Eventually what, Matt? Since I shut you off before—go ahead and finish that thought."

He pulled the truck onto the side of the road, threw it into park, and turned to her, his eyes filled with frustration and pain. Deep, long-held pain that Hollis understood.

"Eventually the miscarriage. That's what I was going to say. *Your* pregnancy, *your* miscarriage, were *you* not thinking? Not thinking about us or about me?"

Hollis lost her breath and then started to laugh. She'd read once that people under extreme pressure often laughed. If this conversation didn't qualify as pressure, she wasn't sure what would.

Matt shook his head. "That's great. Go ahead and laugh. Are you completely dead inside?"

She could tell that he would have taken back his choice of words if he could, but it was too late and maybe he was right. Maybe she'd been walking around all this time thinking she'd dodged a bullet when in fact a part of her had died.

"I'm not dead."

"Sorry. Maybe we should go."

"I wasn't thinking about you. It wasn't conscious, but all I thought about back then was that I was pregnant and when I lost it, yes, I suppose that was my loss too." She touched his hand without even questioning it as if there were suddenly no rules for what she now understood to be their baby. Matt's hand pulled back at first and then closed tightly around hers. He didn't say anything but squeezed her hand.

"I'm sorry," she said, her voice soft. She was desperate to keep the tears from escaping.

"I don't want you to be sorry."

"Then what do you want me to say?"

"It's not a matter of the right thing to say at this point, Holls. I wanted to be there for you. It was our baby and when it was gone, it was *our* loss."

Hollis shook her head. The idea that they were in something together, that instead of the past being about her pushing forward and making a life for herself, it was about her turning him away... that was more than her heart was ready to handle. She didn't want to discuss this right now, not any of it. Getting out of the truck, Hollis started walking.

"Where are you going?" Matt caught up with her and turned her by the shoulders.

Hollis squirmed and he let her go. "I need some air. I don't know why we are talking about this. It's over, has been over for so many years. I don't want to go back there."

"I don't either. I wasn't trying to say that you didn't—"

"It doesn't matter what I didn't do. I was the one who was pregnant. I was the one alone in that bathroom."

Matt looked back at the truck, so Hollis took him by the shoulder this time. "Me, in the bathroom, bleeding and cramping with no one to help. That was me, so I'm sorry if I didn't include you." She somehow hoped her words could explain away what to her adult mind seemed so selfish now.

"You go through things alone, Hollis, because that's how you want it. No one is good enough to ever share in your fear, your pain."

"That is not true!" She pushed at his chest.

"Oh, okay." He threw his hands up and walked back to the truck.

When they were both in, Matt pulled out onto the road. They drove in silence and Hollis wondered if it was somehow possible to slip back into the easy conversation they were having before she brought up baby clothes and Matt had her looking at things differently. In retrospect, she'd hardly given his feelings a thought, which she knew sounded cruel, but back when her entire world went myopic, it was difficult to see anything. Maybe that was a gift time afforded people, some distance to see outside their own solitary experience, but at twenty-two, there was no such view.

Sitting next to him now, she could see the pain. There was no longer anything she could do about it. Maybe he was right and she should have let him in. Hollis shook her head at the thought because it was so easy to do the right thing in reverse. She'd done the best she could, and that had caused him pain. She didn't know what to do with that or with the thought that after all of these years, she still insisted on going through things alone. She wasn't sure where "letting people in" would fit on her long list of things to fix, but it wasn't going to happen anytime soon so she did the one thing that had always worked with Matt: she changed the subject.

"Back to the clock, why is it no one ever says, 'He's all randy because his clock is ticking?'"

Some of the tension simply slipped away, and Hollis wondered if that was because the subject was now no longer off-limits, "the event" wasn't a "shh" anymore. That didn't mean either of them had the strength to sort through their mess, but there was some relief. Glancing at her quickly again, Matt must have recognized the life raft she was offering. His beautiful eyes softened around the edges and true to form, he took it.

"Hold on, randy? No one uses that word anymore," he said with a hesitant smile.

"I do. It's a great word. One of the guests, staying in Lil' Earl, said it at breakfast."

"Was he eighty?"

"I don't care. It's a perfect word to describe men. I'm bringing it back."

Matt shook his head and pulled off again, this time to get gas. "Well, if anyone can bring 'randy' back, it's you."

Hollis hopped out while he filled the tank. "Men are never told their clock is ticking."

"That's because our clock doesn't tick. Men don't have a shelf life."

Hollis felt her temper rise, and then she heard the snicker he was trying to hide behind his sunglasses.

"You're good at pissing me off, you know?"

"I do. Lots of practice." He replaced the pump and they climbed back into the truck.

"A shelf life. Wow."

"I said that to piss you off. I have an entire stash of things that I know will get you all fired up."

"Did you dust those off recently? Why?"

"I have dusted off a few. And because despite my best efforts to ignore, it's nice to... have you back, Holls."

Hollis put her bare feet on the metal glove box of the truck and pulled on one of the baseball caps she found in the truck low on her forehead. "Happy to entertain. Ass."

He grinned as they twisted and turned toward Point Reyes, and Hollis realized she'd missed him. When they were younger, things were simple and the love she felt for Matt, she realized, must have been conditional on that ease because once things became complicated, she'd left and he hadn't followed. The want currently coursing through as the endless coastline once more came into view was different. Cleared of the glitter of youth and chosen snippets of their past, she wanted to know him now, to discover who he had become. In her longing to find out what she'd missed, Hollis almost forgot that things in her life, while certainly not on the same scale as they were back then, were again ugly and complicated.

Her heart quietly asked if he could help, if maybe now she could let him. That single question took Hollis's breath away as she turned her face to the breeze of the open window. Need had remained the one thing Hollis controlled above all else. It made a person weak, gave away the upper hand. As "regimented" as it sounded, the one thing that scared her more than being fired, being found out, was

need. Accepting their past was one thing, but needing him again—
Hollis shook her head as if she were having an actual conversation
with her heart—that wasn't possible.

Chapter Eleven

They grabbed crab sandwiches and chowder from The Crab Hut. There was barely enough room to turn around inside because most of the space was an entire wall of huge stainless steel pots boiling on burners and a short service counter with small plastic cups of sauces, fresh slices of lemon, a stack of napkins, and a homemade pie under glass with a few pieces already missing. This whole area spoke to a part of Matt he thought must be tucked into the corner of all grown men. The idea of being a pirate or a fisherman on the open sea—it was a kid dream for most men and far less romantic for the men who did the work, but that didn't stop the fascination every time he was in a harbor town. Outside the blue-and-white building hung a chalkboard with their offerings for the day and a decent-sized grass area that overlooked the harbor. There were four circular concrete tables with benches.

He'd been here a few dozen times with Hollis while they were growing up, but when it was their turn to order, he wondered what adult Hollis in the tiny shorts ordered at a crab shack. When she'd first come storming back into the cove, he was flooded with memories, but now where she'd been and the person she'd grown into held more interest. They both ordered the crab sandwich, which was nothing new, but then she ordered chowder and Matt had smoked oysters. Old and new, maybe it was the optimism of the day or that she was her most beautiful when she didn't seem to care, but for the first time in a very long time, Matt felt the possibility. His stupid heart overpowered logic and history. For the span of one lunch, his mind allowed him to wonder if one car ride or one Party on the Pier at a time could be pieced together to make a life. There they sat, her watching day-tripping families taking pictures, laughing when the guy with a long beard working the smoker turned and she noticed his T-shirt that read, *Shuck You*, and Matt watching... her. Sun and sea, one of his favorite places, and the whole time he tried to decide if it was a great place or if everything had been great with her. He rubbed the back of his neck and logic slowly brought him back down. *That's enough heart for one day.*

Hollis finished her last spoonful of chowder and stood to throw out their trash. Somehow, she managed to hit the corner of the tray and the red-and-white baskets went flying.

"Fu—dge nuts!"

"What's with that? You've done it a couple of times now. What are you doing?" Matt helped her pick up the garbage and after they managed to get it all safely into the brown plastic can, they returned to the table.

"I'm cleaning up my mouth. I'm not a good example for small children."

"Is that something that's important to you?"

"Yes, I mean it wasn't, but I had to run to Kerensky's for Uncle Mitch last week. I was on the phone and... it's a long story, but I was livid with a guy from work because he was trying to say that... it doesn't matter, the point is that I was cursing a blue streak and when I left the stall there was a mother and her daughter. She read me the riot act and then her daughter told me I wasn't washing my hands properly."

"So you were smacked down in a hardware store by a mom and her kid?"

Hollis shrugged. "I guess. It was weird. I felt like a crazy person.

Completely oblivious that there were other people in the world, and it made me question how I'd gotten to the point where I would talk like that in a public place."

"Kerensky's no less."

"Right. I get in these modes where I'm some sort of a…"

"Bulldog?"

"I guess. Whatever, Mr. Smart-ass. You asked. So that's why I'm saying 'truck' instead of 'fuck' and 'spit' instead of 'shit.'" She whispered the last few words.

Matt looked around. "But there are no children. We're not in the bathroom."

"Practice. I'm practicing so it becomes my new norm. You never know where you'll be. My mother tells me all the time I curse like a sailor." Her brow wrinkled and Matt tried not to look at her mouth or think of the perfectly naughty things he'd heard slip from it. "No way she can be right, so better language is on the action plan."

"Okay, wow, there is so much to take in here. Let's start with 'blue streak?'"

"Isn't that great? The guy who washes all the windows for Uncle Mitch, you know the one with the missing finger?"

Matt nodded.

"I overheard him saying it the other day and I thought it was so clever. I like the image, so I stole it. I'm using it now."

"Just like that, it's been incorporated and added to 'randy.' Okay, next, do you honestly have an action plan for yourself? Tell me that was a joke."

Matt wouldn't put it past her. He used to tease her about her color-coded notes and her incessant use of index cards when they were in school. Sometimes it was a little surreal he was sitting across from her again, like some sort of second chance he'd given up on a long time ago.

"No, not exactly. I have the usual notes and a few timelines." She took the last sip of her soda, dumped the ice on the grass, and tossed her paper cup in the blue recycle bin. The Crab Hut had been recycling since before it was cool, and as Hollis had said, it was habit.

"So, that sounds like an action plan."

"Fine, yes, I guess it's an action plan. They're so darn measurable and helpful."

Matt finished his drink and tossed it too. "I hear ya. I can't get enough of them myself."

Hollis shook her head.

"Okay, last question."

"And then we really need to get going." Hollis stood up.

"The eventual goal with Operation Mouth Cleanup will be to naturally say things like 'funky town' and 'ships sailing' in moments of anger? That you'll transform into a Willy Wonka kind of ranting person instead of a sailor?"

"Yes. Make fun, if you will, I honestly don't care. You didn't see the look on that mother's face. I'm rarely embarrassed, but that day I was embarrassed by my mouth."

"I've always been a fan of your mouth, Holls."

The air left her lungs—he could see it swoosh past and, whether she knew it or not, her eyes went all stormy-seas sexy. Holy hell, she was something. So far he'd been holding his own with the banter, but all this talk about her mouth and his mind drifted somewhere it had no business going.

Pull it together. This is Hollis. Hollis of the saved voice mails on your phone after she left so you could still hear her voice. That one, remember how pathetic you were? Snap out of this, asshole, or you're going right back to Loser Land.

"Did you rewash your hands?" Matt asked as his eyes took their time traveling up to meet hers, and he stood to leave.

"What?"

"The little girl, you said she didn't like the way you washed your hands."

Hollis nodded. "But I'm not adopting that into my life. Three minutes is stupid."

He laughed and opened the truck door for her.

They drove for about twenty minutes. Hollis had fond memories of this drive. When she and her sisters were little, her uncle would load them into his truck, the one before this relic, and drive them to the store for ice cream. There were frozen treats like the ones a kid could get from the ice cream section at the small general store at the cove, and there were special treats. The Tasty Cone was in Point Reyes and they made their own ice cream with cream from the local dairies. It was, to this day, the best ice cream Hollis or her sisters had ever had. She wasn't sure if it was because of that time in her life or if it was the ice cream. It didn't matter. She was almost afraid to see if the Tasty Cone was still around because what if they stopped by for ice cream now and it wasn't as good? Sometimes revisiting the past had a way of messing up the shine, she thought. Maybe that would happen with Matt, maybe after a few more minutes with him, she would realize he hadn't been all that back then and certainly wasn't much now.

Wishful thinking disappeared when she glanced over at him and all her body wanted to do was scoot closer. The bump of the gravel parking area brought Hollis back to reality as they pulled past a sign that read, *Point Reyes National Seashore.*

"I thought we were going to the markets."

"We are, but I thought we'd check out the lighthouse."

"I've never been to the lighthouse."

"I know, me neither. It's something new."

Hollis sat in the warmth of the car as Matt came around and opened her door. "You're not afraid of a little new, are you, Holls? Let's go."

"I'm in tiny shorts and a tank top."

Matt pulled his sweatshirt off, and she caught a glimpse of a dusting of dark hair on his stomach. That was new too.

"Your sweatshirt is not going to fit me."

"Because you are obviously making a fashion statement with the rest of this. Put it on and let's go before this van of tourists beats us to it."

Hollis poked her head through the sweatshirt and in addition to swimming in material, she was drowning in the scent of him. For how many years had women relished, gone completely silly, for the smell of their men? Her man. Hollis didn't have a man. Wanting and having were two different things. Matt had taught her that a long time ago, so she would settle for what was turning into a great day and the warm delicious smell of him because neither of them had what it took for the "having" part.

Matt wanted to tell her she had what looked like a piece of oyster cracker in her hair. He wanted to reach out and pull it from the strands, but even in his sweatshirt, she was breathtaking and he had a feeling touching her at all would lead to complete logic shutdown followed by finally taking the mouth he couldn't stop thinking about. Suddenly, his mind was back to the many pleasures of Hollis's mouth. She liked to talk and whisper, he remembered vividly, as if he'd left her bed that morning. *That's a great idea, dumbass. Let's go down hot-sex memory lane too.* Instead of telling her about the cracker, he did what he usually did—he stood back and gave her some space as they walked toward the lighthouse. She'd eventually find the piece of cracker herself.

They stopped at a section of chain-link fence and looked out at an ocean far wilder than the bay water near Mitchell's Cove. The wind was howling as they walked down the cascading stairs that led to the lighthouse. Succulents and grasses clung to the rocky coast. A foghorn sound vibrated from the lighthouse and for a moment, Matt wondered if he could live in a 137-year-old lighthouse. Did people still live in lighthouses, or had that—like most things solitary and romantic—died?

"No," she said from behind as he read one of the placards.

"No, what?"

"No, no one lives here anymore and no, you could not do this. Even you, an only child, would lose your mind."

Matt turned to face her and she did not back up. They were face-to-face and he quirked a brow in question.

"What, you think you alone possess the I-know-what-you're-thinking mind trick?"

He nodded. "How?"

Her windblown face bloomed into a smile, and she reached up and touched his forehead. "I've known you for a long time. Even after a few years, some things don't change."

"A few years?"

"Feels like yesterday sometimes, doesn't it?"

Yeah, it does, Holls. "Sometimes."

"Anyway, Parks and Recreation keeps up the lighthouse now, so your dreams of wearing a turtleneck and smoking a pipe are dashed. You'll have to seek out one of those desolate posts no one wants."

"Would you come with me?"

Matt could count on one hand the number of times he'd seen Hollis truly stumped for a response. Looking at her now, he would need the other hand because she was searching for something to say... then her eyes slowly drifted away without an answer.

As her hair blew across her face and she returned her gaze to the ocean, there it was again, the need to touch her. Hollis had always been a beautiful girl, at least to his eyes, and she'd grown into a gorgeous woman, but there was something about the whole package that completely turned him upside down. She was, quite simply, brilliant. The things she took the time to know, the way she saw the world, all of it collected inside a compact, efficient body and hidden behind a face men wrote songs about. She was a deadly combination and no matter how mixed up the signals behind her silver eyes became, Matt never tired of watching to see what was coming next.

"If I were ever going to live in a lighthouse, which is a crazy idea because I love the city and my life, but if there were ever a vacancy and a lighthouse needed me I would... consider it with you, Locke-ness."

"What would our life in a lighthouse look like?" he managed to ask, his heart drumming in his chest.

She turned.

"We'd probably have to wear those scratchy sweaters and eat lots of stew."

She was dismissing him. He wasn't good at noticing it when they were younger, but he saw it now. He'd asked her a question, and she either didn't want to think about it or couldn't. Matt had never been sure where that line was for Hollis, but she was excellent at keeping to herself.

"Christ, let's hope the lighthouse never needs me, right?" Hollis said.

Her laugh was laced with the pain, and Matt guessed it had something to do with the gap that often rested between what was and what could have been. He could have left it there, easily kept walking or read another placard, but the more time he spent with her, easy didn't seem to be enough.

"When did you move on?" Matt asked.

"Sorry?" She turned to face him, the wind doing its best to whip her hair back to the ocean. The piece of cracker came unstuck, and he watched it twirl in the wind and drift from sight.

"After us, when was your next relationship?"

"Honestly? We're at a lighthouse. We're stuffed with delicious crab. You want to talk about this right here, in front of the school tour group?"

"They're in there looking at the aquariums."

Hollis looked out toward the water again as if it held some answers for her and then quickly turned back. "Are you asking me when I had sex again after you or when I went on a date?"

"Either."

She pulled the hood of his sweatshirt up around her neck. "I don't even remember. Two, three years? I didn't date anyone until after I graduated. I was a little... well, it was the furthest thing from my mind."

"Two years after we were finished?"

"Yeah, I guess or two years after we graduated. I can't remember."

"You can't remember, right. You said that."

Her brow furrowed in annoyance. "Why are you asking?"

"I have no idea. I was watching you, and being here with you, it seems like we have a lot to talk about. Then, when we start, it feels strange, like the statute of limitations on it has run out or something."

"It?"

"Closure? Yeah, I have no idea what I'm talking about. Let's get back to reading about the last guy who ran this place before Parks and Rec took over."

She held his gaze for a moment. It was as if she was struggling with some kind of internal debate. She inhaled and exhaled slowly. "I wasn't involved with anyone after you, Matt. The part of you that wants to make that romantic needs to remember what I'd been through physically and that I had a one-track mind back then: finish school and be successful at all costs. I worked for a smaller firm during the last few months of my master's. I was in the break room and there was a paper on the table. It must have been Monday because it was a Sunday paper. Sections folded, things torn out. I honestly can't make this up." She took another deep breath. "One of the sections was folded over to the wedding announcements and I saw your picture. I was sitting there eating my fuc—nky"—she looked around, and Matt felt the urge to laugh but wanted to hear the rest of the story more—"yogurt and there you were with Little Miss Headband. You were getting married, at some country club of all places."

Hollis looked back out toward the lighthouse. He took one step into her because he suddenly felt the space between them grow instead of shrink. "That night, I finally went out with one of the other interns who had been asking me for a couple of weeks. He took me to dinner and I funky towned his brains out."

Matt had no right to be jealous, but that didn't stop it from crawling up his neck. He smiled because this whole cleaning up her language thing was entertaining. And it helped distract him from the idea of her going to town with anyone but him. "Did you two date?"

She shook her head. "No. It didn't help, so I dumped him. I think he's married to one of the other interns from our class, so it worked out for him. Do you want to see if we can climb inside this thing?" She pointed to the lighthouse.

"Hollis." She looked at him for less than a beat and continued down the stairs to the lighthouse. Conversation over. Even though he thought his throat was going to close shut while she was telling him the story, he wouldn't have unasked the question. They were talking about real things again and while every instinct in him said to back up, maybe that wasn't the answer anymore.

Chapter Twelve

The sun was setting by the time they arrived back at Mitchell's Cove. With the parking lot over three-quarters full, Hollis smiled. Uncle Mitch continued to fight her every step of the way claiming he did not need anything more than he already had, but Hollis had dealt with tougher resistance before. The sounds of music and merriment, along with the smell of summer bonfires she loved so much, filled the air before she even left the truck. Whether he needed it or not, Uncle Mitch would do well to understand that people needed him. They needed places like his cabins, his cove, to escape, laugh, and share a moment destined—by virtue of the fact that it's a holiday or time away—not to last. His place was special and she believed it deserved success.

She used to get a rush from finding money, "getting the cookie" as her boss enjoyed chanting during his meetings, for projects and people that were special. In reflection, Hollis was beginning to notice that like so many things, that had changed too. Her work had become about money instead of discovery. She used to work hard finding the hidden gem, and somewhere along the way it turned into taking what other companies had and outsmarting the competition. She was good at it, no question, but until recently, she'd never bothered to ask if what she did was worthwhile, if she was contributing to something important.

The band playing inside the restaurant turned gentler with a lilting guitar and a soft snare drum. Hollis closed her eyes.

"I'll bring this stuff in to your uncle," Matt said as he came around the truck with boxes in both hands.

Her eyes opened and she nodded. "I'm going to take a shower."

When he smiled, she tried not to visualize what the heat that crept into his eyes promised.

"What?" he asked when she rolled her eyes.

"Nothing. Thank you for the drive, the afternoon, and the lighthouse."

"You're welcome. I'll... see you around." Matt looked like he was in some awkward limbo.

"Yeah." She should have said more, but they'd had quite a day already. She turned toward her cabin.

"I was thinking I might get one of Mitch's burgers. It's a great night and I haven't been out to the bait shack on the pier in forever."

Hollis kept her back to him. There were so many reasons she should keep walking, an entire action plan full of better ideas, but he was giving her something and while whatever it was felt scary, she wasn't willing to miss out on a little more time with him — not tonight.

"You hungry?" he asked, still standing behind her, arms full in the parking lot.

"I could eat." Hollis still didn't turn to face him.

"Good. Go get some decent clothes on, will ya?"

She looked over her shoulder at the sound of his laughter, shook her head, and ran to her cabin. It was one night, one burger, and then she'd get back to fixing her problems and returning to work. One night wasn't going to change anything.

Matt delivered the oysters and cheese to Mitch, who was a bit concerned they were already thirty minutes into dinner, but forgave them when Matt explained they'd gone to the lighthouse.

"Incredible, right? I've often thought that would be a great job," he said before running off to give the chef the blue cheese.

Despite their obvious differences, he and Mitch often thought alike. The man was an interesting mix of real world and old world. He had an iPhone and an iPad tablet, but still used shaving soap with a brush. He ordered all of his clothes online and there were some interesting pieces, but he drove around in an old truck. Matt had liked Mitch all along, even when they were kids. Now he loved him like family, which was interesting because up until he agreed to help out when Poppy went on leave, he had not put much time into extended family. But now he was closer to Mitch and saw Greg all the time at The Bean. He had Toro, and even Poppy and Mr. Trumble were a part of his routine. He supposed those relationships were the result of effort and maybe, as his mother had pointed out, giving something of himself even if no one asked. He should probably call his father tomorrow and check on him. He'd think about it, but right now all he wanted was more time with her.

Picking up two to-go boxes with the burgers he'd ordered, Matt grabbed an extra tablecloth and a bottle of wine from the section of the refrigerator marked, "For Hollis ONLY." He hesitated, remembering Mitch said Hollis was "laying off the grape," then put the bottle back. Instead, he slid a water bottle under his arm and took a candle from the basket by the silverware. As he made his way up the pier, his heart drummed in his chest, but as hard as he tried, he could not convince himself this was a bad idea.

The bait shack was situated at the end of the pier. It had a single string of lights on it now, but it was often pitch black. In the summers of their childhood, Hollis and Matt made a deal on the nights that their parents called them home after sunset. Matt's parents' house was on a hill near Mitchell's Cove that faced the water, and Hollis's family was in *Bunny Blue*, which was two in from the pier. They agreed to keep a lookout after dinner, and if one of them could sneak away, she or he would bring a flashlight and point it faceup in the dark little shack. Matt was usually the one who could get away first because his parents had a habit of watching television after dinner. If either Hollis or Matt saw the light, they knew the other was waiting.

He hadn't brought a flashlight this time because she would be there to meet him. Matt set everything down on the rusty and crooked card table in the shack and turned as Hollis, now in jeans and a long-sleeved T-shirt, walked up their pier and toward him. Her hair was wet and gathered at the base of her neck. His mind tried to order things, run through all the reasons he should leave the light that was Hollis Jeffries off for good, but nothing worked. He couldn't take his eyes off her. If she was going to crush him again, that was fine, so long as he had the chance to spend one more evening with her on their pier.

"You managed, though," Matt said, cautiously leaning back in an old chair that was poised to collapse at any minute and crossing his arms over his chest. They'd finished their burgers and were quickly closing in on the fries.

"What does that mean?" Hollis asked, taking a sip of the water bottle that sat on the table between them.

"Exactly what I said. Without me, you survived. You were happy."

"I guess. So did you."

"I think it may have taken me longer." He smiled.

"I'm sorry? You were married two years after I graduated. Married. Are we seriously going to argue over who was more heartbroken?"

"I never said my heart broke."

"Oh, well then I win." She took another sip and seemed to be searching for her feelings again. Matt wondered where feelings went on Hollis's action plan.

"I win because my heart broke and fell apart. What's that nursery rhyme?" Hollis asked.

"Which one?"

"The egg, he sits on the wall?"

"Humpty Dumpty?"

"Yes, like that." She nodded. "I was definitely the egg man—or woman, I guess. I probably still haven't found all the pieces." Her eyes met his and in that moment, the crap they'd been through was right there in the tiny shack with them. He wanted to tell her he was sorry things became so twisted, that he would spend the rest of his life helping her find the pieces. He wanted to say a lot of things, but Matt learned a long time ago that a little thinking before speaking went a long way. So even though the look in her eyes said they could hop in his car and cruise up the coast, stop for taffy, and live forever making the other one laugh in scratchy sweaters eating stew, Matt knew better. The woman sitting across from him was not an adventure to be taken lightly. He'd tried once and failed.

"Your heart broke," she said, cheeks flushed, eyes barely looking as she wrapped her arms around herself to keep warm.

"You think?"

"I know."

They sat listening to the muffled sounds and music from the restaurant. It was as if they were somewhere else, some other state or country even. All alone, floating out on a strip of wood.

"Remember second year of Junior Sailing?" Hollis asked.

"Ninety-five?"

Hollis nodded. "We had to partner up and Taylor Britton wanted me to be on his boat. Because of my mad skills, obviously."

Matt shook his head and snatched the water bottle from her.

"You put up a little fight, but the counselor said whoever ran to the boat yard and back won me as a partner."

Matt nodded. He knew where this was going.

"You rolled your eyes and told Taylor he could have me." She pulled her legs into a crisscross on her own wobbly chair. "You sailed so hard that summer. Protests, shouting, you were intense. Won the whole damn series, remember?"

He did.

"If your heart was hurt over losing me to Taylor, I'm guessing it broke, at least a little when we..."

She appeared at a loss for words, so he helped her. "When you left?"

Hollis nodded, and Matt needed a release from the cruel pain that hit him in the chest. He couldn't tell her that when he'd lost her, his heart didn't break, it died. He wasn't ready to face that or tell her that since she'd been back, instead of feeling the distance of so many years, he felt like they were more real, more honest than they had ever been before. He needed a way out or he'd drown in her, so he went with light and easy.

"First of all, if memory serves, I kicked Britton's ass because he sucked even with you on his boat."

Hollis laughed. "Sure looked like maximum effort out there."

"Yeah, well look what it got me. You danced with him at the End of the Series Dance."

"One dance. He was my partner. You weren't even willing to run to the boat yard for me, and I danced twice with you."

"He ran track. He would have won."

"You could have tried."

Their eyes met across the warmth of the candlelight and even though Matt had spent so many years feeling like the one kept from the story, for the first time, he wondered if he had it all wrong. God, he'd hated Junior Sailing.

After the candle had burned out, they sat on the pier. The dinner crowd must have been finishing up because people started spilling out into the gravel parking lot. Hollis was amazed how time still managed to fly when she was with him. She'd been on dates, good dates, where the conversation was stimulating and the guy was fun, but nothing had ever come close to being with Matt. They moved from one thing to another seamlessly until by the time one of them had to go home or go to class, they were talking about something else entirely. Hollis normally said more words, but Matt's insights tended to be more interesting.

Watching the fish glide through the glow of June phosphorescence, Hollis wondered how she had ever let him go. It seemed impossible that she cut off a part of her world that at the time felt as vital as her next breath. But she had—she'd left and never looked back.

"Humpty Dumpty... surprisingly childlike for someone like you," Matt said into the darkness.

"Someone like me?" She let the question hang between them, knowing his response could hurt her, but wanting it anyway.

"Yeah, calculated, precise."

"What kind of way is that to describe a person?"

"It's accurate when it comes to you, Holls. You are a driven, push-to-the-front-of-the-line kind of a person."

"What? How do you know that? The last time you saw me, I was twenty-one."

"Oh come on. Look at you. You *are* success. Your body is perfect, you dress perfectly."

She tilted her head in confusion because it had been so long since she'd felt even close to perfect.

"Well, with the exception of what will probably be a brief period of... downtime. You're meticulous. Your action plans have action plans. That type of person is a force. You're a force."

Something shifted in his voice. It was like they'd been out playing all day and Matt quickly realized it was time to go home. Maybe he thought they only had one day. Maybe that was all he wanted. Hollis couldn't tell, but he was no longer playful and flirty.

"Force? You make me sound like a computer or the Terminator."

He raised his eyebrows as if to say, "If the shoe fits."

"Then why are you sitting with me? Aren't you afraid I'll bulldoze right over you?"

Matt grinned and lay back on the dock. "Been there, done that."

"I did not bulldoze over you." The stillness was now stifling. "Matt?" She lay back beside him.

"Let's leave it at you being a force, a powerful one. Okay?"

He stared up into the night sky and Hollis suddenly needed to prove him wrong. She wasn't a machine. She had feelings and emotions, so many of them slamming into her lately, and she wanted him to know. Reaching out, she found his hand and focused on the stars.

"If we lived in a lighthouse, I would bake fresh bread every Saturday and I'd want a cookie jar. I'd wear Wellies all the time, worn-out jeans, and sweaters. Not scratchy ones."

Matt turned his head slowly. She could see him out of the corner of her eye, but she kept gazing up in fear she would lose her nerve.

"Big soft sweaters and a down coat with a fur-trimmed hood. When we come in from the wind and surf, we will leave our boots at the door, hang our coats on a polished brass hook, and walk around in our socks." It was all right there in the dotted stars of the sky. She could see them together. "We would eat soup and stew from big bowls with torn pieces of the bread I made. And stock up on cherries and ice cream. No computers; we would write letters by hand. And none of our dishes would match."

"Holls." He squeezed her hand.

She closed her eyes. Somewhere in her heart, she wanted the dream. She wanted to show him now what she was too selfish to show him before. "We would never miss a sunrise if we lived in a lighthouse. We could take walks and have tea in town."

"Where would we get our food?" he asked, his voice right above a whisper.

"On Wednesdays, we would ride our bikes to the small store for groceries. We would always have music." She felt the tears warm and melt around her closed eyes but she didn't care—she kept holding his hand.

"On Sundays, I should probably oil the banister of the staircase and clean the windows," Matt added and when Hollis turned to him, he reached across and wiped her tear away. "Why did you stop?" He smiled. "Let me guess... because it was your story to tell and I messed it up?"

She smiled, but then grew serious. "I'm not a robot."

"I know." He looked back up at the stars and let go of her hand. Maybe the idea of the lighthouse being more than a passing comment was too much for him.

"Why haven't you left town yet if you live in the city?" she asked, sitting up.

"Poppy is back part-time for now and my dad had hip surgery. It slowed him down so I've been helping out."

The wind chime outside the bait shack tinkled and knocked as the pier rolled with the movement of the water.

"So you don't live here."

He shook his head.

"And you don't work at the coffee shop."

Again, he shook his head and added, "I'm filling in, but no, it's not my job."

"Why would you let me believe you were working there?"

He shrugged. "I guess it was easier."

"What do you do then?"

"I'm a programmer."

Matt stood abruptly. Hollis guessed show-and-tell was over, which struck her as odd; she tended to be the one to shut down, but it was getting cold and she had shared more with him in one day than she had with anyone in the twelve years they'd been apart. It felt like taking a deep breath, but as she stood, Hollis was reminded that she didn't live in a lighthouse with Matt. She had a laptop waiting for her and a very real problem to fix.

"Why are you here?" he asked as if he'd heard her thoughts.

There was a cold punch to his question that shattered what remained of her lighthouse story.

"I..." Suddenly, it was easier to talk about sweaters and soup than it was to rehash poor choices and things she hadn't even shared with her family. "I've had some stress at work. I'm pushing too hard and... I needed a break."

Matt didn't believe her, she could tell, but he didn't ask for a different answer and she didn't offer. They had been quite a pair, push and pull, bend, and eventually break. Walking up the pier, Hollis felt the empty space between them. A moment ago she was holding his hand in the moonlight. Now, it felt like they were on opposite sides of the bay.

"Goodnight, Holls," he said, facing her as the wind picked up and his hair blew across his forehead.

His hands were full of the items he'd brought out for their dinner, so Hollis instinctively reached up and moved the hair from his eyes. Even though her breath caught, she stayed there and touched the side of his face. Her palm was cold compared to the warm stubble of his skin. Matt's eyes met hers, and Hollis could have sworn he leaned into her hand. As her touch slid down the side of his neck, she could feel his pulse and when Matt dropped what he was holding to the ground and pulled her into his body, she knew he saw everything. Everything she'd put behind the wall of a different life, a different choice.

Chapter Thirteen

The first time Matt kissed Hollis had, not surprisingly, started with an argument and finished with a bet. They were in the water holding on to the dock. It was the week before school started and they were both thirteen. Matt remembered it vividly because it was the first year Hollis wore a bikini, one that didn't look like a sports bra. This one had strings and in the span of one summer, he had gone from imagining kissing her to figuring out how to make that happen. It had been the summer of PlayStation and the first time he'd ever heard the word Yahoo. Hollis started watching *Friends* that summer. He remembered because years later, when they themselves were in their twenties, Matt had been standing in their tiny kitchen when he yelled, "Yeah, well I'm sorry this isn't like *Friends*." She had slammed the bathroom door and he'd slept on the couch that night. But back in 1994, she'd seen two episodes, they were suntanned from a summer well spent, and all he wanted to do was kiss her before they had to go home and start different schools on different sides of the bay.

"You can't hold your breath for more than sixty seconds. No way, you barely made it to forty last summer."

"So."

"So"—she splashed him—"nothing has changed. You still have the same lungs."

"They've grown."

She snickered, her braces glistening in the last afternoon sun.

"Fine. If you pass out, I'm not saving you."

"Fine."

"Good. What's the bet?"

"I hold my breath for sixty seconds or more and you... you kiss me."

"What?" Another splash. "Quit screwing around Locke-ness, what's the bet?"

"That's it." He switched positions, still holding on to the dock and facing her.

Brows furrowed, Hollis was about to splash him again when he took her hand.

"Why?" she asked quietly.

"Why, what?" He was still holding her hand, surprised her wrist was so much smaller than his.

"Why do you want to kiss me, stupid?"

"Because when I hold my breath that long I get dizzy and if I'm gonna do it, I want something good."

She shook her head. "Well, I've never kissed anyone so I'm probably not going to be good at it and besides, I have braces."

"So."

"So, pick something else. Then next year, after I get my braces off and I've practiced on a few boys, then that can be the bet. It makes no sense to make that your bet right now. Sixty seconds, you could have anything. An ice cream. I... I could buy you a burger or candy. I mean, who wants to touch lips with some girl who's never even done it before?"

"I do." He moved in closer, nervous and unable to control his body in the water. His leg bumped into the slick smoothness of hers and Hollis's eyes grew to almost perfect circles.

She inhaled, exhaled, took a wad of gum from her mouth, and stuck it on the dock. Their eyes held and Matt remembered being that mixture of nerves and excitement seldom recreated after thirteen. Looking back on it now, he wished he'd paid closer attention, but no one ever did that.

After a few ripples in the water and one more bump of her leg, Hollis said, "Do you know what you're doing?"

"I'll figure it out."

"Okay, well let's go."

"Don't you want me to hold my breath under water first?"

Hollis huffed and pulled him into her. Matt put his other hand on the dock so he could hold on in the water, facing her. He would remember forever the sensation of her other hand leaving the dock and wrapping around his neck so that she was suspended, holding on to nothing but him. His thirteen-year-old heart thundering in his chest, he noticed every detail on her face, the freckles, the droplets of water on her eyelashes, everything. When he finally tilted his head to lean in and kiss her, Hollis closed her shining silver eyes and the moment before his lips touched hers, she whispered, "Be careful of my braces."

It was the first of many kisses and Hollis had been right, they both became much better with practice.

"Don't love me," she said, the moment Matt drifted from his memory and realized his body was gloriously pressed against a stunning and unsure thirty-four-year-old Hollis Jeffries. He was inches from the breathtaking familiarity of her wide and waiting eyes.

"Too late," he whispered into the side of her neck, drinking in the smell of the night air tangled in the still dampness of her hair.

Hollis smiled. "Now what kind of defeatist attitude is that?"

His breath gently met the untouched skin behind her ear. "There's no sense in fighting it anymore. I won't win."

"I'll bet you could if you tried." Her head fell to the side, giving him more of her neck.

Matt smiled. She remembered too. Their first kiss, the one that he supposed had brought them to where they were right now. He traced his lips down the long curve to her collarbone. "All bets are off tonight, Holls."

Their eyes met as he checked to make sure she was with him, ready for what this one kiss was going to do.

As her eyes fell closed, Matt wondered if their second first kiss would be enough. He doubted it, but he kissed her anyway.

The kiss went from questioning to craving in less than a breath. He'd been foolish to think that after all the years he would need to relearn her, which seemed absurd now that her body was in his arms. She was a little different but so much of the same that he almost didn't remember to breathe. The woman confounded him when she was thirteen, so Matt knew this older, snarkier version would surely finish him off. A moan from her lips glided past his and as simple as anything else on a late-summer night, he remembered what it was to want.

Matt had spent the past twelve years wanting for very little. Life after Hollis was almost enough but never full, and that was how he survived, he guessed. The minimum was easy, less to lose. But as her mouth searched his, enough turned insatiable.

Hollis didn't believe in the yin and yang of things. The concept that every life was comprised of good and bad was something more in line with her sister Sage. Hollis believed in stamina, pushing through and making her own good. That rarely involved the influence of something otherworldly or kismet, as so many of the romantic movies Annabelle made her watch espoused. Things worked out or they didn't, based on decisions, choices, and recently, after several late-night talks with her uncle, "how a person rises after falling." Life was tactile for Hollis—she was in control, in charge of her destiny. And then she wasn't.

The kiss started with the hesitation of a man about to jump off a cliff he knew would kill him and then it turned to falling into the warmest, sun-drenched water under a crystal-blue sky. There had to be something to fate—she'd believed in it when she was little, hadn't she?

When she was thirteen, she was given a book of mythology. The Greeks believed that humans were first born with four legs and four arms. Zeus feared their power, so he split them apart, which explained why people search for their other half, their split-apart. She'd known the moment she read that story that Matt was her other half. When they were together, even when they were fighting, she was convinced that she was complete.

That's what she told him the night he walked her back to her cabin after their first kiss.

He'd smiled. "Whatever you say, Holls," he said and tried to kiss her again.

She had let him, twice, and before she closed her front door, she said, "I still don't believe you can hold your breath for sixty seconds."

He had laughed and walked back to his house. Hollis crawled into bed and closed her eyes, but her heart stayed up all night.

Was it possible she was less aware of herself now than she was at thirteen? Anything was possible at this point because she'd lost the ability to stand when Matt's hand had slipped under her T-shirt and touched the skin of her back. His arms kept her from melting into a puddle and slipping through the slats of the pier, and when he whispered, "I've missed you," she knew it was real. She wasn't reliving some memory or dream she allowed before shutting that all off in the name of survival; she was there in the dark of a summer night kissing the one man who made her feel whole and this time, she didn't have braces.

Hollis kept her eyes closed when their lips at last parted and she tried to think of something pithy, clever as she had when she was a teenager, but nothing popped into her foggy mind. She simply opened her eyes to a home she'd been away from for far too long.

"I missed you too."

Matt looked taken aback, as if he'd expected her to push instead of pull. She supposed that was a valid expectation, and she found she loved surprising him. They were safe standing there under the stars and nothing was going to swoop down and steal it away from her, at least not yet.

Chapter Fourteen

Hollis sat outside the restaurant in the red-and-white sling chair that looked like it was left over from another time. She tested the material to make sure she wasn't going to break through the center like *I Love Lucy*. There were a few people wheeling bags on the sidewalk to check in, and one lady had a wide-brimmed yellow hat Hollis coveted for herself. She looked down at her nails, and for the first time since she'd left her office and driven straight to her parents' house, Hollis thought she might be ready for a manicure.

Mitch was too distracted greeting guests and trying to figure out how to use the new scanner Hollis had ordered for all of his receipts to worry about finding another karate kid task, so she took a seat. The sun was almost directly overhead, and she shaded her eyes to look up at the cotton-white clouds hanging in a blue sky. Hollis was again reminded of her sisters and the summers they spent lying on the beach arguing over the pictures made in the clouds. Sitting alone, Hollis told herself there was a mouse, a turtle and... maybe a mail-man. She smiled. It was a gorgeous day, so she closed her eyes and tried to quiet her mind enough for a short nap.

"Excuse me," a Jersey accent, pinched too tight at the nose, zipped across the distant hum of beach traffic and Hollis kept her eyes closed, hoping it would go away.

"Hello! Honestly, these beach places are kitschy, Fred, but the service is awful." Claps sounded inches from her face this time.

Hollis had dated a guy from Jersey once. Mo, great guy with an even better family. She had spent four days with them. She and Mo had gone to a seminar titled, "Spots Aren't Only for Leopards." She would remember that title forever because it was awful and so was the seminar, but afterward, Mo's mom and dad took them to Passaic River Falls. Hollis had loved his family and New Jersey, which was great news for the woman currently tapping her cheap wedge sandal. Had it not been for Hollis's previous love of the "Garden State," she would have made this woman cry.

"Is there something I can help you with?" she asked in her calm, conference-room voice once she opened her eyes.

"Ah, yeah. We only have four towels in our little bungalow, and Fred asked for extra towels when he booked online. Didn't you, Fred?" She turned, and Hollis noticed the gold necklace sort of burrowing into the folds of her neck. The poor bastard who was obviously married to Miss Congeniality nodded.

"And"—her eyes widened as if she had exciting news. Hollis highly doubted it—"we used a Groupon that promised a welcome basket. We don't got a basket."

Hollis silenced the grammar police in her head and smiled. Years of dealing with people had prepared her for this moment. The woman was so close to the edge of the water that all Hollis would have to do was brush past her with a quick elbow to the ribs and the nasty hag with way too much hairspray would need more than towels.

"I am so sorry to hear about this. Which cabin are you staying in?"

"There are seven cabins. Is it that hard to keep your guests straight?"

"I... let's start over. My name is Hollis. And you two are?"

Fred hesitated for a minute, as Hollis was sure he'd done his entire marriage, and stepped forward to take Hollis's extended hand.

"We're Fred and Sue Morris."

Hollis liked Fred.

"Yes, of course, you are in Big Earl. It's your anniversary. Welcome. I will bring the towels to your cabin right now and the basket. I apologize things were not ready for you. I'll include a bottle of wine on the house and some fresh flowers. Are you two heading out?"

Bad Shoes nodded in that stunned way Hollis loved when she'd cut bad attitude off at the knees.

"Okay." Hollis guided Fred and his unfortunate wife down the path toward Toro's place. "Have fun and we'll look forward to welcoming you back."

Fred nodded and his wife barely managed a smile. Hollis turned back toward her chair and saw Uncle Mitch with a big smile on his sunburned face.

"Wow. I did not see that coming. The Big Earl couple is... challenging. When I heard her voice, I thought by the time I came out here you'd be burying her in the sand."

Hollis smiled. "Not today. I'm in a good mood and I happen to like New Jersey, so she was safe. Besides, challenging people are my specialty." Hollis sat back down in her chair and crossed her legs.

"You should have sunglasses on out here."

"Said the man who is the color of a lobster." She shaded her eyes and looked up at him. "What happened, by the way, did you forget sunscreen?"

Her uncle shook his head. "It's stupid. I took this paddleboard yoga class Toro was offering and I was so tired, I fell asleep on the beach after."

Hollis held his eyes for a beat, trying to figure out if he was joking. "You do yoga?"

He shrugged, waving to a lady walking two almost-identical miniature fur-ball dogs toward the beach. "Not usually, but I thought I'd try. Last time. I think I pulled something."

"You should probably start with yoga on land first before attempting to balance on a board, don't you think?"

"Probably. So what did Big Earl couple want?"

"They had legitimate complaints. No extra towels and they didn't get a welcome basket."

"Shoot, I was meaning to tell Candy."

"It's all right. I told them we'd fix it right away and I gently guided them away from my gorgeous day."

"You threw in a bottle of wine and flowers. I heard. You're good at this, Tots."

She laughed then realized her uncle was serious. She was on a fine line with seconds to respond before she appeared to be a snotty elitist. Maybe that wasn't who she really was, but prior to getting her feet back in the sand, she had been accused of such behavior.

"You think?"

"I do. I mean I know you're crazy educated, but what you did with that woman is not found in a book. You're genuinely concerned about people."

"Let's not get carried away. It's more of a kill 'em with kindness philosophy." Hollis stood.

"Well, it works. You're incredible, you know."

Hollis was stunned. "I don't these days, honestly. Thank you." She kissed her uncle on the cheek and before she cried or jumped into his lap and asked him to read *Where the Wild Things Are* with the voices and all, she turned and ran right into Matt.

"Perfect, you're here. I'd like to take you somewhere. Are you free?" He steadied her.

Hollis looked back to her uncle, who was sporting an interesting pair of tie-dyed pants and collared shirt that in no way matched. "Will you take care of Big Earl for me? You can grab a bottle of wine from my now-neglected stash and I put some larkspur at the hostess station, so you can have Candy put those in their room."

Her uncle saluted and waved her to go.

Hollis turned back to Matt, still remembering his mouth on hers but not wanting to be obvious. "It seems Mr. Miyagi is letting me go. Where do you want to take me?"

"It's a surprise." He took her hand and led her to the parking lot.

"Once again, I'm"—she looked down at her striped shorts and flip-flops—"not exactly dressed for a surprise."

"You are for this one." He opened the passenger door of a black SUV and climbed in to drive.

"Is this yours?" Hollis asked, putting her seatbelt on.

"I hope so." Matt pulled onto Highway 1 with the sun now dropping lower in the sky. "We need to hurry up."

"Why? Is this a Mercedes G-Class?"

Matt turned briefly then focused back on the winding coastal road. "You know cars?"

"I know this one. Something doesn't make sense here. Either your parents are supporting you, which I find hard to reconcile given what I know about you, or this mystery programming job pays extremely well. What's going on?"

"It's an old one. I think it's like 2010 or somewhere around there."

"Uh huh."

"It was a gift." Matt smiled.

"From who?"

"A lady friend." His brows wiggled, sending his glasses up and down.

Hollis laughed. "Oh, so that explains it. You have a sugar mama."

Matt nodded.

"Well, you are kind of hot, so I can see why the older country club gals would want a piece of that."

He took her hand and kissed it as if they'd been together forever. They had in fact, but not like this. The road stretched out into the bay then curved back in, and Hollis was mesmerized. The beauty of the area was never lost on her, and she could get used to the calm pulse of her heart.

"It never gets old," she said, turning her face to the wind. "Are you seriously thinking I'm leaving this conversation with the explanation that you're some rich woman's boy toy?"

"Yeah, I really like that. It sounds like the perfect thing to send my parents right over the edge. It might make them wish they'd bought a puppy instead or that I'd been in that car instead of John."

Hollis was stunned as the memory of Matt's family rushed back to her. In their isolated dance to find one another, she'd forgotten. "That's not funny. Take it back."

Matt shook his head. Damn him, he never took things back when she asked.

"How are your parents?"

Matt was no longer smiling. "I told you, my dad had hip surgery and my mother is perpetually disappointed that I didn't at least produce one grandchild before getting divorced and shattering her dreams."

Hollis had to remind herself that he'd been married. It was part of his life now, part of their adult histories. Their stories had evolved and when she looked back at Matt, she realized he was older. Sometimes when they were this close to the ocean, she forgot.

"Is he in pain?"

"He's still sore, and yes, he's still *a* pain. I spoke with Toro, though, so we might try to get him in the water."

"That's a great idea."

"We'll see. I might have to use a tranquilizer gun."

They laughed and drove for a few more minutes before Matt said, "Your sister is getting married?"

"She is. In a little over a month now."

"Do you like Garrett? That's his name, right?"

"Yes and yes."

He smiled at her one-word answers. Hollis shared pieces of the Sage and Garrett story. Caught him up on the rest of the Jeffries sisters and mentioned that her parents were planning a trip to India for their anniversary.

"Wow, most couples go to Paris."

Hollis smirked. "Not mine. Every time, it's someplace new."

"I remember that. Does that bother you?"

"Does what bother me?"

"That they're so... accomplished. I've always thought they cast a fairly big shadow."

"No. I don't mind." With the weight of discussing their families, she couldn't tell why, but she took her hand back and looked out the window as they pulled into a parking area.

She had never been to Lawson's Landing—another first. She'd been clamming before, but never on Tomales, which was strange because she and her family had spent so many summers here. It felt intentional on Matt's part, as if he was continuing to add to their present in the hope it would somehow dilute the past twelve years. So much of their history swirled around this area that it was difficult to be original on a date. *Date. Is that what this is?*

It took less than an hour before they were slopping around the dark black mud in their waders. The guy who set them up had asked if they wanted one bucket to share, and Matt shook his head and snatched up two buckets before Hollis even had a chance to answer. He knew Hollis. Had he not grabbed an extra bucket, she would have insisted. They each needed to have their own because that was the only way to know who picked the most clams.

Sometimes, he wasn't sure Hollis was even aware that she naturally made everything a show-up event; all of life's experiences turned into a contest of sorts. Hollis worked her own clam tube and shovel. Matt knew there were men who would be annoyed or intimidated by her ability to grasp and conquer, but he found it incredibly sexy. After about an hour, the sun was starting to set and they came together to see if either of them had reached the fifty-clam limit.

"Thirty-six, thirty-seven. I've got thirty-seven, you?" Matt asked.

Hollis had a smudge of sand across her cheek and a face that said she did not have thirty-seven.

"Did you stick your tongue out at me?" he asked as he reached out to wipe the sand off her face.

"Sure did." She backed up, bucket in hand.

"How many did you get, Holls?"

"Enough. I didn't go over. Are you ready to leave, because I should get back to—"

He faked like he was going to walk away but turned and grabbed her around the waist. Hollis dropped her bucket as he swung her around. The sun was creeping lower and they did need to get back, but her cheeks were flushed and her clothes stuck to her every curve... and those waders. Matt had never noticed how sexy waders could be. God, she was like the difference between the cloistered air conditioning of a San Francisco boardroom and the fresh cool ocean breeze.

Still holding her, before she could say anything, argue or debate, he kissed her, ran his hands along the sides of her breasts, and when her own hands began to travel his body, Matt allowed himself to feel all of her. Maybe he would regret this later, tell himself he should have pulled back after kissing her. That was probably how it would play out. Instead of having her for the rest of his life, messy, complicated, and so capable of making him feel everything, she would return home. Once the novelty of the cove wore off and she returned to her expensive shoes and even more expensive men, he would again be the fool.

Not this time, his stupid heart whispered. *Every time*, his mind whispered back. Matt watched Hollis break free of his arm and try to run in her waders and decided not to listen to either. He grabbed his bucket and couldn't manage to wipe the smile off his face. Whatever way this thing played out, he had created a new memory. The sound of her laughter and those waders would surely carry him a few more years.

Chapter Fifteen

*L*awson's Landing had a shower, but the mere sight of his clinging T-shirt was enough to shut her brain down, so Hollis was certain a shower scene after the great afternoon they'd had was a bad idea. That had not kept her from spending most of the drive home imagining ripping his clothes off and finding all that sand. When they pulled up to Mitchell's Cove, Matt grabbed both buckets from the back and contributed even more to her fantasy as his arms flexed under the weight.

"Oh, look at you two go. Special change," Mitch called over his shoulder to the chef in the back. "Okay, now get out because dinner starts in an hour and I don't want sand on my floor."

"Seriously?" Hollis was about to shake her hair and send the sand flying but decided to behave. Instead, they backed out, careful not to shake the wrong cuff or jiggle the wrong pocket. Obviously not ready to say good-bye, they settled themselves on a concrete bench off to the side of the entrance.

"I got more clams than you," Matt sang quietly as he leaned over and kissed her neck.

Hollis shook her head then grabbed his face and kissed him. It was sort of a punishment kiss, a thin line between love and hate type of thing. Even playful, his lips weakened her knees.

She was so lost in him she didn't realize they had company and certainly didn't feel the sleaze that was Reese. Sort of like those puzzles in the Sunday paper that asked, "What's Wrong with This Picture," when Hollis opened her eyes, her mind posed the same question.

"I heard you liked it rough, but jeez, you're a mess." Reese whistled, all of his class plainly on display.

Hollis felt like the earth had skipped a beat on its axis as her two words collided in an instant. She stood up and brushed at her shorts. "What do you want, Reese? How did you find me?"

"I want to know when you're coming back. If you're done playing... sand castle with whoever this guy is?"

She glanced quickly at Matt then took Reese's arm and led him back toward her cabin. "Your asshole is showing, let's get you indoors."

Reese laughed. "Strangely, I've missed you, Hollis."

"I'll bet."

"Seriously, it's been two months now. No one fired you, so what the hell are you doing here?"

"Finding myself."

He appeared puzzled, as if the concept was foreign. "Are you finished?"

"No. I need a couple more weeks. I've been checking e-mails, staying on top of everything. Christ, this morning I was on a teleconference with a guy from Spain."

"I know. I was there."

"Then what the hel"—Hollis pictured the crazy mom—"What are you doing here? The consultants are working with Zeke. I received an e-mail last night and they're optimistic about progress. I'll be back when I'm ready."

"Megan is getting awfully cozy with Corning."

"Oh, who cares. It's not like he'd be the first boss Megan's ever slept with."

"Ouch." Reese took a piece of her still sandy and crazy wavy hair. "I like this version of you. Kind of wild."

Hollis cringed because no matter how many times he tried to turn on the sexy, the idea of ever getting wild with Reese was out of the question.

"Time to go, Reese. Head back and tell Megan that I'm fine and if she or Corning need anything, they have computers." She led him back to the parking lot and noticed he had a driver waiting. Her eyes went wide.

"A driver, huh? Are they paying for your lunch and dinner too?"

Reese winked and climbed into the seat offered by the uniformed man now holding open the back door. "Hurry back," he managed to get out before the door closed.

Hollis found she was ill equipped to deal with Reese or anything work-related with sand in her shorts. Or maybe that was simply a metaphor for happiness. It was entirely possible, she had started to realize that happy and her life back home didn't go hand in hand at all.

Matt was still sitting on the bench outside the restaurant when Hollis sent the mystery man off in some car and walked toward him, still covered in sand. He would have smiled, but her face told him the smiling portion of the day was over. It was dark now and the bugs zapped at the two lights above the wooden sign that read *Mitchell's Cove* in sprawling blue script.

"You like it rough?" Matt asked, part genuinely curious and the other part sarcastic.

"I do, rough and cold." Hollis sat next to him with a vacant expression on her face as she ran her fingers through the sand on her leg.

"Hasn't been my experience." Matt smiled when she finally glanced over.

"That was a long time ago."

"Not that long ago. Who was that... really great guy?"

"Reese Winterford."

"Wow. He sounds like he's from *Game of Thrones*."

"That's Winterfell." She smiled, which was a good sign, but it was nowhere close to reaching her beautiful eyes.

"I stand corrected. He sounds like a spinoff of *Game of Thrones*. How does he know you like it rough?"

"He doesn't."

"Seemed like he might."

Hollis shook her head. They'd both now resorted to one-word answers, and Matt could feel himself wanting answers to pieces of her that were no longer his business.

He watched her fingers thread through the sand on her skin. "We were having a perfectly great sunset until Mr. Creepy appeared and screwed the whole thing up. Let's talk."

"He's a colleague."

"Sleep with a lot of colleagues, do you, Holls?" Matt knew it was harsh, but he wanted a reaction, something.

"Fuc—"

"Ah, ah. Think of the children."

Her jaw clenched as her eyes told him exactly where he could go without a single spoken syllable.

"Truck you. I don't owe you an explanation for anything." Hollis sat up straight, as if that somehow gave her more power over the situation.

"True. Can I have one question?"

She inhaled and exhaled, and he could tell she was biting down on the inside of her bottom lip. Some things never changed. "What?"

"Were you in love with him?"

Hollis laughed a full hearty laugh and shook her head. "Matt, I haven't been in love in a long time. No. I did not, do not, love Reese. He's a complete ass... ociate."

"Okay, then how long?"

"How long what?"

"How long since you've been in love?"

"Is this the part in the romantic comedy where I look deep into your eyes and say, 'Not since you, Matt?'"

He didn't flinch, didn't show fear. He waited, hoping whatever outer shell she'd put up at the sight of that guy would wash away and sandy, happy Hollis would float back to the surface.

"I don't do love anymore." Her eyes melted a little in the glow of the overhead lights. She stood, brushing her hands together as sand continued to fall off, and turned to leave.

He reached for her arm, but the words stuck in his throat when she turned back. She was thinking about the last time she'd been in love. He couldn't blame her—so was he.

"Me too, Holls. Me too."

Their gazes held for a moment as if it were some other summer, some other time when exactly what they needed was right there in a stolen kiss or holding hands. Hollis shook herself free from everything he could tell was rushing through her and punched him in the shoulder.

"Ouch."

"Cut it out, Matt. No one likes a soft, whiney guy. Man up."

"Okay." He pulled her into him and relished the total shock on her face for a split second before he kissed her. The outer shell was still there, but by the time he could taste the salt on her tongue, her hands climbed into his hair and they were back in their moment. Matt tried not to think about anything outside of the way her body responded to him, but he had a feeling things were about to get complicated. If they were in a "romantic comedy," as she'd called it, this next part was his least favorite.

Chapter Sixteen

The following Monday, Hollis felt like she was drowning in paper. She had sifted through what felt like hundreds of invoices, receipts, and unopened pieces of mail that were all mixed together with cryptic notes scribbled on torn pieces of paper her uncle couldn't even decipher. She put everything on his desk first thing in the morning then grabbed three empty boxes and began sorting. By the time Uncle Mitch entered with a tray of iced tea, she could see the wood of his desktop. When he tried to set the tray on top of one of her boxes, Hollis almost growled.

"How's it going in here?"

"That box is file, that one is scan, and the one over there, the one that is overflowing, is garbage. You honestly can't keep living like this."

"Like what?"

Hollis blinked the dust from her eyes and spread her arms, trying to encompass the entire ordered mess. "Like these things aren't important, like this is all easy. It's not."

Uncle Mitch picked up the cat that was once again back on the other chair and took a seat.

"Why do I feel like the tables have turned and I'm the karate kid?" He smiled and propped his feet up on the corner of the desk opposite Hollis.

She shook her head and smiled a little. Tension pulsed at her back, her jaw clenched, and Hollis recognized her foul mood had more to do with her recent visitor than it did with some stacks of paper. She'd enjoyed creating some order, but Reese had been to the cove, her cove, and that made her uneasy. Not that she couldn't deal with him, because he was a "minor player" even according to his own boss, but it was the blending of the two—past and present—that was bothering her. Maybe that's why she hadn't returned in all these years... because she was somehow encapsulating this time in her life, their life.

"Okay, so this is the last pile." Hollis gestured to the largest pile in the center of the desk. "I've fixed the scanner, so you can get back to making these receipts disappear, but you also need to go through this stack."

"Great. I'll look that over." He poured their iced tea.

"Now. You need to look over it now so we can finish this. Also, I've set up a karaoke night in the bar for Saturday. We'll rent a machine for the first few nights, see how it goes, and if it sells, you should invest in your own. They're not that expensive. Did you hire those two servers we interviewed?"

"Yes. They can both start tomorrow."

"Perfect. They should be ready to go by Saturday. Trial by fire."

She switched seats with him, getting him back behind the desk that was, she would at least admit to herself, looking much better. Uncle Mitch huffed and tried to share another story, but she kept him on task and he began reviewing the pile under her watchful eye. Filled with a simple sense of accomplishment that, if she was honest, she hadn't felt in her own job for years, Hollis took a sip of her iced tea and sat quietly as Uncle Mitch sorted out his... well, she supposed it was his past. The idea had her shaking her head as she opened her own laptop and wondered what surprises awaited her. Maybe she could somehow sort and shred a path through her dilemma too. The first e-mail read *Mandatory Meeting*. Hollis let a slow stream of air exit her lungs and highly doubted it would ever be that easy.

Refilling their glasses of tea almost an hour later, Hollis had responded to several e-mails noting that she would be back in the office by ten o'clock the next day for the meeting. The investors were preparing to exercise the part of their agreement that allowed them to bring in oversight. Hollis could not let that happen. One of her other e-mails gave her a measure of hope: Zeke was having a "bit of a breakthrough," as one of the consultants had put it. At last, a glimmer of good news. Now, all she had to do was hold off the circling suits for a little while longer.

"This is all going to be okay," she told herself, but it must have been out loud because Uncle Mitch looked up from over his reading glasses.

"If you say so, Tots. Is it time for lunch yet?" He shook his head and sent another piece of paper through the shredder.

She nodded despite the knot in her stomach. Closing her laptop and shutting her eyes, Hollis rubbed her temples and was reminded of a time when she quite literally slipped.

She had thought she was drowning for a minute back then too. This was it, she was going to sink to the bottom of Tamales Bay, she remembered telling herself, which was as fitting a place as any to die even at sixteen. So much of her life, the happy parts, had been spent on the pier, so she might as well end it there too. Granted, it was a mere twelve feet at the high season, but people drowned in bathtubs, so this wouldn't be quite as embarrassing as her teenage mind had thought.

When she had slipped off the pier and fallen into the water one early morning after an argument with her parents about taking honors classes and her "inability to see the big picture," Hollis hadn't even bothered to frantically paddle or lunge back for the pier. She simply sank, allowing the weight of her body to fall past her shoulders and down to her feet. She watched as her dark hair swirled around her like one of those mermaids in a movie. The growth beneath the pier, filled with bright green and seashells, was so inviting, so alive, and yet all hidden below the surface. She reached out to touch it, but she was too far away. Water separated her and the life teeming below the pier. She wondered how long she had been underwater along with whether or not she'd twisted her ankle and what that might mean for field hockey practice, which was due to start in less than a month.

Images of her sisters, her mother, and father passed by her as frozen snapshots of her brief teenage life. Hollis remembered smiling and feeling her body jerk a little, as if it had decided all on its own to swim to the surface. She needed to decide at that point if she was really going to die because her lungs began asking for breath, pissed they had to hold out so long. Arms stretched overhead, Hollis felt the water slide through her fingers as she pulled toward the blue-green surface, toward the early morning sunlight. It was so quiet. Her feet instinctively began propelling her upward. She'd almost reached the surface, stopping to drag her hand along the green life that had all but masked the below-the-surface wood of the pier.

She was young and things weren't so bad. Besides, she was far too selfish to end her life on her own. People needed her. Heck, the world needed her. She reached her hands toward the surface and then saw a burst of bubbles and what looked like underwater smoke as someone or something plunged into the water beside her. Someone had come to save her, probably Uncle Mitch because her parents were most likely still inside figuring out which boarding school they should ship her off to, she'd thought. Her uncle wasn't much of a swimmer, so she should probably grab him on her way up if she was going to avoid a real Jeffries family tragedy. Reaching out, she held the muscled, water-slick arm. It was warm in the summer water, coursing with as much life as the algae, but smooth and strong. The arm wrapped around her waist and instead of feeling trapped, Hollis relaxed and instantly stopped paddling as if she'd already made it back onto the dock.

Breaking the surface, her lungs clamored for breath as her skin prickled in the cool morning air. Her would-be rescuer was still holding her, his other arm outstretched and holding the dock. Having caught her breath, she blinked her eyes free of the droplets of water and lifted her arm to the dock in some minuscule effort to help keep them above water. Without a doubt, he had them, the both of them, but even back then Hollis was never one for being rescued. The instant she turned to face him, the moment he tossed the dark wet curtain of his hair off his face, she felt herself go back under. It was as if he'd let her go and she now had cement in her lungs. She became hyperaware of his body and that he was holding her, and her heart did one of those scrambling-and-backing-up routines she often saw in scary movies, right before the villain grabbed hold of an ankle and reduced the cast by one more. That morning, as Matt held her, she knew what it was to be loved outside the bonds of her family. He knew her, frequent fights and all, but when she'd slipped, gone under, he was somehow there and while she still liked knowing she could kick herself to the surface, she held on.

"Okay, that's the last one in this pile," Uncle Mitch said, pulling Hollis from her memory.

She opened her eyes, blinked up at the slowest ceiling fan she had ever seen, and wondered for the first time in a long time if Matt saw her now, knew she was drowning this time.

Chapter Seventeen

*H*ollis arrived at The Bean the next morning and Matt almost didn't recognize her. Her hair was silky and straight down her back. She was in a black skirt and stockings. Like the lovesick idiot he was, his eyes followed the length of her sheer legs and wondered where those things ended and the lace began. Hollis had never been a lace kind of woman, she was sexier in cotton, but looking at her, now he knew this Hollis worked the lace. Her blouse was starched white and buttoned up the front. She was at least four inches taller thanks to heels that again conjured up the lace and her and... *Jesus, what are you, a teenager? Help the next damn customer, Coffee Man.* Hollis was three people back in the line and on the phone.

"No. That is not how this is going to go. I will be in by ten and I want everyone in the conference room." Hollis shook her head. "I am not on fu..." She looked around.

Matt smiled.

"I am not on vacation. I have been working this entire time, and I'm not sure why Reese or anyone else for that matter... Right. Right. I'm done discussing this over the phone too. I'll be there soon."

She touched her phone to hang up, threw it into her bag, and then smiled at Poppy.

"Great bag."

Hollis let out a breath. "Thanks. I'll give it to you, but you have to take the phone too."

Poppy laughed. "I'm okay. I just had a baby, so whatever drama is on that phone is all yours."

"That's right. Matt showed me the... that is, I saw pictures of her. Hannah, right?"

"Yes." Poppy's face beamed as it tended to do when she was discussing her new daughter. "Do you want the usual?"

"Yes, please."

Poppy turned to give Matt the order and he already had it made. He walked around the counter and gestured for Hollis to join him off to the side.

"You're wearing a bra today," he said, and for a moment wished Hollis blushed. He had a feeling she would be gorgeous if she ever allowed herself to blush. The thought was amusing as if blushing was something a person could turn on and off. If it was possible to control it, Hollis had it locked down.

She shook her head and took her coffee.

"Where did you even find these clothes?" He looked her over and when their eyes met, he felt the heat he'd missed but was still a little hesitant to let in the door.

"I keep a backup in my car." She took the lid off her espresso and took a sip.

"Where're you headed?" Matt tried for casual, but the truth was at the sight of her all cleaned up and shiny, his heart had surged with a familiar rush of panic. He had nothing to panic about. They were not together and she likely could and would leave when she chose to leave. He was being stupid, but all rational thought he tried to send through to his head was blocked by his heart, which kept insisting that she'd come back and maybe...

"Yes, I've been given a leave from my summer detox program for the afternoon. The monkeys at my circus are trying to take over, so I need to go into the office." Hollis smiled and it barely turned her lips. Each time she brought up her job, there was a weight between her eyes and Matt wondered if that was the mystery reason she'd come back. It had something to do with work.

"Kind of defeats the summer program, doesn't it?"

"I guess." Her phone buzzed and she looked like a child crossing the street, not sure if she should check her phone or finish their conversation.

Matt wanted to help her decide by pulling her in and kissing her right there in front of everyone. He wanted to tell her that he had enough money for the both of them. Show her that they didn't need to live in a lighthouse to bake bread and walk around in their socks. They could do that from some great flat in the city. Maybe they could work together on a project, or she could start her own firm and pick what was worth late nights on her laptop and what wasn't. He wanted her to know that he wanted a life with her, no matter where it was. He wanted children. But instead, he said nothing, only rolled his shoulder as if he could somehow wash all the want away, and turned back toward the counter.

"I"—Hollis threw her phone in her purse—"have a few minutes before I need to leave. Do you want to talk about anything?"

She stepped into him and smelled incredible, but expensive, and her white blouse appeared too stiff over what he knew was soft, sun-warmed skin. She was ready to go, ready to return, and the thought of losing her again almost brought him to his knees.

"Nope. I'm good. Drive safe." He placed his hand at the small of her back and led her to the door.

"Right." Hollis stood taller as they walked outside but somehow came across less sure of herself than she was before. "Okay, well I'm off." She climbed into her car and he closed the door.

Matt could see her shoulder rise and fall in a breath before she pulled away from the parking lot. As he returned to the coffee shop, he realized her white shirt wasn't starchy at all. It was soft when he touched her. He didn't know why it mattered, but as he collected two empty cups and repositioned chairs around his parents' place, it seemed important.

Dobbins Capital had several hundred employees and sixteen vice presidents. Of those vice presidents, three were women and Hollis was one. She'd been given the promotion that brought her from the thirty-first floor to the thirty-second a couple days shy of her thirty-second birthday. It was an honor, a huge accomplishment that she immediately called her parents to report. Annabelle had taken her out for lunch to celebrate, but when Hollis arrived home that night well after eleven, she had never felt more alone in her life. It was kind of like the day she and her family went to the Louvre in Paris the week before she left for college. Hollis had wanted to see the *Mona Lisa* since she'd first been drawn to the painting's eyes in some picture book she had when she was little. She had a postcard of the portrait among the ticket stubs and snapshots around her mirror in her bedroom and eventually an Andy Warhol version as her screen saver on her first laptop.

Finally getting to see the *Mona Lisa* was a big deal, so on that trip when they followed the crowds along the giant white stone walls of one of the world's most celebrated museums, her heart was pounding with expectation. Her father read the map and told her "Mona" was in the next room. Hollis was anxious but patient as what felt like thousands of people moved in the same direction. She knew it would be worth the wait when she made it there, when she saw what she'd been waiting to see all her young life.

Her family in tow, Hollis turned into a room that was about the size of their entire house, and her father pointed to the far wall. Hollis saw two things: What looked like a relatively small frame tucked behind a glass or plastic enclosure and a sea of people all standing about, mobile phones in the air snapping pictures as they chatted and pushed their way about the room. Hollis stood frozen in her letdown. She'd had visions of this, walking along and suddenly coming upon the *Mona Lisa*, standing for hours marveling at the brush strokes and wondering if the rumors were true and what the smile truly said about her. But this mess of people climbing over one another simply to chronicle that they'd seen the painting was not what Hollis had in mind at all. In the end, she'd turned around and left the room, moved on, and looked at other paintings, because even as an eighteen-year-old, she wanted nothing to do with something so absurd.

About a month into her promotion, she'd felt the same way, but there had been nowhere to turn and no other room to view, so she made the best of it and learned to live among the crowds and their mobile phones.

Having survived a four-hour meeting, Hollis now sat in an office she hadn't seen in months and again realized two things:

One, she was running low on time. In less than a month, she would need the complete man-child she was stuck with to fix his damn chi and become one of three grown-ups heading Pretty Boys Gaming. It was a ridiculous name, she knew, but they had a great logo. Wilt and Liam were geniuses at spinning, but they were nothing but, well, pretty boys without Zeke. They needed Zeke, and so did she if she was ever going to erase this nightmare before anyone figured out how and why she offered this company up to their investors without securing their resources. She'd already talked to Liam, told him he needed to fix this, but he'd responded that his "hands were tied" with that stupid little wink that would haunt her for the rest of her career.

And two, if and when this was all over, she needed more. She used to love her job, still loved a challenge and finding the next best thing, but now she also wanted a life. Her life at Dobbins Capital was "a circus," as Farmer Garrett had said. The clothes, the conference rooms, it was like being an actress, and somewhere along her climb up the ladder she'd left her makeup on. Staying in character, never having downtime, was eating away at her. Maybe that was why she'd lost it months ago. Maybe it was a coping mechanism that said, "Hey, you're eating yourself, idiot."

Hollis pulled up her phone. No texts and no calls. She'd sensed something weird when he'd all but pushed her out the door of The Bean. Not that she could blame him. One minute she was kissing him silly and the next, she was cleaned up and prepared to hop back on the high wire. Lately, the contrast was startling even to her eyes. Hollis turned off her office lights and stood in the doorway for a minute, looking out over the scattered city glitter shining through the enormous windows behind her desk. She used to recognize this job, this life with all of the bells and whistles. It was never the *Mona Lisa*, but it still meant success, a win in her column. Now, having spent so much time at the cove with her uncle and being with Matt, it suddenly felt like the costume had shrunk; it was too tight and she didn't know how to ask if someone could take out the waist a little.

He was her deep breath, a warm splash of water on a clean face, and in that moment, she needed him more than she had ever needed a single person in her entire life. There it was, that word again. Need. Hollis had accepted the want, there was no denying it anymore. She loved him, always had. But she had joined the circus and even if she could find a new painting, how would they ever find a lighthouse?

Chapter Eighteen

att put the standard weekly reports in his bag and quickly took
some pictures of the longer table he'd placed against the back
wall of The Bean. He also took a picture of the display case that
now had lights so customers could see the options during their evening
hours. His father was still complaining of pain according to Matt's mom,
but she thought it might get his mind back on track if Matt could,
instead of calling, come down and "give him a little in-person update."
That's how it was presented. He had an early afternoon meeting in the
city with a potential client looking for an app that allowed his clients to
try on his specific hairstyles. The guy had some specific ideas and the
project sounded fun. Matt had learned, mostly through trial and error,
how to navigate the industry, but he still sought out fun. His father was
another story, but Matt agreed to stop by for lunch after his meeting.

Handing over the hydrangeas he'd brought this time, Matt kissed
his mom and took a seat in the living room. When she returned with
iced tea, he pulled out his phone and shared the latest round of
pictures from Poppy.

"Oh, now that's adorable. I haven't seen that one yet," she said,
holding his phone and looking at a picture of Eddie holding Hannah
by the shore of the bay.

Matt smiled and his mom flipped through a couple more shots.

"Look at that sweet hat." She turned the phone so he could see. "She's precious."

"She is." Matt took back his phone.

"Who is?" his father asked from the other room.

"You'll have to come and see for yourself," she responded.

Matt rose to offer whatever help his father would accept, but his mom touched his arm.

"Leave him," she said barely above a whisper. "The doctor advised that he needs to want to move at this point and do it on his own. He'll get in here eventually. The curiosity will eat at him."

Even though Matt had been stretched a little thin managing the shop, filling in for Poppy and his father and keeping an eye on his own company for the past three months, he didn't envy his mother one bit. She looked tired. When his father joined them for lunch, it was clear why.

"It's nice you bring pictures of other people's children. Not like we have any grandchildren. Don't you think that upsets your mother?" It was impressive that his father managed to get out all that anger in between bites of his sandwich.

"David," Matt's mother tried, as she did a lot lately, to ease the acid of her husband's tongue.

"It's okay, Mom. I'm not sure how not having children is my fault, Dad. Did you want me to run out and get someone pregnant?"

His father huffed and took a potato chip off his plate. "Would have been nice if you'd stayed with your wife and made a family."

Matt shook his head and was no longer hungry. He stood to clear his plate.

"I have cookies, Matt. Please stay."

Taking his plate into the kitchen, he attempted to calm the frustration he felt when he was around his father. Everything, every single thing was Matt's fault in his father's eyes. Matt wouldn't be surprised if their air conditioner went out and it was somehow made to be his fault too.

"Mom, I need to get going," Matt said, returning to the living room and reaching in his bag for the reports. "Here's the current inventory report and the sales for the past two weeks. Poppy is back part-time and should be ready to take things back in a month."

"Well, I'm sure you're happy about that," his dad said.

Matt looked to his mother, who shook her head, her eyes pleading for patience. "It will be nice to get back to work," Matt reluctantly replied and braced himself.

"Sure, what we do isn't work," his father said under his breath while flipping through the pictures of the baby on Matt's phone. "What the hell is this?"

Matt put the reports on the coffee table and walked around to the back of his father, who was now sharing the picture with his mother.

"Oh, that looks great," she said. "Where is that?"

"That's our shop. He put a table in my shop." He flipped to the next one. "And what? Why do we need lights in there? Those cases were fine as they were."

Matt didn't know why he bothered, but he tried anyway. "Dad, the table allows for more seating, and I dropped electric below so people can use their laptops. I also upgraded your Wi-Fi. It's so much faster, and you know how Mrs. Higgans loves to shop on eBay while she and her husband have coffee. She's thrilled."

His father huffed. "There was nothing wrong with our service before, and what are these lights?"

Matt hunched over his father, hoping somehow getting closer to him would help, and pulled the lighting picture back up. "They're small lights, and I ran them along the trim so no one can see them. The light runs up the case during the evening hours so people can see inside."

His father didn't say a word and gave Matt back his phone.

"Thank you, Matt. I think it looks lovely." His mother cleared the rest of the lunch dishes.

Matt sat back down and pushed the reports across the table to his father.

"I don't get why you forever need to change things." His father's face twisted in discomfort as he shifted his weight in the chair.

"I've never changed anything in your shops, but I've been there awhile and I thought I'd put some effort in, help. They're improvements, Dad, meant to make things better."

"I don't care if it's better. I want things to stop changing. Change is never good. When you left, that was not good. When your brother died, again not good." His father's eyes began to well up and Matt took a deep breath. The doctor said he would be emotional after surgery, but he would never get used to seeing his dad cry. He'd come to appreciate his grouchy disposition. At least he could argue with grouchy.

"I didn't leave, Dad."

His father held up his hand and winced when he adjusted again. "And this damn thing." He gestured to his hip. "If I'd left the front path alone instead of putting those new pavers in, I would never have tripped. One more change that has messed me up."

"The pavers were uneven."

"They were fine," his father almost shouted. "I like things the way they are. I liked when you were little and you used to follow me around. Now, now, look at you off doing something that has nothing to do with your family."

His mother poked her head in from the kitchen, and Matt held up his hand to ask for a minute.

"I'm not having this argument with you again. I love the shop. I thought by doing a few things, I was showing you that. I've taken good care of things while Poppy was away, but I'm not going to apologize for choosing my own career."

"Of course you aren't, Mr. High and Mighty. That's fine. I'll be good as new soon." He shifted and struggled with the pillow at his thigh.

Matt wanted to reach out and help him but saw no point. Whether his father was fueled by anger or pain, it didn't matter. All of it was directed at him. Any minute now, his father would finish with something about his dead son being better and that would be Matt's cue to leave before he said something he couldn't take back.

"I'm sure John would have been perfectly happy to take over the shops."

And there it was. Matt stood as his mother returned from the kitchen with some cookies. He leaned down and kissed his father on the cheek. His dad tensed but allowed it. He always did. No matter how far away from understanding each other they grew, the kiss was the last word. It had started when he was little being dropped off at school and it survived through his teenage years. The kiss said, "I might not like you, but I'll always love you," and came from his mother, who was half Italian on her mother's side. Italians were big kissers and even though his father's family were not big kissers, his dad tolerated the kiss and sometimes enjoyed it.

Matt kissed his mother good-bye without another word, afraid what might come spilling out of his mouth if he wasn't careful, and left.

Hollis left the office late, which used to be second nature but now felt strange. People had dinner after work or went home and spent time with their families. Some met friends for happy hour or even went to a movie. Most people made it home right as the sun was setting; they weren't leaving the office chasing dawn. She could have been in her pajamas by the time the evening news was over. She should have gone back to her apartment, but she didn't.

Driving through Point Reyes and back to Mitchell's Cove, Hollis looked at the clock on her dash and realized it was after midnight. The streets were empty. Even the light above the entrance of the restaurant was out. She pulled off the road and noticed Matt's house was dark. He was probably asleep already. Again, most people were tucked into their homes by now, she thought.

Hollis glanced at the Locke family bungalow one more time and noticed the tree in the center of the small lawn, leaves brushing in the evening breeze. She remembered when Matt and his father had planted that tree. He'd been pissed because he wanted to kayak that day. They were freshmen in high school. She'd seen him that morning and when he complained about having to plant a tree with his dad,

Hollis had said, "work before play." Matt had stormed off, but later that day she brought them both lunch and sat in the yard reading while they grunted and argued the tree into place. She'd done the same the year they had summer reading or the time Matt had to go to the dermatologist to have a mole removed on the back of his neck because he never wore sunscreen and burned his neck every summer. "It's not skin cancer," he said. "I'm not going all the way to the doctor—it's a pain in the ass." She'd gone with him, and it had not been skin cancer, but Matt's mother was relieved, which was worth the trip as far as Hollis was concerned.

Things came easy for Matt. He rarely studied. He didn't like hassle, which used to annoy Hollis, who ardently believed in hard work. Matt enjoyed mental conflict, discussion, and debates, but something in his nature made him choose to give in when the physical world, or maybe his emotions, became mixed up. Hollis smiled at the tree. It was huge, a perfect shade to his parents' front windows, rooted and almost winking at her in appreciation for keeping Matt from his fun that afternoon.

The moon was a little over half, but giving off the glow of a full moon, and the wind spun the weather vane on top of the restaurant and tinkled the chimes on the outside of the building as Hollis made her way to Mr. Boots. Stopping at the pier, she looked out over the bay, pulled her blazer closed, and stepped up onto the wood. The water buckled and waved as she shook her hair loose from the elastic, wanting the wind in her hair, to feel her place, their place. Matt was most likely asleep and she didn't want to bother him. She would turn on the light in the name of tradition and enjoy the evening chill by herself this time. After the day she had, she wanted to feel alive. Hollis was certain not a single person in that conference room remembered what it was like to be young and sneaking up a dock under the light of a half-moon. Hollis took her shoes off and smiled as her bare feet touched the damp wood.

When she arrived at the bait shack, she turned on the flashlight she'd taken from the side of the restaurant, the one Uncle Mitch kept under the circuit box for emergencies. The wide beam cut through the darkness of the shack and when she set the flashlight in the middle of the little table faceup, she took in a breath of sea air, let it out, and closed her eyes.

"You'll be fine. You're home," she heard the wind say. Hollis thought maybe the wind had been telling her things all her life, but at some point, she became too noisy to listen. Pulling the blanket she'd found in the back of her car from her bag, she laid it on the pier. She had meant to check and see if their initials were still etched in the wall of the shack, but the meeting at Dobbins Capital was still spinning through her mind and she was so tired. Her last thought was one of surrender. She certainly didn't want to be found out, but the desire to continue doing battle had passed. She no longer wanted to call someone "our win" in the way it had come to mean. She wanted peace and more than at any other time in her life, she wanted to be happy. Hollis tried to take in as many stars as her eyes could hold and then she fell asleep.

Matt had fallen asleep on the couch in the living room of his parents' bungalow reading some crime novel he'd almost given up on. The story jumped between three different time periods and was virtually impossible to follow, but he'd decided to give it one more try since it was a distraction from the argument with his father. Did what happened at lunch even qualify as an argument anymore? The same thing kept playing on a loop these days each time he spoke to or saw his dad. Not in the big bursts of a full on fight, but more like smaller jabs and heaving sighs seeping with ambivalence.

His father was in pain, Matt reminded himself, and that did explain why things felt so heightened, but the core of his issue with his father was deep, rooted in years of seeing things differently. Closing the book, Matt sat up and made his way to the bed right as his phone vibrated. He pulled it from his pocket, hoping it was Hollis, deflated when it wasn't, and then panicked to see the call was from Officer Hernandez, Greg, a little after midnight.

"What's wrong?" Matt answered, sounding like his own mother.

Greg's laughter spilled from the phone and Matt let out a deep breath.

"Aww, man, you can't do that. It's after midnight. I thought something was wrong with you or your kids."

"And being a cop and all, I'd naturally call you first?"

Matt closed his eyes. "Fine. Then why are you calling me?"

"To tell you that I was right. I love it when I'm right. She is still your girl."

"Seriously? Are you drinking on the job? Can't we discuss this tomorrow?"

"No, sober as a judge, but I was getting off shift and noticed the light coming from the bait shack."

Matt's heart raced.

"When I drove by, I noticed your girl on the pier. The light's on, so you should probably get your ass out there." He laughed again.

"How do you know about the light?" Matt was surprised and wondering why Hollis was at the bait shack.

"Oh, please. You two have been playing flashlight forever. Who do you think was keeping an eye on you when you crossed over Highway 1 in the dark?"

"After you realized I wasn't breaking into someone's house?"

"Damn straight. Now, quit jabbering with me and go get your girl before she freezes out there."

"For the hundredth time, she's not my—" The call died and Matt went to the front window and pulled back the curtain. There it was, a faint line of light that almost appeared to cut through the night and light the moon.

He grabbed a sweatshirt and walked to the pier.

Hollis was huddled under a blanket in what looked like the same white shirt from that morning. The wind blew, swaying the dock a little as he finally made it to her. Her shoes were off and tossed to the side and she was asleep, head resting on what looked like a balled-up blazer. He carefully sat down next to her and for a moment watched her sleep.

"Sometimes people don't know they need you. You have to show them." Matt heard his mother's voice. He felt a knot in his chest as he pushed the hair off her cheek. She was sleeping so soundly, as if she were in her own bed at home. Maybe she was, he thought.

They used to have an ice cream truck in his neighborhood growing up. It would tinkle down the street shortly after school let out and by one on Saturday. Matt would get money from his parents, and he and his friends would chase down the truck and push into some semblance of a line. His best friend, Tim, routinely bought an ice cream sandwich. He would sit on the stairs to their house and lick all around the edges until there was only ice cream in the center and the chocolate cookie threatened to fall onto the sidewalk. Then, and not a moment sooner, he ate the cookie part.

Matt bought the Strawberry Shortcake, and every time it was either soggy or smushed into the wrapper. He knew before he ordered that it would be smushed, a pain in the ass because he'd have to lick the wrapper and inevitably go back in the house to wash his hands before he and his friends went back out to play. Most of the kids in his neighborhood chose the Firecracker. It was easy to open, held together even in the heat of summer, and was refreshing. He told himself any time they ran after the green-and-yellow truck that he should get The Firecracker, it was the easiest choice, but time after time he paid for the Strawberry Shortcake and sat next to his best friend and made a mess, enjoying every bit of goodness.

Hollis was Strawberry Shortcake. He had no idea why he kept coming back. That wasn't true. He knew. It was exactly as Greg had said. She was his girl, always would be, even if that meant she was a mess or she made him work harder than anyone else. She was still a goodness he would never find anywhere else.

Matt stretched out behind her. Resting on one arm, he wrapped the other around her waist and pulled her close. Hollis stirred for a second then settled into his body as if she had never left.

"Psst... Holls."

She grunted.

"You're going to freeze out here."

Her eyes fluttered open like they were in some big fluffy bed on a Sunday morning instead of on a damp pier in the middle of June.

"You're here," she said, her voice heavy with sleep.

"You put the light on."

"I thought you were asleep and things were awkward this morning, so I walked out here alone." She rolled to face him and Matt finally understood. It wasn't that she didn't need him, she didn't know how to need him.

"The light goes on and if we can sneak out, we sneak out. Those rules haven't changed and whether you want me to or not now, Holls, I'll always come for you." He kissed her cold nose. "Bad day at work?"

"You told me to be happy when I left, remember?"

"I do, and I added recently that I was secretly counting on you being miserable."

"Right. Did you mean that? Do you want me to be happy?"

"I do." The idea that being happy somehow meant her leaving again had him sitting up. Hollis joined him, crossed her legs even in her skirt, and looked at him as if he might have the answers she was looking for.

"I want to be happy."

"Okay. What does that mean? Is there some kind of plan for happiness?"

She shook her head. "I don't think so. I mean there are things I need to clean up, to simplify, but—"

"Can we talk about your plan inside? It's cold out here and you"—he noticed the balled-up material was her perfectly pressed blazer from the morning—"should put this jacket on." He put it over her shoulders and she took his hands again.

"Do you have any hobbies, Matt?"

He was used to these random changes of subject. Hollis had downshifted and changed directions for as long as they had known each other. Matt attributed it to her lightning-speed mind and loved how she pulled her thoughts and ideas seemingly from nowhere.

"I... well, I'm reading this bad book right now, so I read. I paddleboard and kayak, summer stuff around here, but I'm not sure what you would classify as a hobby."

"Do you play checkers?"

He smiled because she suddenly looked like a little girl wrapped in a grown-up's jacket. "I do. We used to play all the time, remember?"

She nodded. "I love checkers and backgammon. I used to make bookmarks and those friendship bracelets."

"I remember."

"And even when we were in college, we rode bikes and went on hikes. We did things. Oh, and I used to make cards for people."

It was good that she kept talking because he could barely breathe. It was like layers of whatever she'd gone through since they split were peeling off her and underneath was the young woman who sent him to the drug store in the middle of the night. He was sure those layers would go back on, but sitting there with her on the pier, he wanted to simply say, "Hi, Holls. Welcome back." Instead, he sat there watching her find her way.

"Anyway, the point is, I want to do things again. I want a life and not just a job. And this thing with us, I think it's because we are split-aparts."

Matt raised his eyebrow, waiting for her to go on.

"When I was driving back tonight, I remembered the story, and split-aparts are supposed to be like this. I mean they shared a body and then they were separated—that's violent messy stuff. So, we need to remember that. You know?"

He met her eyes and tried to think of a one-word response, something to tease her with, but instead he decided to give her the honesty she'd asked for weeks ago.

"I love you. I love you so much, Holls, I'm not sure I ever stopped."

Her hands stopped flailing and she came to a complete stop, staring at him. *Crap!* There he was again out in the breeze with his heart in his ever-hopeful hand.

Hollis leaned into him and took his face in her hands. "I love you, too," she said quietly, looking farther into his eyes than he'd ever thought was possible. "I have... always loved you too but I have a mess. I'm a mess and I need to fix that first."

He pulled her into him like a child snatching something he wants off the shelf before anyone else can take it and kissed her. He would never have enough of her.

"I don't care if you're a mess. Whatever it is, we can deal with it in the morning."

"I can deal with it. I mean I am dealing with it, but before you say you want me, you need to know—"

Matt kissed her again and picked her up in his arms, blanket and all, before she could say another word. "Too late again, Holls. I want you. I love you and right now more than anything, I need you."

Hollis said nothing and kissed him again, so he carried her to Mr. Boots.

Chapter Nineteen

*T*he last time Hollis and Matt had made love, it was tender and in the middle of the night after their second pizza during finals week. It was another seemingly uneventful moment she'd looked back on over the years and wondered if she would have done things differently had she known it was going to be the last time he touched her like that. Like everything else in the past, there was nothing she could do about it. Now, here they were again, and whether this was the first of many times to come, or the last one, she was going to cherish him this time.

Matt kicked the door closed, leaned down, and she locked it. At first, when he'd whipped her into his arms like some great pirate, her heart had jumped in her chest, but now, in the darkness of her cabin, with no more than the light of that half-moon and the dim streetlight at the boat ramp, her heartbeat was deep and content. Eyes locked on one another, Matt set her down so they were both standing by her bed. Hollis brought her hands to his chest as the power of his breath moved through his body. He was a force all on his own, and after a day of being someone she no longer wanted to be, she was playful and pushed on his chest. Matt fell back onto the bed.

"You know a lot of guys have a hot corporate woman fantasy. Not you, though, I bet." Hollis suddenly felt a different kind of power as she flipped open the top button of her blouse.

Matt was propped up on his elbows as a slow, sexy smile spread across his face and his eyes shifted to her blouse. "Nah, it's never been my thing."

Hollis could feel his eyes on her and the thunder of his breath as she unzipped her skirt, which fell to the floor, revealing her garters and stockings. Matt's hands clenched and opened as if his sense of touch had recently been restored. Hollis kept her heels on because they made her feel powerful and if she was going to strip off her costume, who she'd decided to become when she left him behind, she needed a few more minutes of courage.

"Well, that's good you're not into something so cliché, so typical male." She stepped out of her skirt and returned to unbuttoning her blouse.

Matt stood from the bed but still kept his distance as he brought his hand to his face and brushed over a day's worth of stubble, his eyes glued to each button like he was about to make an important decision. Hollis opened her blouse and let the sides of silk slide off now-golden shoulders. Her boobs were never a big reveal for Hollis when she'd gotten undressed for other men, but she knew Matt. She knew what he liked and didn't, what turned him on and drove him crazy. He loved her, all of her, and even though she barely filled out an A cup, as her blouse hit the floor, he closed the space between them and Hollis held on tight.

"There are some"—he kissed down her neck, undid her bra—"benefits to this fantasy. I can see that now."

Hollis laughed and at the warmth of his hands, his mouth dancing across her skin, she let out a moan. Matt swept her back up into his arms.

"Is this part of the fantasy? Do you take me on a conference room table now?" She kissed his neck and felt him suddenly still. He was looking at her as if she might disappear.

"There are some in the drawer," she said softly, refusing to allow the huge wave of all their yesterdays crash over them.

Matt put her gently on the bed, opened the drawer, and put a condom on the nightstand.

"Are you—" he started to ask.

"No, I'm not. I'm not at all sure. Does that have to make a difference? Do I need to stop you if I'm not sure?" Hollis closed her eyes because she needed a break from looking at him.

"No." He kissed her softly, flipped open the garters, and started gliding the stockings down her legs.

She opened her eyes to his smiling, mischievous face. "It's only us. It has always been us. Shut the rest of it down for a while, for right now. You can analyze it all tomorrow, I promise I'll listen, but for now, right now, I'd like to have you screaming at me for a different reason. Is that okay?"

Hollis nodded and felt her own playfulness return. "Some men like to keep those on."

Matt smiled, set the last stocking aside, and kissed his way around her legs. "I've been trying to tell you this for years. I'm not some men, Holls. I'll choose your bare skin every time."

Dear God, the way he said her name was erotic all by itself. One more smile, a gentle nudge of her legs, and Hollis lost all memory of anything that had happened before. It might as well have been the first night they'd made love on the tiny island in the middle of the bay. Like some sort of implosion, everything fell in on itself and the one thing that mattered was what he was doing to her, his tongue, and the unguarded heat each time she touched him. Matt made his way back up her body and Hollis felt like they were in water, swirling and gasping, their lungs straining until their bodies finally took hold, pulsed through the waves, and floated above the surface like the best out-of-nowhere afternoon rain.

Matt sat on the small patio of Mr. Boots and could make out the faint outline of the two islands that sat watch in the center of Tomales Bay. The largest, Hog Island, was about two acres, and it was where he took Hollis the summer they turned eighteen. The closest side of the island was a protected seal sanctuary, an important fact Matt forgot when they were in his kayak and making their way toward the island with blankets and Oreos. Hollis loved Oreos and somehow his eighteen-year-old mind thought cookies might help ease any nerves. After seeing the *Keep Out* signs with his flashlight that night, they paddled around to the other side of the island, which was a little creepier and not exactly the most romantic place for a guy wanting to have sex with his girlfriend for the first time, even with Oreos. He smiled at the memory now and the awkwardness that moved their lives one step closer to each other.

The other island, Duck Island, was much smaller. Matt had wanted to swim out there as a kid and find out once and for all if Hog and Duck were one island or if they were split apart. Split-aparts, he thought, smiling again and remembering Hollis's words on the pier a couple of hours ago. While his entire body was still humming, Matt couldn't help but wonder again about the "mess" she had mentioned again. *What is this big mistake?*

"Did you know that the San Andreas Fault runs right through our bay?" The screen door squeaked open and Hollis, wrapped in a blanket, took the seat next to him and looked out toward the water. "In fact, rumor has it that the earthquake of 1906 is what separated the two islands."

"That's a rumor."

She looked at him, and the moonlight danced on her bare shoulders. She was flushed and so stunning, it was a good thing Matt was already sitting down.

"I guess," she said softly. "They're not really separated, you know?"

He didn't know.

"There's a sand pit that connects them so even though they look like two separate islands, they have perpetually been joined under the surface."

Matt knew in that moment why nothing ever worked after her. How could it? It was possible, he thought as they sat in the quiet night, to love someone first and for so long. To be connected all the while appearing singular. He wasn't one for symbolism. In fact, the first time Hollis had told him they were split-aparts he'd thought she was a little crazy, but she was right. They were and would forever be connected even if they couldn't manage to make things work above the surface. Even if he lost her again and a thread was all he had to hold on to, he would because they were one.

Hollis started laughing.

"Laughter is good, but rarely after sex," Matt said.

She kept laughing. "Don't you think it's ironic that the first time you and I made love it was on that island right there?"

"Hog Island. I know, why couldn't I have picked Desire Beach, a little up the way. That would have been a much more romantic story."

"True, but I meant Fat Pigs. Fat Pigs, in a roundabout way, has brought me back here with you."

They stopped laughing. She obviously realized she'd said more than she meant to and he was busy trying to pick up the breadcrumbs.

"Fat Pigs the game?"

Hollis nodded and offered nothing more.

"Would you like to elaborate on that?"

She shook her head and looked so beautiful and sad at the same time that he wasn't going to push it.

"I never realized how important pigs were in my life," he said, taking her hand. She smiled and he could see her return from whatever it was she was trying to again handle all by herself. The little she had let slip had Matt thinking. He couldn't help it. Fat Pigs. How had a simple game caused this much trouble?

Hollis brought his hand to her lips in a gesture he recognized as, "Don't worry about it. I'll be fine." God, how many times had he heard that either through words or actions meant to keep him out? In all the years he'd known her, Hollis Jeffries had not once ever handed over the reins, fallen, and let him or anyone else help her up. He wasn't sure how to tell her that she could save herself, but he'd like to help, so he held her hand and looked out at the islands.

Without a word, Hollis stood and led him back to bed. This time, her lips, her breath had brushed over every turn and ridge of his body, until he'd all but lost his mind. When it was his turn, when she was writing beneath him, softly pleading his name, he slid past everything that distanced them during the sunlight hours, shattered them both, and prayed to the moonlight that she would let herself need him, at least this once.

Chapter Twenty

*H*ollis woke up, wrapped in a very real adult Matt Locke, and proceeded to panic. She quietly padded to the bathroom and pulled on a T-shirt and a pair of sweatpants she'd left hanging on the back of the door. Grabbing her phone, she saw it was almost five o'clock. Hollis was on autopilot, she knew she was, but could do nothing to stop it. She needed air, room, so she pulled her hair through a Mitchell's Cove cap and rooted in her bag for her keys. She stopped at the front door of the cabin to glance back at Matt's naked sleeping body then stepped into the early morning mist.

As she backed out, she noticed her uncle's old truck. She'd grown to love the warm vinyl smell and the bounce of the clutch. Sitting in the plush leather of her car again, she felt like an imposter, but like those con artists down by Fisherman's Wharf, she no longer knew which life was real and which was the fake. It had been so easy mere hours ago with Matt, but now it was morning and none of what she promised seemed possible without the moonlight.

Her skin still warm from his body, Hollis rolled down her window, started up Highway 1, and began to cry. Oh God, how long had it been since she'd cried like this? She found being pissed and getting even were more productive in her world than any kind of crying. But as the tears seeped toward her neck, she was awash with guilt that reached down deep. All the pain she'd pushed away came rushing to the surface, and her crying turned to sobs. No wonder after they broke up she never went back to the cove. It was a survival instinct that kept her away because she was no longer that girl. She'd become something else, and now she was trapped.

She took the road that eventually dropped her into Bodega Bay as the sky began to brighten. When she'd first woken up next to him, drowning in him, she thought she might go home. Some screwed-up part of herself had chimed in while she was getting dressed and even suggested she should check on her apartment, maybe get some fresh clothes. By the time she climbed in her car, she'd reminded herself that her housekeeper texted her every few days and that she already had all of the fun, beachy pieces of clothing in her wardrobe. Besides, what would that do to Matt when he woke up and found out that she had gone back to San Francisco? Why did that thought, the introduction of Matt's feelings, still feel awkward and new to her? Hadn't she thought of him before, wondered what it was like for him?

Hollis knew the answer was no; they'd already covered this and she had not considered his feelings, but now that he'd held her, made love to her, she couldn't reconcile it. The idea that she could have been in a relationship with him for so long and loved him at times to desperation but somehow not care how he felt was too much to take. If she was able to admit that to herself, what did that make her?

She tried to quickly change her thoughts, but she'd never been good at squashing something until it was thought into the ground, so she found herself wanting to remember what had happened the day she left—or did he leave first? Jesus, she couldn't remember. All she knew now was the more she tried to recall who she was back then, the more images of a young Matt flooded her mind.

"Do you need anything?" he had asked when she called him over Christmas break to tell him she'd lost the baby a little over three weeks after taking the tests.

"No. I'm fine."

"Should you go to the doctor?"

"I drove back to campus and went to student health. I'm fine."

"You went back to school? Why didn't you call me?"

"There was no reason. What, did you want to hold my hand? I'm not pregnant, it went away on its own, so I didn't see the point in bothering you."

"Bothering me?"

Hollis said nothing because she was numb.

"What are you doing, Holls?"

"I'm... trying to figure some things out."

"Like?"

"Like what I want and where I want to go in my life." The emphasis was on the "my," Hollis remembered, and she was all but certain she'd never asked him how he was dealing with everything.

"Okay, well try to get some rest. I'll come see you tomorrow."

"I'm not going to be home, so maybe next weekend."

The line was silent and she remembered hoping in that stupid twentysomething push-pull way that he would say something, but Matt wasn't the kind of guy to push, so he said he loved her and that he'd call her later. After that, all that remained of their relationship were long periods of silence sprinkled with the occasional argument. That summer, Hollis graduated in under three and a half years. Matt moved out of their apartment on the day of her graduation and left Stanford the following week. Something that had started so simply on the pier at Mitchell's Cove and had grown over so many summers took a mere few months to unravel. And there it was, turning in her stomach as the memory faded. She hadn't thought about him, not once and what was worse... she'd never even thought about—

She was going to be sick if she didn't stop. She'd stopped thinking about all of this years ago for a reason because when she allowed any of it in, she realized she was a monster.

Hollis parked on the dirt road behind Vern's Crabs and walked toward the marina. Most of the boats were already out for the day and the seagulls began circling in anticipation of visitors. The tears had let up as she finished shoving each moment back where it belonged, but her heart kept telling her to get back in the car and crawl back into bed with him. She had never been more full of feeling and empty at the same time. Hollis wiped her eyes and then felt him at her back.

"Is that a Mercedes?"

Somehow, often when she was so mad and didn't want him to, Matt managed to make her laugh. She looked over her shoulder. He kissed her on the top of her head and sat next to her on the bench.

She'd been crying, and Matt didn't know how to make the feelings racing through him stop. When she'd snuck out of bed, he had let her go, once again not knowing why she was leaving and still no closer on how to make her stay. They sat on the bench side by side and watched the sun greet the harbor.

"Talk to me, Holls," he said at last, his voice sounding scratchy even to his own ears.

"I would have had an abortion."

After all the time they'd spent together, not much that Hollis said set him back on his heels, but that did. They hadn't talked about her pregnancy except for the early morning when she took the test, a few cursory conversations before she left, and a less than five-minute conversation after she'd had a miscarriage. They'd never discussed what they were going to do now that she was pregnant. He'd intended to ask her to marry him then spend the rest of his life with her, making babies and feeling like the luckiest man ever.

Hollis had different plans and three weeks after they'd taken the test, so had Mother Nature. Matt knew it was selfish, but he'd been disappointed when she'd called. He should have been relieved. They were young and had no business having a baby. They would never have planned to have a child while still in school, Hollis certainly would not have. But when that pink cross appeared in the small window of the test all three times, Matt would have never said it to her stricken face, but part of him had been excited. Hollis was his person, there was not a doubt in his mind. He saw the pregnancy as simply speeding up the inevitable while Hollis saw it as — hell, he had no idea how she felt back then, but the look on her face now suggested he was about to find out.

"Okay. I'm not sure you know that for sure, but okay." Matt tried to sound unfazed.

"I do know. I researched clinics and—" She started to cry and right when he thought she'd broken his heart into hundreds of pieces, she found some random piece still intact and broke that.

"This is another hypothetical. What, are you going to blame yourself for decisions you might have made, but didn't? You need more guilt or misery? Why?"

Nothing. She sat next to him and sobbed. He wanted to put his arm around her, comfort her, but he knew Hollis all too well. She didn't want his pity or his comfort, not right now anyway. She was in "give me some space while I figure this out" mode. He'd first seen this side of her when they were eleven years old and her dog's paw was caught in some wire. By the time Matt had run home and returned with wire clippers, she was sitting with Pilot, petting him and talking to him. He'd presented the wire cutters to her as if he had saved the day, only to have her brush them away. For the next hour, he sat shifting the cutters from one hand to the other while she carefully unwrapped Pilot from a snarl of wire with no visible beginning or end. She patiently lifted, bent, and twisted Pilot free and was rewarded with a big kiss across her face before he ran off to find trouble again.

His eleven-year-old mind hadn't known it yet, but that one moment said so much about the woman she would become. Hollis Jeffries didn't want the easy way or to be rescued. She wanted space to make her way, to find an answer that was true for her. He'd thought it cool at the time, fascinating as they became older and grew into adults, but eventually, he realized that in giving her that space, in letting "Hollis be Hollis," as her father often said, there somehow wasn't any room at all. Not for him anyway.

Hollis stopped crying, sniffled, and wiped her eyes. "I should have asked you. At least listened to your feelings, and I didn't. I don't know, there were too many things in my head and all I knew was I wanted it to all go away."

"And it did, all on its own. Nature, God, whatever you want to call it, had a different plan. I don't know why that's not enough for you. What, are you pissed off you didn't get to make the decision?"

"Yes."

Matt turned to meet her eyes. "Seriously?"

She nodded. "I think that's part of it. Someone or something snatched that choice away from me and I felt powerless."

"Welcome to the human experience, Holls. I mean there's all sorts of crap we have no control over, didn't you know that?"

"Not when I was that age."

They stared out over the water, the street behind them silent except for the squawk of the occasional seagull.

"I didn't want any of it after I... lost it."

"I know."

"How could I have turned like that? Turned away from something that felt like everything."

"You were scared."

"Were you scared?"

"No, but I didn't have as many things I needed to do. My life plan was a little less ambitious."

Hollis nodded.

"And, I wasn't the one who was pregnant. It was our baby, but it was your body. I was happy. I wanted to marry you anyway at that point, so moving that up was no big deal for me."

She turned to him.

"Yeah, I know I had no clue how to live that life so young, but I'm telling you how I felt at the time. I guess I see how it's different, though. I could still do what I wanted and come home to a sweet baby. You would have had to go through the pregnancy, give birth to her. It wasn't part of your life plan, and that scared you. I get that now."

"Her?" Pain filled her eyes.

"I don't know why, but when I think about the pregnancy, it's a her. I'm sorry."

"It's fine. I never thought about it. 'It.' I guess the baby was an 'it' to me. What is wrong with me?"

"Nothing. You were young. We both were and at the same time, I thought having a baby would be fun. You saw it as a trap. Maybe we were both wrong. Maybe the truth is somewhere in the middle."

She took a deep breath, and he hoped she felt the same lift he was feeling. It helped that they could talk about it now, that almost like a release valve, the ache was eased by the truth.

"Why didn't your marriage work?" Hollis asked.

Matt knew then that she must feel some relief because her thoughts were moving on. His answer was something he'd only recently figured out.

"Because I was broken. I had no business getting married."

"That's insightful."

Matt laughed and when Hollis turned to him, her smile almost reached her blotchy and somehow still stunning eyes.

"Yeah, well I realized since you had an action plan and all that, I should probably figure my life out too."

They sat listening to the water lap against the scattered boats and in the spirit of honesty and huge mistakes, Matt let the memory in as he attempted to explain to Hollis where his marriage went wrong without sharing with her exactly what his "programming job" was. There was no point in sharing that piece of his success while she was at such a low point.

Matt married Stacey Kempley the week after he turned twenty-five. When he quit Stanford, he found a job with a company called Four Blades. Their logo was four green bars like blades of grass. He was a zombie back then, but it was nice to be out and free from the classroom. He'd convinced himself that the outpaced coding he was learning at school was going to be all but obsolete by the time he graduated and tried to find a job. Leaving, moving to Silicon Valley, the great Oz of the tech world, would put him on the fast track. And he supposed he was lucky because it did.

Hindsight tended to be smarter and more critical. Matt saw now what he'd been doing. As long as he kept moving, he could fix it all, or so he thought. Stacey was a year older than him, and she worked in implementation. Four Blades mainly developed back-office applications, so she brought new products on board and trained client staff. On their first date, she gave him a slice of banana bread she'd made.

"I made too many, so I thought you might want one," she'd said when she handed him the block wrapped in tin foil.

She had two older brothers, parents were divorced, and she loved sports. She was one of the kindest people he had ever known. He said that when she told him she wanted to write their own vows.

"Stacey is the kindest woman I've ever known." And like that, he'd stood in front of their family and friends and told her she was... kind. When they separated, her brother had told him he was a "complete tool." He'd been right.

When Matt had asked her to marry him, it was almost an afterthought. They had been to Coronado Island with her parents and on the flight home, she had been talking about houses. Flipping through a magazine and telling him she wanted a house with a wraparound porch and lots of grass for kids. Three. She wanted three kids and a porch. When the captain turned off the "fasten seatbelt" sign, Matt had twisted his drink straw into a ring and dropped to one knee in the aisle. He'd mumbled something about getting her that house, and the entire plane cheered and the flight attendant bought them both another drink. The story was told over and over again at parties, when they went to drinks with friends, and anytime Matt was introduced to another new family member.

"So romantic." That was the town response and each time, his stomach turned. He'd been drunk and stupid, but they couldn't see that. Eight months later he had bought her a proper engagement ring and married her at a country club in the Pacific Palisades. Matt left his job and struck out on his own with Bradley Parker. They'd met at Stanford, reconnected through a mutual friend of Stacey's, and together they developed "Call Ahead," an app that allowed customers to preorder coffee shop drinks and pastries. Basically, anything the store offered could be selected on their app, sent to the store, and would be ready for pickup when the person arrived. They sold it to

Starbucks for millions right around the time Stacey started talking about wanting to have a baby.

He and Bradley formed Pilot Programs two months after the sale, and that was the beginning of the end. Matt was never home. The morning Stacey left her wedding ring on their bathroom counter, Matt had had an early meeting. He had not even noticed it was there until he arrived home sometime in the wee hours of the next morning and she was gone. Her trip back to pack up the rest of her things had ended in an argument and before she slammed the door, she said, "You never loved me!" and she had been right. Stacey was the kindest woman he had ever met; Matt simply didn't have a heart to give her in return.

When he was finished giving Hollis the short version, they sat listening to the water lap against the shore and the rhythmic slapping of loose rigging against the boat masts bobbing in the harbor.

"Huh, well it would be silly for me to say I'm sorry you're divorced, but I will say that I'm sorry you had to go through that. I guess it was your own doing and at the same time she should have—"

"Holls?"

"Yes."

Matt stood up and took her hand. "I think we've covered enough for one morning."

"Are you hungry?"

Matt nodded, opening the door of his car. "You?"

"Yes." Hollis walked to her car.

"You could come with me and we can get your car later." Matt smiled because suddenly standing in an empty parking lot with two cars felt like one of the overarching metaphors his English teacher tried to explain when they read Hemingway his senior year in high school.

"How about I drive my car now and meet you at Mitch's for cinnamon buns?"

"Jesus, can you say cinnamon buns more often? That was sexy."

Hollis laughed and shook her head. "Get in your car, Locke-ness."

"You should come with me. I bet you I'll get there before you."

"Oh, you're on." Hollis opened her door.

"Hey, Holls."

She looked up.

"I love you."

"I love you, too. I'll still beat you to Mitch's, but I love you."

Matt laughed and jumped in his car. Hollis pulled out first but pulled into Mitch's last.

She bought breakfast.

Chapter Twenty-One

After another Tuesday morning teleconference during which yet another consultant droned on about the dire situation Pretty Boys had found themselves in, Hollis felt the end was near. She'd called Zeke, who had returned from Mexico, and again listened to his voice mail, if the greeting that played in her ear even qualified as voice mail.

"If you're not plugged in, you don't count." That was all it said and then a beep. Jesus Christ, she should simply march right into Dobbins and declare she'd invested millions of their dollars in a figment of everyone's imagination. There was no way this guy was a functioning adult who went to the grocery store and picked up his dry cleaning like the rest of the world. He was a mirage and a good one at that, because in less than two weeks he was going to destroy her, bring her career to a screeching halt, and embarrass her beyond what she thought imaginable a few months ago. This was a train wreck. It was a matter of time now and she needed to start preparing for impact.

She was in her swimsuit because prior to the "emergency meeting" text she received, she had planned on asking Matt if he wanted to try the paddleboard yoga. After the meeting, she needed a nap, so she crashed on the couch outside her uncle's office while he finished scanning his receipts. Hollis didn't know how long she'd been asleep when she woke up with her face smushed against one of the perfumed-over-mildew cushions, but she rolled onto her back. Half-asleep, she found herself in a memory so vivid it was as if she were that person again—young and fearless.

Her parents bought her a used white Honda for her sixteenth birthday. She'd wanted a Jeep, but she learned quickly that any car was better than no car. The Honda brought her the one thing she could recall craving since birth—independence. In the flash of blowing out candles and trip to the DMV, Hollis was no longer at the mercy of the schedule or the whim of someone else. She'd become her own person, able to go her own way—that's how she saw it. Short of landing her first job at Dairy Queen, her Honda was "that moment."

Once Hollis started making money and could go where she wanted to, her mind began spinning with endless possibilities. As she grew older, it slowed a little bit, but for the most part, she'd chased off nearly every boyfriend she'd ever had because like something battery operated, Hollis didn't slow down. She'd wanted to make her way, make her parents proud for as far back as her memories could take her. She'd never been sure if the activities she chose were hers, or cleverly planted by her parents, but the day Hollis walked on the Stanford campus, none of it mattered. In her eyes, she had arrived. Dipping cones while her friends were at the beach and driving that Honda to the library or guest lectures even after the air conditioning went out had all paid off. She had followed the rules and been given the cookie, the gold star.

She and Matt had dated on and off throughout high school, but most of their time together was summertime at the cove. Even though they both lived in the San Francisco area, Matt lived in the city and Hollis lived in the suburbs. She went to a private high school and he went to public. Hollis had gone to one of his proms but missed her own because she was in Washington DC that weekend for a competition with DECA. They were both busy even though Matt never came across as much more than casual. Hollis took two prep classes and scored 1520 out of 1600 on her SAT the first time. She graduated from high school a semester early and was accepted to Stanford. Matt took the SAT twice, scored less than 1300 on the second try, but wrote an incredible essay and joined her at Stanford the following semester.

Hollis was happy they had both been accepted but would later realize she resented Matt getting the same cookie she did for less work. She spent a few months with a therapist after the miscarriage dissecting and, for the most part, dismantling what the therapist coined "the cookie theory."

"There are no guarantees in life," she'd said. "Just because you follow all the rules, you can't expect to be given this cookie. Life doesn't work that way."

At the time, Hollis thought that sucked, but it had been years now and she was an adult, one who rarely craved cookies anymore.

Hollis sat up, her neck sweating from the afternoon sun, and checked her phone. It was after one and she'd slept for almost two hours. The cushions left a maze of marks on her bare legs. She went to check on Mitch's progress and found him sitting in his standard position, legs propped up with the scanner on his knees as he fed it narrow strips of paper.

As she entered, he looked over his glasses at her. "Thank God, someone has come to rescue me. Is it lunchtime?" His chair let out a moan as he set the scanner on the desk, brought his feet to the ground, and stood before Hollis had a chance to answer. He was still wearing red-white-and-blue shorts even though the Fourth of July had come and gone last week.

"Looked like you were on a roll there. Maybe I should bring the lunch to you. You could have a working lunch?"

"Isn't that an oxymoron?"

She laughed as he led her back out onto the patio before disappearing, soon reappearing with cold salads, bread, and drinks.

"How's Matt?" he asked, sitting next to her on the couch.

"He's Matt."

"Evasive, interesting."

"I'm not being evasive. I'm providing factual information in response to your question."

"Ah, okay. I can play. So, have you and Matt hooked up again?"

Hollis laughed and ate her salad. Mitch was waiting for a "factual response." She should have known better; her uncle was a slippery one.

"Hooked up? I'm not sure what you kids call hooking up these days, but no. We have talked a few times, cleared the air if you will, and now things are... well, he's Matt."

He made the sound of a buzzer. "I'm sorry, but we are going to call bullshit on that response."

"What do you want me to say? I'm not kissing and telling. How's that?"

"So you have kissed him."

"Dear God. Yes! He kissed me and I kissed him back. It's a... curiosity thing."

"Huh, you know I'm curious about a lot of things, antique stringed instruments at the moment, but I rarely have sex with them."

"Can we be done now?"

"Okay, no denial on the sex reference either. Wow, things are progressing along splendidly. Quick story." He held up his hand as if that would keep her in her place.

Uncle Mitch had a habit of telling stories, some of them entertaining—complete with voice impersonations—but most of them with a hidden message. When she and her sisters were younger, they would scatter at the phrase "a quick story," but as they grew older it was a respect thing. Resisting was futile and hard to do without hurting his feelings. Mitch was the single nicest person she knew. No way she was going to hurt him, so she sat.

"When you were... I guess around eleven because Meg was going to start first grade the year after that summer. Maybe you were twelve?"

Hollis gave him a look she hoped asked, "does it really matter?" It must have worked, because he moved on.

"Anyway, you girls used to play business, which was typical for the

Jeffries overachievers." He laughed. "Sage wanted to own a garage so she could be a mechanic or a baker. Interesting combination, but then again, so is Sage."

They both laughed.

"Annabelle was always a—"

"Bookstore," they said together as Hollis joined in on the memory.

"Meg wanted to be a pilot or run a safari."

"God, remember the safari hat she used to wear?"

Her uncle nodded. "That thing saw plenty of adventure. I wonder if she still has it."

Hollis laughed. "I doubt it. Unless she can fit it in her pack. She's probably upgraded to something more... functional."

"Do you remember what business you used to play?"

Hollis shook her head then said, "Banker or lawyer, maybe? Huh, it's weird I don't remember."

"It's not all that weird. When you were little, it was 'richest woman in the world.'"

"That's right." She laughed.

"Until you were about twelve. That year you said you 'ran a partnership.'"

"I did not. That's not even a business."

"That's what you used to say. 'My partner and I have big desks and they face each other. And we have paintings.' That's what you'd say."

Hollis tried to remember being so silly and wondered why her sisters had not laughed at their big sister's vague business plan. "Did we do anything?"

"That was my favorite part. 'We help people during the day and at night we sit on the pier and talk,' you said."

"No fu-nking way!"

Her uncle nodded. "That one year, that is exactly what you said because I remember thinking despite all the pressures your parents put on you that you would be perfectly fine."

"That year? What business did I run the other years?"

"Oh, you went back to richest woman in the world the following year, but for that one summer, you had such potential." He smiled.

Hollis searched her memory and vaguely remembered the desk. She had pictures of that perfect desk in her mind and her partner sitting across from her. So weird. Where had that piece of dreaming gone? Hollis stood to leave.

"I need to get the towels from the dryer before your guests check in at four."

"Look at you being all hospitable. I might have to keep you."

She laughed. "Not going to happen, and you are in the home stretch with all those tiny pieces of paper. Back to it."

"Eh, come to think of it, maybe I don't want you. No, I do. Even though you've killed most of the perfectly innocent dust in my office, I like having you here, Tiny Tots."

Hollis smiled and turned to leave.

"Hey, before you go. What summer did you meet Matt?"

She didn't bother turning around. There was the lesson in the story, delivered with a punch. "You already know."

"I do. Might want to remind yourself is all."

She shook her head, not wanting to give anything away. Walking back to her cabin, Hollis found herself with that nagging need again, this time, though, without all the talking.

The air smelled of lilac and Matt could hear the buzz of distant bees as the moisture from his beer bottle dripped around his fingers. He loved summer. Loved it even more now that she was around. The stupid grin on his face would not go away. He knew there were still hurdles to get over, that he wasn't guaranteed anything more than a summer, but sipping his beer, Matt didn't care. He let the warm day take him back to another all-important summer.

Hollis had made sure to point out every bad tack and rigging mistake he'd made that first week of Junior Sailing as if they were training for Olympic trials instead of floating around on dinghies with a ragged sail that had seen far too many summers.

She liked to hit his shoulder and he liked to tease her. She would pop up at the general store or on the beach. They were friends, and then they turned thirteen. That summer, her hair was long and mermaid wavy, at least that was how his newly minted teenage mind saw it. She'd starting wearing cutoff shorts he knew had not been worn during other summers and gauzy tank tops the colors of Starburst candy. She worked at the sandwich shop and used to jump off the pier with her friends until they collapsed on towels and giggled their way to the ice cream parlor. Her friends were attractive, now that he thought about it, most girls were pretty as soon as Matt turned thirteen, but Hollis was beautiful and fierce. That was the summer he held her hand for the first time while he walked her back to *Bunny Blue* after she got off work. Hollis's parents had money, but she worked. She relied on no one, even back then.

There were nights on the pier when they would stay up until four in the morning. He told her his parents fought about not being able to have another baby and she told him her parents had lost a baby in between Annabelle and Meg, but nothing like his brother's death. She teared up when he told her about John and she was the first person he could remember ever saying to him, "That must have been hard on you."

The summer they turned thirteen was the "Summer of Knowledge," as Matt liked to call it. They'd messed with each other up until then, teased, but that summer things were different. He knew even back then that Hollis was special and a guy met one, maybe two, girls like her in a lifetime. When she'd kissed him for the first time that summer, he would have traded his entire comic book collection to be around her forever.

Matt fell softly from his memory and back into watering his parents' rosebushes. He must have missed the knock at the door over the rush of the hose because the side gate opened and Hollis walked through wearing nothing but bathing suit bottoms and a white tank top. Her feet were bare and her hair was pulled off her face. She had more freckles on her face than she did when she'd first arrived back at the cove.

"Hey." Matt turned off the hose.

She walked straight toward him, took the beer from his hand, and set it on the small patio table his parents had bought at a garage sale when they first moved into their bungalow at the cove. Each time Matt looked at the table, his mind confirmed that was the garage sale table. Weird the way the mind worked, he thought, right before his completely shut down because Hollis lifted the hem of his T-shirt, pulled it over his head, and threw it on the garage sale table.

"I folded the towels," she said, running her hand along his shoulder and kissing her way along his back until she was standing behind him. "And my uncle is almost done with the receipts."

At least that's what Matt thought she said when her arms snaked under his and moved along his chest, her body pressed against his back. She smelled like coconuts and fabric softener and he tried to find his words, but her lips were on him again. The sun was warm. Matt closed his eyes.

"The kitchen ran out of butter. Can you believe that?"

He groaned, not at the question but at the way his body danced when she went up on her toes and took his earlobe between her teeth.

"I took the truck and bought butter and then I thought I'd come get you for paddleboarding." Her hands moved down his stomach to the waistband of his board shorts.

Matt's brain tuned back in for a minute long enough to yell, "Hell, yes!" then went fuzzy again.

Hollis pulled the Velcro at his waist and moved back around to face him. Her eyes bluer than silver, at that moment they almost matched the sky.

"Then I had a stupid conference call"—she kissed his chest and Matt felt his shorts drop around his ankles—"I had lunch with Mitch and he told me a story, of course. When I was walking back to my cabin, I started thinking about you... inside me, our bodies warm and pressed together." Her voice was barely above a whisper and thick with a need Matt knew all too well. "I thought it was a memory, maybe something from the past I was revisiting, but then I realized: it wasn't." Hollis slid her fingers into the sides of her bathing suit and

Matt thought he might stop breathing right there. Was it the butter or the conference call that got her like this? Whatever it was, he could get used to this.

"I was remembering the other night" — she slid the suit off her legs and kicked it aside — "and for the first time in so long, my present was better than my past."

Finally able to use his hands, Matt pulled the tank top over her head. The minute he lifted her onto the garage sale table and sent the beer bottle flying to his parents' grass, he knew exactly what she was talking about. They'd moved beyond their past. It was still a familiar friend, the glue that connected them after all of these years, but the present, even with all the mess, was where they wanted to be. Hollis arched her back and Matt ran the palm of his hand through the center of her most perfect breasts, right down to her stomach. When they slid from her afternoon fantasy into making another memory, he was suddenly grateful for every minute he'd been without her if all of that brought them here.

Chapter Twenty-Two

Matt woke to Hollis wide-awake on the living room floor of his parents' bungalow. She was gloriously naked and under the same blanket he'd grabbed off the couch when he realized they weren't going to make it to the bedroom. The sun had set and while she looked thoroughly loved tucked in next to him, she was staring up at the ceiling. Something was wrong and he didn't know how much longer he could wait, so he tested the waters.

"Why was your conference call bad?" Matt asked, sitting up and clicking on the light next to them. Her legs were outside the covers, and he noticed she had no toenail polish on. In all the time he'd known Hollis, save maybe when they were younger than thirteen, he had never seen her toes unpainted. Something about the bareness of it, the vacancy in her stare, told him she didn't need an interrogation, so he changed direction.

"I need to find a new dentist."

Hollis looked up at him.

"I mean, I've had the same one for a few years now, but the last time I went in, his assistant said they were not using happy gas anymore for cleanings."

Her face softened as she raised her eyebrow. He kept talking.

"As you know, I'm scared of the dentist, even the cleaning, so that is not going to work for me. Have you ever had happy gas? I don't think we've ever talked about this. Are you scared of the dentist?"

"No."

"To both?"

Hollis nodded, and Matt thought he could see the slightest upturn of a smile. He kept going.

"I hate to do it because they're so close to my house and the office too for that matter, but I need the happy gas. I searched Google and checked to see if I could bring my own—yeah, that's a narcotic." He laughed. "Then I tried to turn on the charm with the assistant. I used the eyes and asked if she could make an exception."

Hollis sat up.

Matt shook his head. "It didn't work. She was immune to the baby blues. So I'm not sure what I should do. This guy at work says he tried acupuncture to get over his fear of the dentist. Have you ever tried acupuncture?"

"No." She was definitely smiling now.

Matt was glad because he wasn't sure what was left to say about his dentist. Being the talker was hard, but then Hollis leaned over, kissed him, and climbed into his lap. He thanked his dentist and her bare toenails for letting him help. Scooting over until his back was resting on the back of the couch, he turned on the television.

"Have you seen the *The Karate Kid*?" she asked, turning so she was now facing the television and between his legs. He was going to need to put some clothes on soon or he wasn't going to be able to think, but he didn't want to move.

"I have. Have you seen the second one? I think there's a third one too."

She looked over her shoulder at him. "Really?"

Matt did eventually get up and put some sweats on while they made popcorn. They watched *The Karate Kid, Part II* and *The Karate Kid, Part III*, agreed they should have stopped at two, and when she fell asleep in his arms, he carried her to bed and held her until the sun peeked through the blinds in the morning.

Hollis did most of the talking, the work when they were younger.

She was the effort and Matt was the ease. She planned and he helped her calm down. Most relationships were that way, one person more something than the other, but tonight the roles were reversed and Matt found that babbling whatever was on his mind helped settle the thing that was making her so crazy. In the years since they'd last seen each other, he'd learned some things too.

Hollis woke up the following morning to coffee, a still-warm sticky bun, and a note that simply said, "Gone to find a new dentist." She laughed and sat up in bed. Taking the lid off the coffee, she thanked the gods and sipped herself awake. It was Thursday. Hollis loved Thursdays. It was well into the week, but there was still enough time to get things done before people started winding down for the weekend. When she used to work sixteen-hour days, Thursday was the sweet spot. She pushed her hair off her face and took such a large bite of the sticky bun that she had to scramble from bed for a napkin because she couldn't reach all of the stick on her mouth with her tongue. Crawling back into bed, she leaned back on the pillows and thought about Matt talking her down last night. He knew what she needed still, and for some reason, she let him help. Hollis had never climbed into anyone's lap other than her uncle's, and that was a long time ago. She was learning to let someone help and finding it was all right for Matt to see her knocked off her self-imposed pedestal.

Right as she finished her coffee, her phone vibrated. It was seven in the morning, and Reese was already calling her. God, she hoped it was good news, that her long-held appreciation of Thursday would remain intact after she hung up.

"I should have known you weren't playing around," his game show host voice said before she even greeted him.

"What is it, Reese?"

"Matthew Locke. I knew I recognized him. I thought you hated tech. You said after the Fat Pigs thing, and I quote, 'I'm going back where I belong.' Guess you changed your mind."

"Still waiting for you to make sense." Getting the feeling Reese was simply calling because he liked to hear himself speak, Hollis put the last of the sticky bun in her mouth.

"The guy you were playing sandbox with. Come on, don't play coy, Jeffries. What are you two working on?"

Hollis swallowed and felt that rush she rarely experienced anymore of not being in the loop. She could count on one hand how many times she had any kind of a loop issue. She checked and double-checked to make sure she was never caught with her big-girl pants down. She wasn't sure what Reese was talking about or how he knew Matt, but she wasn't going to tell Reese that. "Fake it till you make it," her first boss at Dairy Queen had said. Turned out that was awful advice because there was a right way and wrong way to make a Blizzard. However, in this case, it was perfect advice.

"I... I'm gonna need to call you back." She hung up to Reese scrambling like a rat for more information.

Hollis pulled out her laptop and googled Matthew Locke. Coffee, some half marathon, a puff piece on a new The Bean location, hardly WikiLeaks. Maybe Reese was mistaken. Yeah, that never happened. She searched Matt Locke, Matthew E. Locke, Matthew Everly Locke. Nothing, nothing, and nothing. *Damn it!*

Hollis tapped the end of her pencil on her laptop as her corporate-killer instinct roared to life. Challenge, she loved a hunt. The idea hit her, and she smiled and called Reese back.

"Hey, can you do me a favor?"

"Do I get half the bonus?"

"Can you spell Matthew's company? I keep entering it wrong."

"He's with you, can't you—"

"Reese, please don't give me sh— a hard time on this. He's meeting with two strategists right now and I'm not going to interrupt him to ask him how to spell his company. Cooperate, or I'll tell Megan, your tight-ass boss, that you screwed her mother."

Silence.

"Are *still* screwing her mother."

Hollis heard a huff over the phone and smiled.

"It's not like it's hard to spell, genius. It's Pilot Programs. P-I-L—"

She disconnected and dropped the phone to the bed. She googled Pilot Programs and found a website and articles from every major tech and financial newspaper in the world. She'd heard of Pilot; they were involved in some project she'd sat in on. *Which one was that?* She searched her brain and remembered it had something to do with software for school cafeterias. She couldn't remember which side she was on, but she remembered the company because her favorite dog... had been named Pilot.

Hollis felt the air exit her lungs that same way it had when she was tripped by some kid the year her dad wanted her to try soccer. The little bitch stuck her foot out and as hard as she tried to recover, Hollis had landed chest first in the scratchy Bermuda grass. It felt like her lungs had given up, collapsed, and left her gasping. She was right back there now, but without the grass. What was he doing? And why had he let her think he was some dropout working at a coffee shop? Why had he let her tease him?

Oh, God. Hollis grabbed her wallet, left her cabin, and held her hand up as she rushed by the nothing-is-ever-as-good-as-home couple that had checked into Red Rover yesterday afternoon. No way she was dealing with them now.

Matt knew that look the minute she blew through the front door of The Bean a little after nine. He'd left her early with coffee, sugar, and a note. The woman in shorts and his sweatshirt currently gesturing for him while he handed a tourist her latte didn't seem like she woke up to any of those things.

Matt smiled at Hollis; nothing in return. *Not good.* It was Thursday, her favorite day. He hoped whatever it was could be fixed and fast.

At last, when he was able to get away, he approached her and noted Hollis looked like she'd already taken a ride on the crazy train. Her hair was barely hanging on to a knot, bun, something that looked like a runaway ball of yarn at the base of her neck, and her eyes were wild.

He could feel the thoughts spinning and when he was within arm's reach, she tried to grab him but missed and ended up pulling him to the corner table by the sleeve of his T-shirt. There was no one sitting there, thank God, because she plopped him down in one of the chairs and joined him by practically throwing herself into the other. This was not going to be a good Thursday.

"What is going on?" she asked.

"I... could you be a little more specific?"

"Sure. Who the hel-lo are you, and why are you lying to me? You, and I'm not sure whoever else is in on your little charade, have been leading me to believe you are one thing when it turns out you are someone else entirely."

Despite the ranting and slightly insane head bobbing, Matt knew exactly what she was talking about. He'd had a feeling this would come up at some point, but not right this minute. Wasn't it often that way, when you least expected it? Songs were written about irony for a reason.

He tried the silent, confused treatment first. It was his "go-to."

When he said nothing, she leaned across the small round table until they were face-to-face.

"You made me think you were— God we did... things and now I'm... it was all a lie. You are a lie."

That was about enough, Matt thought. "I am not a lie. How I make money has nothing to do with who I am, who we are."

"Oh, really? Well, I have to disagree with you there considering you named your fu—dging company after my sweet dog and you are not a 'programmer.' This all feels personal, Matt. Is this some kind of game? You know, like I left so you're going to make me want you again and then break it to me that it was a joke?"

"What are you talking about?"

"I'm talking about feeling like a complete loser last night. Crawling into your lap," she whispered that last part, and he almost laughed. "Then I wake up this morning and miraculously, my sweet innocent programmer who plays coffee man on the side turns out to be a CEO of an up-and-coming incredible company, and he's loaded." More whispering.

"I am not sweet, nor am I innocent. Please don't say that again. About the rest, isn't that a good thing? I'm sure books have been written about this exact scenario."

"No, not the books I read. This is not a good thing."

"Why? Because I didn't tell you, or you're more comfortable with me being the coffee dropout."

"Both."

This time he laughed. "Holls, I'm guessing you've dated some successful men in the past twelve years. As much as I try not to picture that, I don't get how I'm any different."

"Because you are," she said much louder than he was expecting. "You're... you. You're this part of my life, the part where I smell like ocean and..."

"I'm no longer one part of your life and you are not one part of mine. You came to the cove to deal with your life. There was no reason for me to discuss what I do for a living. It hadn't come up yet. That's not the same as lying."

"You told me you need to find a new dentist. I feel like the fact that you own one of the most talked-about tech companies in the country is a few notches above that on the catching-up scale."

She went to stand and he took her hand. "Why does it matter?"

"Because this, this is all pressure. You are worth more than I'll ever make in a lifetime. I... don't like that."

"Christ, aren't we too old for this? I love you. This isn't a competition. What's the problem? I'm real, not some easy summer fling?"

She laughed.

"You can't simply leave now? Is that it, Holls? I'm a solid investment."

"What the fu—dge pops are you talking about? I've never denied your success. I'm the one who said you were crazy to leave school because you were brilliant."

Matt stood. "I don't need to justify this to you or anyone else. Yes, I run Pilot Programs. It is a complete coincidence that my company is named after your dog. Bradley came up with the name. Yes, I didn't tell you because you're going through some stuff and I didn't want to rub your nose in something. I know how you are."

"You know how I am? How I... I am not this!" She stood back, her hands flailing in an up-and-down motion. "I don't need you to hold things back from me. I'm not a child, and I have my own success."

"Sure. I know you do." Matt realized the minute the words came out of his mouth that she would take them as condescending, but this was ridiculous.

"Don't patronize me."

He shook his head. "I give up."

"Oh, well that's nothing new."

Letting her have the last word, Matt went back behind the counter because there was no winning this one. By the time he looked up, she was gone.

Chapter Twenty-Three

*H*ollis had helped herself to two large glasses of wine that she decided were long overdue because she wasn't a drunk and if she was, that particular challenge would need to get the hell to the back of the line. In the midst of drinking, she had texted Annabelle. It was a long diatribe against the double standard for women in the workplace and from what she could tell, now looking at her phone, a string of mostly illegible comments about Matt not being the coffee man or some programmer and how she was ready to leave the past behind. It wasn't her finest hour, she would admit, but Anna replied that she would come for a visit. Now that they were tucked into a booth at the restaurant at the cove, Hollis forgave her momentary trip into digital stupidity.

"What does that mean? He's not a programmer?"

"He owns the company. He and his friend Bradley developed the app so people can preorder their coffee and then it's ready when they get there."

"Oh, I love that. Starbucks has that."

"They bought it from him."

Anna's eyes grew wide. "Really? Well, that is news and exciting. He's successful. That's great."

Hollis said nothing and took a bite of the crab dip delivered to their table.

"I mean... that is *not* a good thing?" her sister asked.

"No. I guess it is, but he lied and made me think he was... not as loaded or well respected as he is."

"Did you ever ask him what he did?"

Hollis chewed another chip and dip as she nodded. "I did, and he said he was a programmer."

"Which technically is not a lie."

"I think it's a sign."

"Stop it. You're self-sabotaging again."

"Holy sh—in splints. Did Sage say that? It sounds like something that would come from one of her Be a Better You tomes."

Anna laughed. "Tomes, great word. Crossword?"

Hollis shook her head. "Discovery Channel last night because I couldn't sleep. It is a good one, not used enough."

"Agreed. No, I did not get that from Sage—it's my own. You're screwing up your happiness because... I don't know why, but believe me, the pickings are slim out there and you, of course, are pissy with your man because he's made some money and has a career."

"It's not simply a career, it's impressive."

"Better than yours?"

"Yes."

"Well, there it is. You're a study, Hollis. Can't you be second?"

"No fu—dge cake way you get to do that to me. You know the IQ score of every friend you have."

"That was research for my thesis."

"Uh huh. Remember when you were drunk after you graduated?"

Anna nodded as if she already knew where this was going.

"You rambled them all off and then told the whole bar yours was higher."

"O thou invisible spirit of wine, if thou hast no name to be known by, let us call thee—devil!" The words slipped from her sister's mouth like an easy exhale and even though Hollis knew it was Shakespeare, she understood their meaning. That was Anna's talent, she was brilliant at bringing language to life for her students, for everyone come to think of it. Not that Hollis would tell her that now. She was too much fun to tease.

Hollis scrunched her face. "You're so weird."

"I know."

"Bill—"

"Will."

"Whatever, he's not going to have some pearl of wisdom that's going fix this. What am I even doing here? I had to have known on some level I was going to see him, right?"

Anna nodded.

When her mother had insisted she visit Uncle Mitch, Hollis felt her heart sort of rolled in her chest. The idea of returning to a place, a time when things made sense had appealed to her since much of her present life felt marred by one fateful decision. She'd been embarrassed and worst of all, made to feel foolish. All she could think to do was run home and when her mother opened the door, Hollis took it and ran back to her pier, her sunlight, and on some level, who she was when she was with Matt.

How could a time hold so much possibility and so much pain all at once? She'd loved him with her whole heart and once she had broken his, she did the same to her own and never looked back. She hadn't wanted to be a young mother, or a mother at all for that matter, back then. All she wanted was to win.

"Are you going to take him to the wedding?" Annabelle asked after they ordered chocolate cake.

"Probably not." Hollis took the first bite.

"You're stupid."

"You're stupider."

Her sister laughed. "Don't screw this up, Holls. Ask him about his job, be an adult for Christ's sake. Maybe you two need to leave this place and step out of the postcard. Instead of being pissed he's successful, go see what his life is now."

"Hey, whose side are you on?"

"I think I'm on his," Anna said as they took their dessert to go and waved to Mitch on the way out.

As they left the restaurant, Hollis stopped. "Maybe I'm a lie too."

Annabelle took her hand and they kept walking.

"Well, have you told him why you're here? Does he know what happened at least?"

Hollis shook her head.

"That's crazy. Why not?" Annabelle asked as they made their way to Mr. Boots.

"Because I'm fixing it and he doesn't need to know. I know it was wrong to shut him out the first time, but this is different. This is my work."

"First time?"

Damn it! Her big mouth had talked her right into that one so once they were in the cabin, Hollis told her.

"I got pregnant my junior year in college." She could see the shock and then the hurt run across her sister's face.

"Why didn't you tell anyone?"

"Because right when I was going to have to make some hard decisions, I had a miscarriage."

Annabelle pulled her into her arms. "Why do you do this? Why do you keep us at arm's length? People want to love you, Hollis."

"I'm working on it."

"Yeah, maybe you need to work a little faster."

"I'll get on it right after I keep my job."

"Do you want to talk about that, the job?" Annabelle sat on the edge of the bed and took her shoes off.

"Oh, I'm sorry. I have a one-dramatic-reveal-a-night policy," Hollis said.

Annabelle laughed, but her eyes were still concerned. Hollis hated that. She was supposed to be the big sister.

"Can we start the slumber party now?" Hollis turned toward the bathroom as her sister crawled into bed.

"Hey, Anna?"

Her sister looked up.

"Velcro," Hollis said and closed her door.

She smiled when she heard her sister laugh and say, "Oh my."

They watched romantic movies because Annabelle was the expert on all things made up and too perfect for real life. Before she fell asleep, Hollis reviewed her to-do list for the following day. Closing her laptop, she clicked off the light and knew there was one thing she needed to fix that wasn't on the list. She needed to apologize to Matt because her sister was right—damn it—Hollis was being stupid.

Matt watched his feet hanging above the surface of the dark water the next morning, suddenly struck by how much older his body was. It was an odd thing to notice as the sun slowly climbed into the sky, warming the back of his neck. He wasn't a kid anymore, but sitting on the dock made him feel young and, of course, reminded him of her. Being barefoot reminded him of her too, even when he was back home. Several things had brought her freckled nose and those storm cloud eyes to his mind, despite his best efforts to forget. Days with big fluffy clouds because after Hollis, he tended to notice the shapes, driving with the windows down, any dock or pier, anywhere. Hell, even grilled chicken brought her to mind, reminded him of all the moments he knew she was his, knew he'd never love anyone the way he'd loved her.

A drop of water slipped from his hair and ran down his cheek. He shook his hair the way he'd done as a kid and watched the excess water fly onto the dry dock. He'd had a good swim, but now it was time for him to head into the city. His schedule was packed with meetings and then he was meeting Toro to try to get his dad in the pool.

He'd wanted to call her last night, but no matter how much he loved her or needed her, he would not apologize for his success. He'd spent so much time downplaying things in an effort to gain his father's acceptance or keep the peace. Not with her; he wouldn't do it anymore. Not that he had any clue how to keep her either.

Matt checked his phone. No messages. *Shit!*

Hollis Marie Jeffries, he could hear her young voice introducing herself to him all over again. It was the summer he turned twelve.

The summer his parents had finally started seeing a profit on their three coffee shops and decided to open one along Tomales Bay, about a mile up the road from a place called Mitchell's Cove in the town proper of Mitchell, California. They'd driven up from their home in San Francisco and rented one of the cabins—it was Red Rover.

Matt now smiled at the memory. They'd arrived in the early evening and when Matt ran to the back patio of their cabin, he heard singing. That was the first time he saw Hollis Jeffries, a big long braid down her back, braces, and a small plastic bucket as she walked through a little under two feet of water looking at whatever she could find and singing something Matt didn't recognize at the time. She would later tell him it was the fight song of her private grammar school. He had not introduced himself that day and simply watched her. The following Monday, they were both enrolled in Junior Sailing. It was the summer when his favorite Vans were finally broken in to perfection and he'd wanted to learn how to kayak, but his father had insisted on sailing... and it was the summer he met Hollis. He used to imagine telling this story to their children and adding that they had become friends that day, but that would have been a lie.

The slap of a seal's tail as it swam by pulled Matt from his thoughts, and he was grateful. Standing, he slipped his feet back into his shoes and pulled the now damp T-shirt back over his head as he started back up the pier. There was time for a quick shower before he had to leave. Glancing at the cabins, he thought for a minute they needed to talk, but then he realized he had nothing to say.

David Locke went to physical therapy as planned. Matt had originally thought it wouldn't be necessary, but Toro felt it was important not to disrupt his routine until they were sure the pool was going to work. His mother had a baby shower to go to, which was perfect because it was the two of them for lunch and then Matt would bring in Toro.

After picking up burgers and the almost-silent car ride back to the house, they sat eating and wiping their mouths in silence.

"Mom says you need to take some ibuprofen after you've eaten."

His father grunted.

"I'll get those for you." Matt set the remaining half of his burger down and stood. "Where are they?"

"How should I know? Can you turn on the television?"

"No. Dad, where does Mom keep the medicine?"

"Same place she kept it when you lived here. What do you think, when you move out to become fancy that we moved the medicine?"

Matt inhaled, slowly let it out, and walked to his parents' bathroom. The Advil was right where it usually was and he put two in his hand.

"Here," he said, handing the liquid-filled pills to his father who, of course, ignored him and stared at a television that was not on.

"Dad, take these with our food." He set them on the paper next to his burger.

"Can you get that television?"

"No," Matt said, sitting back down.

"Why not? What are we going to do, talk about all your money? We used to have other things to talk about. See, if you hadn't screwed it all up and—"

"And what?" Matt asked, knowing the answer, but wanting to cut him off before he was allowed to somehow make him feel small again. "Gone to school, found success? Which one of my decisions explains why we have this?" He gestured between the two of them.

"Watch your mouth."

"Sure, right. What should I stop saying, Dad?"

"You have no respect."

"No, I have tremendous respect for you and Mom and what you guys have built."

"We should have had more kids," his father said.

Matt laughed, relieved as some of the usual tension spilled off him. "Oh yeah? You want to be careful with that one. What if little brother had turned out to be... I don't know, a heart surgeon? Or worse, an astronaut? Imagine the shame when little brother or middle child hadn't wanted to learn about roasting coffee. But now, you only have me to pile all the guilt on."

His father grabbed his walker and Matt felt bad. He put his hand over his father's.

"Dad, stay where you are. I'll leave."

"Good."

"I don't know how else to help you," Matt said quietly.

"Help? I don't need your help."

"I think you do, Dad, and I'm tired of backing down, so we're going to see if I can help."

At the knock on the door he was expecting because he'd texted Toro, Matt opened the door.

"Hey, ACM! How's it going?" Toro stepped in and shook his father's hand.

"Toro, I'm... I have a bum hip. That's how it's going. A bum hip and a rude son."

"Said every father, right?" Toro crouched his giant frame down in front of Matt's dad. "So here's the thing, Coffee Master. I have a sister who runs a health club, kind of a rehab place, but there are women in bikinis so it's better. I'd like to get you in the pool."

His father's eyes darted immediately to Matt. "Is this your doing?"

Matt shrugged, knowing anything he said would be the wrong answer at this point.

"Thank you, Toro, but I had physical therapy this morning and it does nothing."

"Don't thank me yet. Let's see how the water goes."

"No." He looked at Matt, stubborn because he knew no other way.

Toro stood and glanced at Matt, who moved to the door. He grabbed a bag of his father's stuff that he'd packed and gave the nod to Toro.

He leaned down and said quietly, "Almighty Coffee Master, your son loves you and you know I worship you, so you'll have to trust us." With that, he gently picked up Matt's father, who was in such shock he didn't even blink until they were out the door.

Chapter Twenty-Four

The following night was karaoke night at Mitchell's Cove. Hollis spent her morning helping to get things set up and went back to her cabin to shower. She hadn't seen Matt and guessed he'd gone back to the city, although Poppy told Hollis this morning when she went to get her coffee that she wasn't coming back full-time until next week.

The music was loud and the restaurant was packed with locals and tourists. Hollis tried to tell herself a little space was good and if he was back home, then distance was good too. They certainly couldn't stay in the "postcard" forever, as Annabelle had put it. Now that she knew what Matt really did, she imagined his life was busy. That was fine; hers was too. Hollis laughed at the thought because about an hour ago she was testing out the strobe light above the karaoke machine. Oh, how the mighty have fallen, she thought right as Matt walked in and sat on one of the bar stools Uncle Mitch had saved for his guests. Hollis took the stool next to him.

"Is there any way all of this could be your fault?" She leaned in so he could hear her, and he smelled so good she almost spun off the stool.

"I..."

"You know, since you have a penis. You could plead the Fifth and the whole thing could be your fault."

"Will that fix this so I can get back to waking up next to you? Because if so, my penis is all yours, blame away."

Hollis laughed and right as Mr. and Mrs. Trumble started singing, more like screeching "Bad Romance" by Lady Gaga, she took Matt's hand and pulled him out to the patio.

"This isn't exactly a slow dance song," he said, settling his hands on her hips.

"I don't care. I'm sorry. I was stupid and it's great that you are successful. Do you forgive me?"

Matt nodded.

"What color is your couch?" she asked.

"My couch? You've seen the couch at my parents' place."

"Your couch at home, where you live now. What color is it?"

"Black. Yours?"

"Mine is a red and orange color. It's not quite a sectional, but it has a little chaise piece on the end. I like to sit there on Sundays and read."

"My couch is kind of small. I should get a bigger one, but I don't spend a lot of time on it."

"Do you have any plants?"

"No. Well, I have a Christmas cactus that my mom brought over when I moved in, but it's barely hanging in there."

"I don't have any plants or pets."

They stood in silence.

"What kind of toothpaste do you use?"

Matt laughed.

"I think it's Crest. There are some kind of beads or whiteners in it because it's a little crunchy when I brush."

"Paste?"

"As opposed to?"

"Gel. Is it blue or white?"

"White."

"Paste." She turned to face him, wrapped her arms under his, and flattened her palms across his back, resting her head on his chest.

"Do... you use paste?"

"Yes. I think we might have the same toothpaste. Crest Whitening. It works. Are you happy with your toothpaste?"

Her eyes met his and she knew Matt could see she was asking him to give her something. Once again, he didn't quite look like he knew what that was, but he played along.

"I am. I've had the blue kind before and I like this one, I like the grit."

"Me too." Hollis smiled.

"Since we are finally getting down to the nitty-gritty."

"Ooooh, great phrase. Can I have it?"

"Sure. Since we are in the nitty-gritty, we should probably discuss toilet paper. I can't use Charmin, it's too soft," Matt offered, visibly enjoying himself now.

"Me neither. You know, I'm not sure what my toilet paper is. I'll have to look when I get home."

"When you get home, yes, you need to do that." His mouth hovered over hers and when he kissed her, soft and capable, it triggered something in her. A desire to keep him safe, which she knew sounded weird, but she didn't want anything to ruin it this time.

"What about trash bags?" she asked, her head still swimming as their lips parted.

"I have no idea—whatever's under my sink."

"You should know this information. Maybe we should check on your trash bags now."

"That is a good idea. Do you want me to take you home, Holls? We could go to my parents' place or back to your cabin."

"I want to see where you live. I want to be there."

Matt pulled her toward the exit—stopping at some point behind a couple debating whether they should sing Stevie Wonder or Neil Diamond—and bent to kiss her again as if he couldn't quite make it to the parking lot without one more. On their way out the door, her uncle walked in carrying more popcorn.

"We need to check on Matt's trash bags."

Her uncle smiled and nodded. "Absolutely. You two get on that."

They drove with the windows up and the quiet of the car. The isolation, as opposed to the open sea air, made things different already. As they crossed the bridge into San Francisco, it felt sort of like returning from a long vacation and having to check the mail and buy groceries. Those were things they hadn't done together in a long time and as Hollis sat next to him, for the first time since she had returned, Matt wondered if they would work outside of the cove.

Matt had never put much thought into his apartment. He bought it after his divorce and thought of it as a conveniently located place to sleep and visit with the occasional friend. After his divorce, most of those "friends" had been women, but that became old quickly. He would admit his place was stereotypical single guy, but he'd never thought of it as cold until she was standing in the entryway. It didn't feel like the right place for her and yet he wanted her there, in his life. She'd asked and they'd set aside so many things, skipped more conversations than they should have. She wanted to be in his place, and now they were. If she chose to stay one day, he had no doubt she would fill every room with love. After a quick tour, during which Hollis commented that he needed more artwork on the walls, Matt took her into his bedroom, and later, when they'd fallen asleep in one another's arms, she was restless. He wasn't sure if she was dreaming, but it certainly wasn't a fairy tale. He'd rolled over to find her gone at some point in the middle of the night and heard noises in the kitchen.

"Holls, what are you doing?" he asked, buttoning up his jeans.

"I'm making brownies." Hollis was stirring batter in nothing but the button up shirt he'd worn hours before.

"It's two in the morning."

"I know, I had an urge."

Matt nodded. "Are you all right?"

"Yes. I like your home," she said, still not making eye contact as she began pouring the chocolate into a waiting pan.

"Thank you." He sat at the counter. "Do you need some help?"

"No."

"Why are you stressed?"

"Who says I'm stressed?"

"You bake when you're stressed. Of course, it was cut and bake cookies back then, but I'm assuming it's the same thing with better… skills."

She laughed and used a spatula to get the last of the batter.

"So?"

"Would you like to go to my sister's wedding with me?"

"Yes."

"Okay, good. So, it looks like I'm going to be fired, well, maybe not yet, but soon. I'm sure they'll give me a chance to resign. I mean there were other people who could have vetted Zeke along the way, you know, up the chain. So, they'll give me a chance to resign. I'll update my resume. I've been with them for eight years, but there are some things"—she put the pan in the oven and began washing the dishes—"things that were not right there, so I'm trying to look at this as a learning opportunity. Another one." With the water still running, she leaned both hands on the sink.

"Do you want to tell me what happened now?"

"I screwed up, that's what happened. I screwed up." She began to laugh. "Quite literally, or would that be screwed down? I'm not sure." And then she started to cry.

Matt stood and even though Hollis held up her hand as she tended to do to indicate she was fine, he went behind her and wrapped his arms around her. After a gentle squeeze, she turned in his arms and held on. Matt tried to steady his breath, so unfamiliar with Hollis letting go that it took him aback for a minute.

"Can I help?"

"No. I'll be fine. Will you go to the wedding with me?"

He leaned back and lifted her chin. "Of course I'll go with you."

"It's next Saturday. We need to go to the ceremony at the farm and then fly to Napa. It's a weekend thing."

"That sounds like a good time."

Hollis nodded. "Thank you."

"For what?"

"For going with me."

"What is wrong? If it's work, tell me what happened. I run a damn company, Holls. Other people let me fix their mess. Let's figure this out."

She shook her head. "It's not something... I've tried to work it out, and I think it's time to walk away."

"Okay. Then you'll find some other great job. Do you want to be my partner? I could use someone with an MBA."

She huffed out a breath, but Matt was happy to hear a little bit of a laugh.

"I'm sorry," she said, touching her head to his chest.

"For what?"

"For leaving you, for being so... me. I'm sorry for being anything other than thrilled that you're loaded."

Matt laughed and held her tighter. "I am far from loaded."

"If that's true, then you're not managing things properly."

Hollis seemed lighter from simply talking, and Matt cradled her head in his hands. "Please don't apologize for being you. I've loved you all my life, Holls. That's not going to change."

"Even with my sailor mouth and my second toe being too big?"

"I've always liked the dirty mouth, and you know what they say about big second toes."

"What?"

Matt pulled her into his arms and she wrapped her legs around his waist. "I'm sure someone has said something about big second toes." He kissed her and started back toward the bedroom.

"Wait, I need to check the brownies."

He turned off the oven and continued into the bedroom while Hollis laughed, almost back to normal.

Much later, it started to rain and Matt watched her sleep. Something was wrong. Hollis only baked when things were wrong, and he guessed "wrong" took on deeper meaning as she grew older. He was officially worried now and annoyed he didn't know the full story. This was becoming some kind of stupid game, sort of like holding their breath, but Matt worried that this time, Hollis was going to pass out before admitting she needed help. He hadn't been this worried about her since, well, for about twelve years.

Chapter Twenty-Five

Reese called the morning before they left for Sage's wedding. The guy had impeccable timing. She'd spent last week calming the waters and it appeared, after talking with a consulting company, there might be a way to fix the game in less than a month. Megan had argued during the conference call that followed that she didn't like the consultants they were working with and she "highly doubts you're going to pull this one from its tailspin." Hollis had hung up more determined than ever. Megan's bitch face had that effect on her.

"They're pulling out," he said before she had a chance to say "hello."

"What? It's not the end of the third quarter." Hollis instinctively threw the covers off and climbed from bed. She needed to be dressed for this conversation.

"Someone has a wild hair and now all the rest are following. Time is up. If they don't have a finished functioning game by the end of next week, they're done."

This was it, she thought, the moment had arrived, the "dark place" as her uncle had said. She couldn't figure out how to respond to Reese. She certainly wasn't going to share her fears with someone who wore suspenders and a belt. Hollis took in a slow breath and tried to steady her voice. "Okay, well then we have the rest of this week, four days, and next week. Let Corning know we will have something for him and the group by Thursday of next week."

"What... do you know something I don't know? Because Megan and I have been racking our brains."

I'll bet you have.

"We can't think of a fix for this. I think we need to let them pull out."

"Reese, I need you to listen very carefully. I will have something for the group by next Thursday. If they don't like what I present, then they can walk. For now, all you need to do is convey the message and mark your calendar. Can you handle that?"

He hated when Hollis brought out her "preschool teacher" voice, so he grunted and quickly hung up. Pulling a light sweater on, Hollis opened her laptop and began sending e-mails conveying the information she'd said to Reese. She learned early on not to trust anyone and to cover her ass. She honestly had no idea how she was going to fix this before next Thursday, and she had her sister's wedding for the entire weekend. Hollis had a feeling this one was going to fail, but she wasn't quite ready to give up the cookie yet.

Scanning her inbox, she clicked on an e-mail from a contact she'd reached out to over two weeks ago. They were asking for specifics about the game structure. Hollis forwarded the e-mail to Reese and copied Corning, requesting that they provide a response. At least there was some momentum, she thought as Matt knocked on her door. Hollis put her laptop inside her bag and threw the covers on her bed. When she opened the door, he had a cup of coffee and Hollis wondered if he'd still love her once the darkness settled in.

"Coffee," he said, looking around her room, seemingly inquisitive and impatient at the same time.

"Everything okay?" She expected him to grunt or offer one word this early in the morning, but he surprised her.

"Well, Toro is working with my dad again today and I think he might actually start speaking to me at some point. The hip is getting better."

"That's great." Hollis snatched up some papers she had been read-ing last night before she fell asleep and shoved those in her bag too before locking her cabin door. Matt took her bag and she tried not to jump, but she was still shaken from her call and her laptop had turned into some strange key to a world she still needed.

"We need to talk, Holls. This can't go on like this."

"I know, but right now we need breakfast."

They climbed into his car. Hollis felt the urge to share her story, tell Matt about her morning, but she would take care of it herself and then they could get on with their future.

"What future?" she heard Megan's nasty voice in her head. The bitch was now in her head too? That had to be one step before the bouncy room and the custom-fitted jacket, didn't it? Hollis lowered her sunglasses over her eyes and tried not to think.

Sage Jeffries married Garrett Rye at dawn in the barn on Ryeland Farms. Hollis had originally thought it was insane to have a wedding so early, but when her sister handed her the bouquet right as the cool blue sky warmed to a shade of pink that seemed special ordered for the event, she changed her mind. It was surreal, Hollis thought, and beautiful on a level she was starting to understand again. After the brief and fairly traditional ceremony, Garrett, who wore a vest and no tie, kissed Sage, and with one hand still cradling the back of her neck, he held up the other in a fist as if he'd won some incredible prize. He had, Hollis thought, giving her sister back her bouquet of multicol-ored roses. Sage was hands down one of the best people Hollis knew and while she'd spent a brief period of time trying to be naughty, it was no use. Sage was a kind person and Garrett had found a way to be worthy, eventually.

Sage wore a vintage wedding dress, strapless with a yellow sash around her waist. Her hair was cut into a pixie so she wore a tuft of tulle pinned to the back of her head and speckled with tiny shining blue stones. That was Annabelle's contribution, her "something blue." The art deco cuff bracelet their mother wore at her own wedding was the "something borrowed," and Meg sent thirteen gold coins since even though she was not able to attend, she was put in charge via Skype of the "something old." There was a note with the coins when they arrived two days before the wedding explaining that arras were a tradition in Spain. The groom gave them to the bride to show he could support her. *Since us Jeffries girls pay our own way, here's a little pouch to keep in your garter. Be nice and she'll take you to dinner, Garrett.*

Sage was upset their youngest sister couldn't make it, but they'd all grown accustomed to living without Meg. Secretly, though, they hoped that someday, when she'd lived each adventure she'd managed to dream up, she would return home. Hollis was, of course, put in charge of the hardest bridal item considering her sister loved all things old—something new. At first she thought of shoes, but Sage already had silk shoes from 1920 with little embroidered blue birds around the back of the small heel.

"Of course you do," Hollis had exclaimed to her sister after racking her brain. She'd offered to buy the wedding dress, but even that wasn't new. She'd thought of buying Sage's lingerie but after the *Nice to Naughty* book she'd given her last year, Hollis thought it best to steer clear. She was left with few options and right when the pressure to find something perfect was starting to get to her, Hollis found the perfect "something new." She'd gone into the city and purchased a pair of Cartier diamond earrings from 1926 and asked the jeweler to mount them on new studs. Sage loved them and technically, the parts touching the bride's ears were new.

"That's cheating," Annabelle had said, no doubt pissed at having been topped.

Hollis shrugged her off. "Anna, your middle complex is showing." They all laughed and Hollis gave her sister exactly what she wanted her to have, a little shy of the rules.

The wedding party included Hollis, Annabelle, and Sage's best friend Kenna, who sat across from Garrett's brother Logan, their father Herb, and Travis, Kenna's fiancé. Garrett's dog Jack was the ring bearer and his niece Paige was the flower girl. Matt, Logan's wife Kara, and Herb's girlfriend Libby, the Jeffries set of parents, and Uncle Mitch were also there to help make sure Sage and Garrett had the perfect spot of morning to exchange their vows and announce to lots of cheers and one "I knew it" from Travis that Sage was pregnant.

Hollis had been pissed at first that her sister kept something so important from her, but she quickly remembered twelve years ago when she hadn't let anyone in. When and where to share that news was personal and should never feel like an obligation, Hollis decided as she hugged her sister and shook her head at Garrett and mouthed the words, "You're welcome." He promptly cracked up, and the entire lot of them boarded a private plane waiting at the airport compliments of Grady and Kate Malendar, Kara's brother and sister-in-law. On the plane ride up to Napa, Hollis learned they were expecting their third child any day after having adopted their first two sons. It was a boisterous and laughter-filled trip to the vineyard resort where they would join another hundred or so friends for a reception and overnight party until breakfast the next morning.

"Lots of happy couples and babies," Matt said as he took the seat next to her on the plane.

Hollis nodded, not sure what to say considering their history and the secrets they were able to keep, though briefly, from their families. The contrast was undeniable, the elephant between them, so Hollis pushed it away and focused on where they were at in their lives now. She leaned over and kissed Matt, who in turn pulled her into his lap and kissed her more.

"Circus lady, word on the street is you're in love."

"Aren't we all, Farmer G, aren't we all." Hollis laughed and Matt pulled her back into his arms.

Chapter Twenty-Six

*M*att spent the morning after they returned from Napa in meetings, trying to remember why he was back in the city even though he could still see her in his bed when he left before sunrise to beat the traffic. His father had his third session with Toro next week, Poppy would be back full-time a week after that, and hopefully Matt would be able to return to his big-boy job within the month. The thought both appealed to his need for calm and stirred a sense of dread. Outside of the cove, back at home, where would that leave him and Hollis? He knew relationships tended to be complicated, but somehow being with her in the suspended reality of Mitchell's Cove made things easy. Matt knew it wasn't exactly adult, but he'd liked easy. "Easy never got anyone anything other than fired," he could hear his father barking.

Yeah, yeah. Matt pulled up pictures from the wedding on his desktop right as Bradley knocked on his office door.

"How was Napa?" he asked, taking a seat across the desk from him.

Matt pulled up a picture of Hollis and her sisters and showed it to Bradley. It was one of his favorites.

"I know Hollis Jeffries," Bradley said, leaning in closer as if to confirm. "She works for Dobbins Capital, right?"

Matt nodded and turned the monitor back around as if pulling her back into him. It was strange hearing her name in the context of her job, the life he knew little about.

"I'm surprised she was able to get away for the wedding or is smiling, for that matter. Dobbins is all but being held hostage."

"How so?"

"Zeke... I can't remember his last name. Well whatever, Dobbins Capital, specifically your..."

Matt flashed him a look that told him to be careful.

"Dobbins, specifically your lady friend there, fed Pretty Boys Gaming to a group of bigwig investors."

"Stupid name."

"Yeah, I know, but they're three friends, met in college."

"Don't we all?"

They laughed.

"The two front guys are good-looking. If Kelly tells me Liam is 'hot' one more time, I'm going to tell her she should move in with him and take her car payment with her. They are the schmooze, super salesmen, but the whole thing hinges on Zeke, who's a total pothead and from what I hear, a prima donna. They wrote Fat Pigs, that's their baby. It's supposed to be the next Angry Birds, but better."

"Okay, so aside from the fact that the one guy could break up your marriage, what's the problem?"

"Things were going great, so I hear, until they dropped it into beta testing and some nine-year-old kid broke it. The game stops after like level twenty."

"Scalability issue?"

"Not sure. It's written in Objective-C, which has issues, but that's the thing. This Zeke guy isn't fixing it. He's not even trying. Meanwhile, they've invested millions in promotion. I'm sure you've heard the ads, 'This September, things are about to get—'"

"Dirty," Matt finished. "Yeah, I've heard it, but I guess I didn't put the two together."

"Well, you've been busy stocking the creamers." Bradley laughed.

"We don't use creamers—local dairy fresh each day," Matt deadpanned then smiled. "So this needs to be fixed by September, or what?"

"I read something last week, and rumor is the investors are already looking to pull and recoup. It's a huge mess."

"Why don't they bring in another programmer, have someone rewrite?"

"The guy is weird and protective of his stuff. There's some clause in their contract that basically gives him the reins to the runaway train. Dobbins is completely stuck unless Zeke puts down the bong and decides to work."

"Do you think he knows the problem?"

"He has to. I'm thinking move the whole thing to Lua and that should fix any issues. It's a better language anyway. Why these guys hang on to the stuff they learned in college like it's the Bible, I'll never know. Investors are threatening to jump ship and their man is baked in Mexico somewhere."

"He's back from Mexico," Matt said. "Let's get some of our guys on this."

"Are we letting Dobbins know?"

"Not yet. Let's see if we can help first. How long before they pull the plug?"

Bradley shrugged. "I'm guessing they're not hanging on for more than another week."

"Well then, let's see what we can offer."

"Are you sure this is a good idea?" Bradley asked, standing and making his way to the door.

"We help people, Brad, isn't that what we do?"

"Not usually people that bite, but you are right. I'm on it."

He left and Matt sat at his desk. If he could help her, he would. The fact that she had again told him she didn't think she needed his help was a discussion for another time. Right now, he was going to do exactly what he'd done with his father: if he had an idea and could help, he was going to barge in and do exactly that.

Hollis had been competitive all her life, but she'd never thought she was competitive with Matt. Obviously, she'd been completely wrong because looking back at their freshman year, it was a competition to see who received better grades. Who ran faster? When Matt dropped out after the miscarriage, had she still been like that? Had she felt that despite her setback, getting pregnant in college, she was going to pull ahead and leave him in the dust? Was she that ugly? Was it possible she needed to be in front at all costs? And if she was that person who tried to ring up her groceries in the self-checkout line faster than the woman next to her or walked faster down the hall than the other women to show she was in better shape... if she was that ridiculous person, how did she get there, and even more pressing as she began chewing on the nail of her index finger, how could she fix it?

She began typing up a proposal, an action plan for how they could transition the programming to a contracted entity in the interim to protect the investment. It read like a bunch of words, and Hollis was certain her boss would see it for what it was—failure. There was nothing she could do now but wait for follow-up, so Hollis focused back on getting her uncle's office, his processes, more streamlined so he could function more efficiently. Function more efficiently—Christ, when did she start believing her own propaganda? Maybe her uncle didn't want to function efficiently. Maybe no one did, for that matter.

Looking around Uncle Mitch's office, she suddenly realized that she had come to him for guidance and tried to change him. He walked in behind her with a bagel and cream cheese and sat behind his desk.

"Are we ready to enter the final phase of cleanup, learning how to use Excel?" he exclaimed sarcastically. "I know I'm excited."

"I think you should leave things the way they are. Forget what I said."

"What?"

"I mean it. I had no right to traipse in here and tell you how to run your place. Obviously, you are doing a great job."

"Did something happen?"

"No. I'm not going to be here much longer, and someone once told me I sort of bulldoze over people."

"Tots, I love what we've done to the office. I can find things. I have a calendar. Please don't pull out now. I need you."

Hollis looked at her uncle and thought about telling him, asking him for help, but she knew there was nothing he could do and besides, she was the helper, not the one in need of help in this scenario. So instead, she smiled and returned to work making his office the best possible version of him.

"Maybe it's time for you to let go of some stuff too before you start talking to yourself and the plants like the lady staying in *The Duke*," Uncle Mitch said as she stood behind him watching him type in his password.

"Holy sh—taki, did you see her yesterday? Full conversation with both of the succulents on the patio. I walked out of my cabin and thought she was talking to me."

"She came in for lunch yesterday and I asked her if she was a writer. You know how weird they are, so I thought…" He shook his head.

"Not a writer, huh?" Hollis laughed and felt less unsteady. Uncle Mitch had a way of balancing things.

"Nope, and she looked at me like I was the nut-o for even asking. I smiled and backed away. What was I going to say, 'So you have no reason for talking to my plants?'" He stood from his desk and poured more tea from a tray Hollis hadn't even noticed on the corner of his desk.

Hollis moved the cat and sat and her uncle dropped down into the new chair next to her. They found it at the used furniture store in Point Reyes. It was bright blue and now that he wasn't drowning in papers, there was room. And it was the exact color of the plastic marlin now hanging over his desk. He took her hand as they both looked out toward the bay.

"Let some of this go, Tots. When you were a little girl and your sisters would piss you off, do you remember what I used to say?"

"I thought you only gave me extra Popsicles."

"Well, I did, but while I was contributing to your future root canal…"

"Be a duck."

He nodded. "Let things land and then roll right off your back. Big sisters can't carry it all, or you'll—"

"Drown. I remember."

He kissed her hand.

"Does it get any easier?" she asked.

"What?"

"All of it. Life, all the choices and turns in the road. It was clear to me, and I can't find a path forward with this shi—mess at work. Maybe that's fine because it brought me back here, but I'm tired of figuring things out."

"You're probably asking the wrong person. I'll be fifty-five next month and I'm still working on taking a multivitamin every morning."

"Have you tried the liquid? I mix mine with my juice."

"Sure, I'll try that, but it's not the point of my greatest uncle speech. Life has no finish line, that's the point. You're never going to be done, not even you, Tots. Right when you think you have one piece figured out, a dam breaks somewhere else and you have to juggle. I'm not sure your parents have ever let you girls see the struggle of the juggle. They make it look so darn easy."

"They do." She propped her feet up on his desk.

"I don't think they mean to seem sickly perfect, but maybe they do. Could be they have all kinds of garbage they're hiding and that's why they work so hard. I can tell you my brother is no 'walk in the park,' as our mother used to say."

Hollis laughed. "He says the same thing about you."

"I'm sure he does," he said, shaking his head. "No one has all the answers. What kind of trouble are you in at work? Can I help?"

Hollis loved that he asked as if he could tell some story or get her an extra Popsicle and things would work out. She wished it were still that simple. "No. It is all but over. This game."

"Fat Pigs?"

Hollis nodded. "The lead programmer is a flake, and I offered up the company to our investors. It's a long story, but the gist is this guy can't finish the game and I should have known."

"So they are going to fire you over that?"

Hollis let out a slow breath. "Not right away, but once they start figuring out how this all broke down, I'll lose my job in stunning failure."

"Okay, so go there, take yourself to the worst-case scenario. Sometimes it helps when I get nervous about things."

"Does that ever happen?"

"It used to when I was younger. I had this technique where I would go to the dark place. Whatever the worst case was, I'd imagine myself there."

"I can't quite get there without wanting wine or a nap."

"That bad? Are we talking jail?"

Hollis laughed. "No."

"Then it's not that bad. So, it's you and me, close your eyes and go there."

She closed her eyes and tried to imagine a conference room full of her colleagues and investors when they found out exactly why they'd invested and lost millions of dollars. She tried to picture the snickers, the behind-her-back jokes. And then she saw herself packing her things. She felt the humiliation.

Hollis was about to hyperventilate, so she opened her eyes and looked out over the magnificent bay.

"Well? Doesn't it help to know you'll survive?"

"I opened my eyes before the end again."

"Why?"

"Because I've worked hard and it will be embarrassing."

Her uncle took her hand and kissed it again. "Okay, so it's that bad. Well, let's go with my other coping mechanism, my backup."

"What's that?"

"I drink myself comfortably numb and then I stick my head in the sand."

Hollis laughed. "I've mastered that. Do I have permission to return to the sand, Mr. Miyagi?"

Uncle Mitch laughed, and they sipped their tea knowing full well the time for drinking had come and gone. This was the end of it. He never pushed or asked for the details, and he didn't judge. He simply put his arm around her and squeezed. She imagined it was easier being an uncle as opposed to a father, but at that moment, Hollis was on Team Mitch because if she'd had the same conversation with her father, she'd be sucking her thumb in the corner. Failure of this magnitude, and as a result of a moment of stupidity no less, was simply not acceptable in the Jeffries household. She had tried for two months. She would go back to her cabin tonight and send more e-mails, leave more voicemails, and find a way to accept the "dark place."

Matt walked through the men's locker room of the gym and out a door to the pool. According to Toro, they were going to be working in the outside pool today. It was a little after eight and one of Poppy's full-time days as she started to make her way back to managing the shop. There were two long lap pools in the front and a secondary "deep end" pool, as Toro had described it, toward the back. The smell of sunscreen and chlorine hung in the air in almost equal measure. There was some type of adult swim lesson going on in one of the pools, but Matt finally found Toro's massive frame crouched down at the back pool's edge. As he made his way closer, he saw his father, bare from the waist up, holding on to the side of the pool. His hair was wet and when he noticed Matt approaching, he did something Matt had not seen in years: he smiled. Matt had given up feeling much more than duty and responsibility toward his father a long time ago, but his chest tightened at the sight.

"Hey, man," Toro said, hopping into the pool next to Matt's dad.

"Hey, this is a great place."

"Isn't it?" his father said. "Thanks for coming down to get me."

Matt was taken aback, and Toro smiled when their eyes met.

"I was telling your dad here about my surfing accident and how pain can put you in a bad mood forever until you get some relief."

"Are you starting to feel relief, Dad?"

His father nodded as Toro moved him off the wall and deeper into the water. Matt sat on one of the chairs poolside and felt tears well in his eyes. They should have been tears of joy seeing his father so fluid and mobile, but they were loaded with so much more. The pressure of his solitary childhood eased and he saw his father as simply a man. In the water, hair slicked off his face, he wasn't the stern taskmaster who put Matt to work after school starting when he was thirteen. "It'll keep you outta trouble," that's what he'd said. But here, kicking and moving the water with his hands, he was something Matt recognized. He was a man in his simplest form working on making himself better, and Matt had never felt closer to his father than he did in that moment.

When they were finished, not wanting to disturb the look on his father's face, Matt let Toro help his father out of the water while he stood and handed him a towel.

"You're looking good, Dad."

"I feel good. I'm almost one hundred percent."

"Ninety-nine." Toro smiled as they all sat around a small white table.

"So how's your girl?" his father asked.

Matt looked to Toro, who shrugged in that way that confirmed they'd been talking about him.

"She's probably packing to go home as we speak."

"Ya see, this is where I went wrong."

Matt could feel the strain creep into his neck.

"I never told you what a catch you are, how lucky a woman would be to have you."

Now shocked twice in the last hour, Matt wasn't sure what to say.

"Does she know you're loaded?"

They all laughed and Matt shook his head. "She knows what I do for a living."

"She knows you're a coffee guy. Does she know the things you've invented? Has she seen your office downtown? These are the things you need to be showing off."

"Dad, you haven't even seen my office."

"I know, and I'd like to."

Matt looked to Toro. "Is there some kind of magic in the water?"

Toro shook his head and left them alone.

"He's a smart man and I've been a good father, but not lately."

"Dad, it's fine. I'm glad you are feeling—"

"Don't interrupt. I am not sure when I jumped off track, but you're all I have, and lately that scares me. We tried hard not to burden you with your brother's death, and I keep bringing it up. Maybe I'm getting old. It's getting hot out here and my trunks are starting to itch, but I wanted to thank you. I also want you to know that I'm so proud of you."

Matt had to turn away because he was going to cry, so he hugged his father. "Thank you."

Both men walked back to the locker room and his father said Toro was "one of those meditating types and he's helping me relax my mind too."

Matt laughed.

"I know, right? Your mom's awful happy about that part too."

He left his dad at the door to the locker room and made plans to have lunch with him in the city, at his office, in a couple of weeks. Matt still wondered about the magic in the water, but he wasn't going to question any of it. His father was making his way back and Matt felt a sense of pride that he'd barged in, picked him up, and helped, no matter how messy it was in the beginning. Matt was no longer on the sidelines waiting for things to happen.

Chapter Twenty-Seven

*H*ollis started packing her things when she woke up around four in the morning on Tuesday. When she'd opened her eyes, her first thought was that time was up. Kind of like exam days in school, when the period ended and the teacher would say in a stern voice, "Pencils down."

She had exhausted her options; the final consulting firm came back with something she hardly understood. There was some key or encryption to Zeke's methodology that he alone could unlock. They all apologized, asked where to send their invoice, and moved Hollis closer and closer to the place she was now standing. Right on the edge of a cliff.

Her phone vibrated right as she finished putting her two sweaters on the top of her suitcase. It was Reese. She tried to swallow the lump in her throat and told herself there was no way he knew. There would need to be an investigation into the failed investment. That's when they would know what she'd done. He knew nothing, she told herself, and answered.

Reese announced he was in the conference room with Corning, Megan, and a few of the investors. Her heart dropped. Hollis greeted the group as if nothing was wrong. There was a brief pause; then she heard what sounded like clapping.

She didn't say anything, wondering if someone else had entered the room.

"That was the best we could do with you still off site, Ms. Jeffries," Corning said.

Hollis was still confused. Fortunately, Corning was a direct man, a trait she admired in her boss, and he got right to the point.

"I have to say, I had my doubts for a minute there, but you have saved this project in brilliant fashion. Working tirelessly under pressure, and remotely at that. Zeke has delivered the finished product and Liam e-mailed the extensive testing results. Things are on track."

"We couldn't be happier," some other female voice said.

Hollis probably would have recognized the voice had she not been more shocked and more confused than she'd ever been in her entire life, and that included the time her Chemistry teacher gave her a D on the final.

Wait, Zeke fixed it? Was that possible?

"And as if that is not good enough, Zeke says he was, and I quote, mad inspired, and has completed two more follow-up games that he would like to show us next week," Corning added. "Hollis, are you there?"

"Yes, I'm here. Still soaking in the relief. I'm so glad things worked out and we made it happen within the time frame. Investors, thank you for your patience." She thought that sounded convincing and heard chattering. Hollis needed to figure out what was going on, so she decided to back out slowly while they were obviously talking among themselves.

"Thank you for the call, but I need to catch another call in five minutes," she lied.

"Okay. Sure. You go off and save the world a little more. When can we expect you home?" Corning asked.

"I need to wrap up a few things."

"Fine, tie up loose ends and we'll see you in the office on Monday. Incredible work on this."

"Thank you."

"Oh, and Hollis?"

"Yes?"

"We've already sent them an e-mail, but if you have a chance, please thank your team at Pilot Programs for their help. Great idea reaching out to them. We'll let you go," he said and disconnected, which was a great thing because she wouldn't have been able to say anything even if she'd known what to say.

Pilot Programs. *Holy shit!*

Hollis felt an avalanche of emotions hit her all at once, and none of them were good. She closed her laptop and left the cabin.

Matt was in the kitchen when he heard the front door of his parents' place open. He knew it was her, knew why she'd stopped by. Bradley had called him last night to give him the good news. He was going to call her, tell her, but decided not to. She was walking toward him with a look that told him he should have called.

"Morning. I was about to call you."

"Really? Why?"

The anger spilled off her. He'd expected it because he'd broken the rules, Hollis's golden rules of distance and space. "Look, I'm sorry. I'm sure you—"

"Don't you dare." She stood, hands on her hips. He'd never seen her so pissed, and he was somehow fine with it because whether she knew it or not, the weight behind her eyes, the worry, was gone.

He stepped into her, leaving no space between them. "Dare what?"

"You do not save me. I save myself."

Matt said nothing yet tried to hold on to her gaze.

"I didn't need your help. I would have figured it out."

"I don't think so, Holls. You needed some help with this one, and I was happy to offer."

"Offer? You didn't even tell me."

"You didn't either. Bradley mentioned something about your firm and the trouble you were having, so you didn't tell me either."

239

"I'm not some charity case you need to ride in on your white horse to save."

"I don't have a horse and I didn't save you. I helped. It turned out to be a coding issue, and some of our guys knew Zeke."

"It's not your right. You had no business—"

"I love you. I have every business."

"Why?"

"Why is it my business?"

"No, why do you love me?"

"Oh, Holls. You were right. You're my split-apart, and you were killing yourself over something that I found myself in a position to fix. I can't help it."

"I left us, left you." She sat at the small kitchen table and he sat across from her.

"So what? That's the past, let it go. Please, this one time, give yourself a damn break."

"I can't because if I let that piece go, then I lose all the rest."

"It's not a package deal. We can shine it up and turn it into whatever we want. Hell, half the world doesn't even know you were pregnant. No one knows you didn't want to be pregnant. It's the past."

"Don't dismiss this, dismiss my feelings like they're no big deal. I'm not some doe-eyed girl in awe of your powers. This is my job, my life. I wish you had respected me enough to give me my space. I was blindsided in that conference call. You stepped over the line."

"I told them you called us, gave you the credit. What line? I helped you."

"I didn't ask. Forget it. I'm repeating myself, and I'm leaving."

Hollis turned and Matt took her shoulders. "No. If you're going to walk out again, I'm going to blow your bullshit wide open. You let people help, just not me? Okay, so when your project hit the fan at work, when you screwed up, how many people did you let help you? Who'd you call?"

"I called my family. I told them everything."

"Everything? Did you? No, you wouldn't have shared the ugly part, the piece you might need help dealing with. Those pieces you keep for yourself. You must have quite a collection shoved down in there by now."

"I hate you."

"That's okay. But know one thing. I know what's happening. I can feel it. You're getting ready to run again, back to your corner, where you can control all the optics, come out as Hollis Jeffries, perfect oldest daughter. I used to be the perfect guy for you because I never wanted a mess either. You said back up and I backed up. You wanted more space and I was happy to oblige because... because I'm probably as screwed up."

She scoffed and turned away from him. He pulled her back.

"Here's the problem with your plan this time. I'm not that kid anymore, Hollis. Know that if, when, you bolt, I'm coming after you. Be prepared for that."

He took her face, cradled it. "Fall on me. Let it all go and let me hold you."

"No."

"Look at me. I will not drop you. I'm right here and no one is looking. Break, Hollis. Let it go."

"I... please leave it alone."

She looked at him, deep into his eyes, questioning if she could once and for all trust him and like a wave about to crest, she pulled back and then crashed.

"The two guys, the ones that run Pretty Boys with Zeke... I slept with one of them. There, are you happy now? Is this ugly enough for you?"

"I know."

"You... what? How do you know?"

Matt said nothing because he knew she would continue and he didn't want to screw it up.

"The worst part is I didn't even want him. Some other partner at our firm wanted him. He could have been her mistake, but instead I wanted to show that I could get him, that I could win. Oh God, that's so screwed up I can't even believe I said it. He climbed into my bed and assured me that his company was on the up and up. I let that influence my decision and I took the deal without meeting Zeke. One look at him and I would have pulled back, I would have known, but instead I was—"

"Distracted."

"Yeah, an amateur move, and I fell for it. That makes me—"

"Human?"

"Oh no, don't pull that with me. 'You're like everyone else, Hollis.' I'm not. I'm worse."

"I don't think that's true."

"That's because you're screwed up too. You... don't see me the way I am. Did you know when we were in college I got back up to study for a couple of extra hours after you went to bed to make sure I knew more than you?"

"I did."

"Did you know one time in Junior Sailing I hid your tiller?"

Matt laughed, he couldn't help it. "That one actually sounds like fun."

"It's true, and one time when I was playing Monopoly with Anna-belle and I was banker, I took two extra five-hundred-dollar bills when she wasn't watching."

She put her head in her hands. "I'm an awful person. I don't know if it's because I was the first, you know, the guinea pig for my parents or what, but something went wrong because I'm awful."

Matt shook his head. "I'm sorry to say it because I know you hate being ordinary, but you're like the rest of us, Holls. You make mis-takes. The difference is you don't let them go. You never forgive yourself, so there's a self-hate thing going on."

Hollis was still crying and made her way to the door. He wanted to pull her into his arms, but this time, he knew what he was doing. He was giving her space, but not much and not for long.

Chapter Twenty-Eight

By the time Hollis walked back to her cabin, she'd calmed down and found some order. Being back had taught her so many things, but now it was time to go. Whether or not she wanted him too was irrelevant now. Matt had saved her ass, saved her job so she could go back to the life she'd worked so hard to create. There was some irony in there, but Hollis didn't have the stamina to figure it out. She closed her suitcase and walked to her uncle's office. He was feeding receipts into the small machine she bought him. His desk was clean, a candle lit, and his classical string music softly played in the background. It looked like a collected, civilized place and Hollis almost fell over.

Her uncle's eyes went to her suitcase then found hers. "Is it time for you to go already? I'm starting to get the hang of this thing." He stood. "I think orderly and responsible looks good on me." As if he sensed she was going to cry, he pulled her into his arms. "I heard things worked out at the job," he said softly, resting his head on top of hers.

Hollis nodded.

"That's good."

They stood and embraced, and Hollis didn't want to let go. She did what moved her forward, closer to the next cookie, but she didn't want to this time. She'd found peace in folding towels, setting up activities, and playing the karate kid. She'd watched the movie three times with him since that day. It was good.

"You'll come back and see me soon?"

She nodded again, almost afraid to speak for fear she'd blubber all over him.

"Quick story."

Hollis started to pull away, but he held her. "Right here is fine. This one will be quick. So I knew this guy once, second in his family of two boys, and he was a badass. Hotshot stockbroker, living the life. He met a gorgeous man who, for some reason, liked him too and so he got down on the proverbial knee to ask him to get married. He said yes and they set the date."

She could feel his breath quicken.

"They were going to go someplace with palm trees and blue water for the honeymoon, so a few months before the wedding, they decided to get certified in scuba. The gorgeous man went for the standard physical and found out he had cancer. Stage four, pancreatic."

Hollis tried to pull back, to look into his eyes, but he held her close while he finished. "He was gone in less than six months." After a few more beats, during which Hollis was sure her uncle was collecting himself so he could finish his story, his arms loosened and his glossy eyes found hers. He held her by the shoulders and softly said, "It is the one thing that matters, Tots. All the rest of this... stuff seems important, but it's not."

"I didn't know."

He laughed and quickly wiped away any tears that threatened to fall. "Do you think you have the market on hiding?" He walked behind his desk, back to his scanner.

Hollis picked up her suitcase.

"Now go put those fancy shoes back on. You should probably get a pedicure too before you return to the circus."

The circus. Apparently, everyone saw it but her.

"I'll be back."

"I know," he said and went back to scanning, lost in his own memories.

Matt had paced around The Bean long enough. Poppy was about to throw him out, so he left and walked toward the cabins. Her car was parked out front and as he approached, she was on the pier. The memory hit him like some kind of epiphany. In all these years, after what they'd been through, not much had changed.

The summer of thirteen, after they became friends but before he'd kissed her, they started jumping off the dock. The first time they stood shoulder to shoulder, toes curled off the edge of the warm wood. Matt took her hand, threaded their fingers together as they were poised to jump. Hollis wiggled her fingers free.

"Don't hold that way. I need to be able to slip free if I don't want to go where you're going once we're in the water."

He could hear her young voice in his head as clear as if she was as close to him as she was now. The woman, even at thirteen, knew how to throw him off center. She had a certain security, a sense of self that Matt had never experienced before, nor did he have it himself at that age. Maybe Hollis taught him how to be a man, how to stop being a boy. He was grateful to her because as he stood in front of a grown-up Hollis, he was going to attempt something far more impossible than a double flip off the pier. He was going to try to make her stay.

"What are you doing?" she asked as he stepped into the buffer of space Hollis liked to keep around herself.

"I need this to be about now. I get that we have a past, but we're not those people anymore. I can help you, love you, and that's all I did." He touched her face. "This is different now and yet you're doing it again."

"What are you talking about? It's not like we can stay here. I need to go back at some point. You made sure I have a job. I suppose I should thank you, but I'm still pissed."

"I know. I'm not talking about going back to the city."

"Then what?"

He took her face gently in his hands as if that would somehow reach her, remind her that this was her life, her home as much as it was his. "When you run this time, Holls, what do you want me to do?"

"Matt, I'm not running. We both have lives. We're adults."

"Answer the question. What do you want me to do?"

"Look, I'm going back. I'll call you."

"What are we?"

"I don't know, okay. What do you want me to say? I'm not running. I'm simply getting back to my life."

"Uh huh."

"Give me a little space to get back and figure things out." He'd heard that one before.

"Space," he repeated.

"Yes, space."

She was already gone. The embarrassment or whatever she had told herself was a reason to leave was placed firmly between them and as before, there was nothing Matt could do. He was getting tired of not having options. She was preparing to return. He'd never known another woman, or man for that matter, so capable of shutting down. Every fiber in his body told him to grab her, make her stay, but that was not a tactic that worked on someone like Hollis, so he did what he swore he would never do. He stepped back and let her leave, again.

Chapter Twenty-Nine

*H*ollis turned toward the window behind her desk and stared out at the other tall buildings. She'd been back a little over two weeks and was finally ready to move Pretty Boys to the "Client Maintenance" file on the corporate shared drive with the rest of her success stories. She'd spent some time at the spa getting all quaffed back to perfect and no longer had sand between her toes. In fact, her toes had returned to their biweekly pedicure schedule. Her hair was blown out and glowing, so it seemed a shame that the tear that escaped messed up her liquid eyeliner. Hollis looked down at her Ferragamos. Silk blouse, pencil skirt, and chickpea salad for lunch, the old Hollis was back. She was whole again, except for one part. It was a vital piece, but she'd once again left it by the cove. Her heart would probably stay there forever this time, and she honestly couldn't blame it.

She turned back to her computer one last time to the picture Poppy sent her of Hannah, who was getting bigger every day, and closed down the pictures of Sage's honeymoon and her ever-so-slightly growing belly. Surrounded by importance and wealth, Hollis told herself life was all about different paths. She was meant to be right where she was and as soon as she accepted that, she would return to her happy.

Hollis had thrown out her broken flip-flops when the doorbell rang. She shoved the suitcase she'd finally managed to unpack into her closet and went to the door.

"Mom. Why are you here? Is everything all right?"

"I don't think it is. May I come in?"

Hollis stepped aside, and her mother walked in with a box in her hand and went straight to the kitchen.

"What's in there?"

Her mother opened the box to what looked like a dozen oatmeal cream pie things, but way better than Little Debbie.

"Oatmeal cream pies?"

"Yes, your uncle told me you were eating those packaged things, and I thought you might need a better version."

"Where did you even find these?"

"There's this little bakery right off of Birch. Divine, you should—"

"So you drove into the city to show me the proper way to eat an oatmeal pie?"

"No. Do you have tea?"

Hollis nodded and pulled down a teapot.

"I drove into the city to tell you that maybe your father and I messed up, but I won't apologize."

"Okay."

"You are a strong, wonderful woman and that is hard to do—those don't grow on trees."

"Did Uncle Mitch say something?"

"He did, but you know him, it's all metaphors and my God, I think the man has fifty of the same Hawaiian shirt. But that's not the point. I'm here to tell you a story."

"Like Uncle Mitch?"

"No, this one is better, and it proves my point."

Hollis settled in.

"When you were little, we had this huge chestnut tree in our backyard. Do you remember?"

"I think so. In the old house before Annabelle was born?"

Her mother nodded. "Yes, so each year birds nested in the tree and sometimes it was windy and tiny birds would fall from the nest. Your father would go out early in the morning and check to make sure there were none on the ground before you girls went out to play."

Hollis made more tea. She had a feeling this was going to be a long one. "I'm listening."

"Anyway, one day you and Sage were out early and there was a baby bird that had fallen from the nest."

Hollis rejoined her mother. "Did Dad get it?"

"No. You found it. It was bigger than the others he found before. It had some feathers and could move its head. It was alive. You came running into the house and made your father come help."

"I think I remember this. Didn't we make a nest for it?"

"Yes, you had learned in school that you needed to leave it on the ground and keep it safe. You did that."

"I remember. And then the bird was gone one morning. Flew away."

"Yes. But after two weeks. For two weeks, you took care of that bird."

"I thought Sage did."

"No, she lost interest after a day. You took care of that bird, watched him day and night, and there was one night we thought he was going to die. His breathing was slow and you slept outside with him."

"I don't remember this."

"I went outside to give you another blanket, and you were talking to the bird. 'Are you listening to me, little guy?' you said. 'Giving up is not an option. You have to fight and get back up in that nest. Do you hear me?'"

Hollis didn't move, not even at the sound of her mother's excellent impersonation of her as a child.

"'We are Jeffries. You are a Jeffries bird because you are in our tree, and we do not fail,'" her mother continued.

Hollis held her hand to her mouth.

"'So, I'm right here with you and we will make it through the night. You are tough and you need to fly.' That's what you said." Her mother's eyes welled up. "That's who you are, sweetheart. You're a fighter and you bring people up, make them stronger. I can't have you walking around telling people you're a horrible person because it's simply not true. You make things happen, Hollis Marie. You're my daughter and I would expect nothing less. Mistakes are merely challenges to overcome."

"Mom."

"No. They're part of life. It's what we do with them, how we survive that makes up who we are."

"But—"

"You found yourself pregnant while you were in college. So?"

"How did you know—"

"Oh for crying out loud, a mother knows these things. I waited for you to tell me and when you didn't, I called Matt. He told me what happened and I let you be. You needed to find your way."

"You are exceptional, my dear. A wonderful force, but you are not a horrible person. Maybe I didn't teach you this, but you need to be kind to yourself, forgive the bumps as you keep going down the road. If you collect them, you'll never make it to my age."

Hollis was now crying.

"That boy loves you, he always has. Now you need to give him a break and stop playing so hard to get. Mistakes aren't the same as failure. You know that. You said it yourself. Now it's time for you to take your own advice."

Chapter Thirty

*H*e had not heard from her in the two weeks since she left the cove. His parents had both come up to check on the store and Poppy was now back full-time. Matt was free to go back to his life and yet, like one of those snow globes his parents bought him one year at Disneyland, he was all over the place.

Sometimes if you want something, you have to take it. The phrase popped into his head as he sat back at his office and finally stopped reading the same e-mail over and over again. If life were as easy as simply "taking it." Outside of the movies, most people who tried to run on in and take what they wanted were shot or arrested. When it came to Hollis, severe body damage was likely. So, Matt worked, bought a plant for his apartment, and tried to find the life he'd managed before a guy named Zeke turned the world on its axis. Matt learned that Fat Pigs was a huge success, and he was sure the follow-up game they were already pushing with the slogan, "Let's get dirty again," would probably be as big.

In an effort to keep her from being humiliated, he'd helped, which in turn sent her away. While that was a sobering thought, Matt wanted her to want to be with him, not simply settle because there were no other options. Watching Hollis fall at the hands of some asshole with a name like Liam was never an option. Bradley had handed him Hollis's blue folder, and Matt had paid the bill and she'd hated him for it.

With a weekend stretched out in front of him, Matt decided to check in on Poppy. He wasn't returning again to Mitchell's Cove hoping Hollis would return. He wasn't that naive anymore. Even though he had plenty of things to do in the city this weekend, he was returning because it had been two weeks and the one way he knew to be close to her was to be there. If that was pathetic, he no longer cared. Every day as his eyes opened, all he wanted was a life with her. If he couldn't have that, if she didn't want him now that her life was back in order, he would love her by being there.

"We really should learn to play a proper card game," Mitch said several hours later as they sat out on the patio drinking beer. "Hollis would lose her mind if she knew this was the extent of our parlor games."

"Old Maid is a proper game," Matt said, discarding a card and trying to breathe at the first mention of her name.

When Matt arrived, tie still dangling from his dress shirt, Mitch immediately put in an order for chowder and settled Matt at the end of the bar with a beer. Mitch had not pried for details or told him he was a fool. He'd simply offered chowder, beer, and now a game of cards, albeit a children's game.

"Do you have any Gary Gophers?" Mitch asked with a straight face and took a pull of his beer.

"Have you heard from her?" Matt handed over two gophers.

"Other than an e-mail with links to virtual tax accountants she wants me to contact, no. Your turn."

"Do you have any... What is this one... Billy Blaze? Christ, how old is this game?"

Mitch laughed. "Old." He handed over one card with a fireman on it. "How are things at home?"

The question struck Matt as odd because for a minute, he forgot this wasn't his home. "Good, getting back to normal."

Mitch raised his eyebrows, still looking down at his hand of cards.

"I'm here to make sure Poppy is adjusting to full-time."

Mitch tossed his last card into the pile between them and declared himself the winner. Matt threw his cards into the pile and finished off his beer. There was a group of people close to the dock having a bonfire. Matt could hear them playing charades and marveled at how normal, how relaxed they sounded. His life had never been relaxed. No matter how hard he tried, there was work or expectation or... Hollis. She pushed in life and while a lot of people would find that off-putting, Matt never minded. In fact, now that she was gone again, he found the drop in urgency depressing. He almost wanted to take up a new hobby or read some ridiculously long book to occupy his mind because when he slowed down, closed his eyes, she was there. He knew from past experience it would get better, but he didn't want it to this time. He wanted her to come back and mess up his life all over again.

So much for the damn split-apart theory, he thought, helping clean up. Mitch shut the lights off behind the bar and walked Matt to the door.

"She'll be back," he said as they locked up and stood in the empty parking lot.

"I'm not so sure."

Mitch nodded. "You told her you were coming for her this time. What are you waiting for?"

"I don't know. I think it's that whole easier said than done business."

Mitch nodded. "The doing is often the hardest part, but she needs you to get her. She would never admit it, but I think she wants the gesture."

Matt wrapped his arms around Mitch and swallowed back the feeling that maybe this was what advice from a big brother felt like. God, if Hollis thought she was a mess, Matt was right there with her.

"Right? That's good advice," Mitch said when Matt let him go.

He nodded because he was afraid if he said anything, he'd make a blubbering asshole of himself.

"Good, so go get her." Mitch patted him on the back and walked away.

Matt had spent his life waiting for a lull in his dad's priorities, waiting for the pain in his mother's eyes to ease into one son being enough, and, of course, waiting for Hollis. In the space of one September evening, standing in a parking lot alone, maybe he was done waiting. He shook his head to clear it and walked toward his car.

Chapter Thirty-One

*I*n typical Hollis form, before he had a chance to snap himself into the "doing," she'd sent the e-mail.

She needed him. Sure, it wasn't some grand cry for help, she hadn't begged him or texted him a million times. Hollis wasn't that woman; she was like one of those paintings Bradley bought for the lobby of their offices. From a distance, it looked like one thing, but when a person moved closer, it was made up of tiny parts of something entirely different. She was intricate like that, so Matt knew exactly what the e-mail he'd received an hour ago meant. It was an article about a lighthouse in Maine that was looking for an innkeeper. One of about a dozen lighthouses still manned, and she sent it to him with the subject—Vacancy. That was it, nothing more.

If he showed the e-mail to anyone else, they would say he was crazy, but as Matt made his way to the financial district, he knew she was asking. Asking him to remember what she had said. "If the opportunity..." He remembered, the pink in her cheeks for the wind and pain in her eyes and the way she brushed it off with a joke. That was Hollis, which was how the woman he'd loved his whole life operated. She offered up these tiny cryptic windows and if—when—he missed them, she moved on without him.

"I don't even know how to change diapers, do you?" she asked him the morning after they found out she was pregnant. He'd been so stunned at the idea of being a father, so wrapped up in the "hows" and "whens" of building a life with her, that he'd missed it. She was asking him the one way she knew how. There was so much in that question. Do you want to have this baby? If you don't know how to change diapers, will you learn? I don't know anything. I'm scared.

Matt had answered with a simple one word: no. Hollis showered and was back in her parents' house in less than forty-eight hours. Window closed.

The lighthouse article was the same thing. It wasn't some interesting piece of news; it was another question. Do you want to love me, scratchy sweaters and stew?

All he needed to do was follow her; go after her. So that's what he was doing as he pulled into the parking garage at 411 Bass Ave. He had absolutely no idea how to "take" Hollis for his own, but he didn't care. He'd start with "I can't live without you" and go from there.

Flawed logic. That's what her decision to leave and return to a world she ran from would have been called in corporate speak. It was at the root of most bad decisions and it was certainly to blame for why Hollis had returned to a place, a job, that didn't bring her any closer to happiness. She'd told Matt when they were back at the cove that she wanted to be happy more than anything and yet she'd spent the past few weeks pretending again, trying to revel in her success even though it all felt wrong.

Matt had not come for her as he'd said he would, which was understandable considering he had saved her ass and she repaid the favor by again running away. She had sent the e-mail and he had not replied. Hollis was sick of herself and her "flawed logic," so she could hardly blame Matt. Besides, she was responsible for her own happy, and that's why she quit her job. After she left her boss's office, she'd had a flash of regret, a feeling of failure even though she told herself she was going out on top, but it was fleeting because by the time she'd packed up her desk and walked past Megan, the snickering bitch, she felt the release of letting go. For the first time in her life, Hollis was choosing herself, her peace of mind over the smoke and mirror show of being perfect.

The doorbell rang as she was packing her books. She stood from her crouched position, and the sunlight glinted off the large window that looked out over San Francisco Bay. For a moment, she was in the center of her half-packed living room and awash with a feeling she didn't recognize. It was sort of like being picked first for a team at recess or being called on in class, but more adult. The doorbell rang again, followed by knocking, and Hollis knew exactly what was racing past her heart: the feeling of being chosen.

Tears flooded her eyes. She knew who was now pounding on her door and she knew why he was there. All those years, had she been waiting for this moment, waiting for him?

The past no longer mattered. Hollis had already taken responsibility for her present, and now she and Matt had come full circle. All of it, the good and bad, had brought them to where they were now—two people, a door, a choice. Hollis wiped her eyes, unlocking her front door to the one man she would ever love.

He was breathless and walked past her before she said a word.

"I'm not sure I want to live in Maine, but—" he blurted out and then looked around her apartment. "Where are you... are you moving?"

Hollis nodded and waited for him to retreat, backtrack because finding her packing was not in his plan, not what he'd expected. She wanted to step forward, tell him she quit her job and exactly how they could have a wonderful life together, but this time, she said nothing.

"Okay, well where are you going?" He let out a breath.

"I don't know yet."

Matt looked a little deflated. "What do you mean you don't know? Don't you have a plan? Color-coded labels or something? Do you have a new apartment yet?"

"No."

He crossed his arms across his chest then uncrossed them and pointed at her. "Don't do that. That is not, we don't do the one-word response anymore."

She almost laughed at his uneasiness, but before she could say anything, he rubbed the back of his neck and began pacing.

"All right, well since you're not offering much, I guess this is on me. If you're packing because you—"

His words fell when Hollis stepped in his path and wrapped her arm around his neck.

"Breathe, Locke-ness." She kissed his neck. "Tell me why you're here."

"I love you." His arms went around her waist. "I don't have an action plan, but that doesn't mean I don't love you. Maybe this doesn't need to be complicated. I'm here to get you."

A smile spread across her face and Hollis felt the world right itself. So many years and there she was, dangling and holding onto him, their hearts pounding and Matt wanting.

"Do you see those boxes?"

He looked toward the window, brow furrowed, and nodded.

"They are packed with books. I never realized how many books I had until I started to pack them. Lots of coffee table books, and even though I sent some of them to the—"

"Holls?"

"Right, sorry. Anyway, those boxes are quite heavy. I bet you can't lift three of them at a time."

The corners of his mouth curved up ever so slightly and his eyes filled with the challenge of a thirteen-year-old. "Of course I can." He held her closer as they both surveyed the boxes.

"Those are packed to the top. You could barely lift the empty keg from behind Mitch's bar last time I checked. No way you can lift three of those." She played along, swallowing a lump in her throat.

Matt nodded. "I've been paddleboarding with Toro. My core is stronger." He released her and patted his abs.

Hollis held back a laugh.

"I'll make you a deal." He stepped into her but didn't touch, instead hovering like they were floating around one another.

"Fine. If you lift three of those boxes, what's the prize?"

Matt's eyes started to fill and Hollis thought she might die right there.

"You are, Holls. If I lift those boxes, will you marry me? I promise we don't need to wear scratchy sweaters."

She leaned into him, their lips almost touching as she wrapped her arms back around his neck. "I'm kind of a bulldog. I've never been married before and as of yesterday, I'm unemployed. Maybe you should wait a while until..."

"I'm done waiting." Matt took her face in his hands.

"Fine," Hollis said. "I'll marry you."

A smile spread across his face as a tear spilled from his glorious blue eyes and Hollis felt her heart swell, taking up the far corners of her chest.

"Don't you want me to lift the boxes first?"

She shook her head and kissed him.

Epilogue

ollis watched as Matt crossed off the last box on the calendar that hung in their kitchen.

"That's three months," she said.

He nodded and kissed her.

"Do you think we're out of the woods?"

"Probably not. I'm not sure this baby-making thing is ever over."

"You know, your honesty is becoming hard to deal with. You do remember that I'm hormonal, right?"

He laughed. "How about I buy you some ice cream? It's probably time to start ice cream therapy."

"Oh, I hear that can be intense. Should we call people? Tell them now?"

"We could take a drive to get the ice cream. I know this great little place by the cove."

"Really, I'm up for a drive. I love the cove."

He stepped into her. "And I love you, Holls." He kissed her, and even though they were a married couple, even though they were most likely going to be parents, his kiss brought her right back to the pier every time. Those summers when she learned to sail, kissed a boy, and found her split-apart.

Acknowledgements

I would like to thank:

Katie McCoach and Nikki Busch because they're wonderful and I enjoy working with them.

Women that make tough choices and pave their own way. I've been inspired my whole life.

My family for putting up with my moods, imaginary friends, and often absent mind.

Readers for inviting me into your lives. The honor is never lost on me.

Tracy Ewens shares a beautiful piece of the desert with her husband and three children in New River, Arizona. She is a recovered theatre major that blogs from the laundry room.

Vacancy is her seventh novel, and the sixth in her *A Love Story* series.

If you would like to keep in touch, you can find Tracy on Facebook and Twitter, or subscribe to her newsletter at www.tracyewens.com.